WEEKEND
ROCKSTARS

by Dave Holwill

In memory of Clive, Eddie and Bowen, without whom I would have known none of this

And for Netty, like everything else I have

CHAPTER 1

The sound of whirring blades eclipsed everything else as George stared unblinkingly into Tim's grinning face. He was powerless to move. Tim laughed maniacally as he swung his arm around George's head, moving his weapon to his stronger right hand, the left now occupied with the headlock that trapped George. George could hear Linda, his twenty one year old daughter, screaming from the other side of the room, but was gripped so firmly that he could not turn his head to see her.

'Do it, for gods sake, stop messing about and take it all off!' Linda's voice screamed above the sound of the blades. He had hoped for more loyalty from his eldest child, but it seemed that his hopes were in vain.

'Well okay then,' Tim said, 'Let's get this done, sorry George, but this is for your own good.' The clippers buzzed loudly against George's skull, almost, but not quite, drowning out the sound of the Saturday night singing show blaring from the television. He looked down to see his hair piling up on the floor, there was a lot less of it than he had expected.

'Oh, that's much better, keep going, all the way, I'll get a razor,' Linda said, leaving the room.

It was George's forty second birthday and he had optimistically invited his friends and family over to help him celebrate. Predictably, everyone had begun making the usual jokes about his hair, or rather, his lack of it. The general feeling had then moved towards him losing what little he had left, and then his dear friends Tim and Matt had grabbed him and taken the decision away from him.

'I reckon it's the Terry Nutkins hairdo that's been holding you back dear,' Tim said as he clipped the last of George's halo of shoulder length hair from the back of his head. 'Everything that is making you so thoroughly miserable, undateable and ridiculous – including both of your divorces – I lay the blame for all of it at your dreadful hairstyle. Now arise, and observe your shiny new barnet.'

George was about to protest that he had still had a full head of hair for his brief first marriage when its progeny returned, 'Hold on!' Linda exclaimed, running up with a bic razor and a can of foam, 'let's finish him properly shall we kids?' she directed this at her little brother and sister, who were in fits of laughter on the sofa, having briefly stopped arguing over who had the biggest slice of cake to watch the assault on their father. Danny and Alice were five and seven respectively, and worshipped their big sister.

Linda quickly tied her own long, brown, almost light enough to call blonde but not quite, hair away from her face and set to rubbing foam into George's head before going to work with the razor.

'Careful love!' George shouted, as Linda's overenthusiastic bic action nearly took off the top of his ear.

'Ok, you can let him go now,' she declared, grinning with satisfaction at her achievement.

Matt and Tim released their grip on George, who gingerly picked himself back up from the floor. He smiled nervously at his three children, who were all gazing at him.

'Oh that is so much better!' exclaimed Donna, Matt's wife, from the kitchen, as she came in with a fresh cold beer for George, to soften the blow.

'Yes, much better,' added Ant, Tim's husband, following in behind her with pink drinks for the children, 'nothing could be worse than that dreadful skullet.'

George walked out into the hall, where there was a mirror. He examined himself, and had to admit that it probably was an improvement. He realised that blindly ignoring the fact that his hairline had receded almost all the way to his neck, and refusing to cut his shoulder length hair had not done him any favours. Maybe his new look would herald a new start for him. He had accepted that he would never be any taller than five foot five and a bit, and that he would never manage to lose the spare tyre that refused to leave his middle. It made him look a little like a deflating beach ball with legs, but at least it no longer had seaweed hanging from the edges of its shiny crown. He straightened his Hawaiian shirt, checked his teeth for bits of crisps, drank deeply from his fresh glass of beer, and rejoined the throng in the living room.

'Okay, maybe you were right,' he conceded, 'I should have just admitted I was a baldy man years ago. Thank you.'

A cheer went up from the assembled masses, and, while Ant carefully swept it into a bag and threw it away, they raised a toast to George's hair.

'Sorry about that old chap,' Tim said, a little later while the two of them were alone in the kitchen, 'but it was necessary, everyone agreed. Sorry if I got a little carried away.'

'It's ok Tim, you were right, time to make a new start.' George had had over three decades to get used to Tim's flamboyance. They had met on their first day at school, and had somehow remained friends ever since.

'Oh Christ, did the paperwork come through today then?' Tim asked, looking down at George, his Cuban heeled boots making him a whole foot taller than him today.

'Yep,' George nodded, 'it's all official now, I have a second decree absolute to add to the collection. Should I have them framed and put on the mantelpiece?'

'Oh yes, that would be fabulous,' Tim smiled, running his hands through his dark brown Elvis-style bouffant to ensure he looked interestingly ruffled, 'shall we go and make an announcement then? More toasts?'

'God no Timothy,' George waved his oldest friend down, 'I was joking, I have already made quite enough of an exhibition of myself today. Besides, Danny and Alice are here, and Joan is still their Mum, so no digs until they've gone to bed.'

'Okay, okay,' Tim spread his midnight-blue-silk-clad arms wide in supplication, 'we'll have to celebrate another time, but you are definitely well rid, and with your new hair it's onwards and upwards for you Georgie boy, mark my words.'

'Hope so, Tim,' George replied, 'I'm going to start a band!'

'A what?' Tim replied, 'are you out of your fucking mind?'

CHAPTER 2

It was the following night, Sunday, and George had had all three children there all day, continuing his birthday celebrations in a more subdued manner than the revels of the night before. Having finally bundled Danny and Alice off to bed, he was looking forward to a quiet evening with Linda.

George's living room was much as you might expect from a man who lives alone. The magnolia walls and hard wearing brown carpets gave away its rented status. There was a second hand sofa, with one very old and well used cushion on it, and an armchair that did not match it, entirely devoid of cushions, both of which faced the unnecessarily large television set mounted on the wall where there might have been a fireplace in times gone past. There were pictures of his children dotted about the place, but most of the wall space was given over to shelves and shelves of cds, records, dvds, magazines and books. And when the shelves had run out, the overflow had been stacked neatly in piles on the floor, well, as neatly as you can manage to pile things on the floor when you have two kids under ten that visit regularly. George was thinking of shelving out the rest of the house to cope with it all.

The coffee table was much stained with red wine, chocolate biscuits, and coffee. All attempts to remove this residue had ended in failure, so George had just decided to call it shabby chic, though he wasn't entirely sure what that meant. He had never really wanted a coffee table, but his mother had insisted on giving it to him some years back, and he had utterly failed to refuse it. It was nothing compared to the state of the old battered footstool in front of the armchair. That had taken decades of Georges size ten feet, and had also been donated by his mother, mostly because he had already ruined it before he moved out of her house twenty five years earlier and she no longer wanted it. Despite their utter mundanity, and complete lack of style or aesthetic, the coffee table and footstool always made George feel at home, no matter where he put them, and they had been in some awful dives over the years. He collapsed into the armchair, and battered the footstool a little further with his beslippered feet.

'Relaxing bath Dad?' Linda asked, putting a large glass of merlot down in front of him.

Linda was George's eldest, born of an ill-advised youthful marriage to a beautiful woman who was clearly out of his league and had gone on to prove it by leaving him and marrying a much better looking, considerably cleverer, older and far more wealthy man. In spite of being George's daughter, Linda had managed to grow up to be a well-balanced, well-read, good-looking twenty one year old psychology graduate.

'Not really Lin,' he replied, 'I had forgotten how much hot water it takes to wash two small children before bedtime, and just how small my water tank is. Twenty regret-filled minutes in a tepid puddle of water does not a relaxing bath make.'

'Sorry Dad, it'll be better tomorrow when we've all gone.' Linda looked apologetically at her father from underneath a fiercely regimented fringe. She had enjoyed a wonderfully luxurious bath, filled with bubbles and happiness before George had gone up.

'You're staying tonight though aren't you?' George asked, a note of panic rising in his voice.

'Of course, I've got you all to myself for once,' she smiled, 'now what's going on with you and your bass?'

Three years previously, George had, in the time honoured style of men rapidly approaching forty, bought himself a brand new, shiny, Candy Apple Red Fender Precision Bass Guitar, under the mistaken apprehension that it had to be easy, what with only having four strings. He had then learned the main riff from Cream's 'Sunshine of your Love', and that bit from 'The Chain' by Fleetwood Mac (you know, from the formula one theme tune?) discovered that playing the bass really hurt your fingers and left it to gather dust in the corner of the dining room.

Then, a year or so later, when Joan had left him, calling him a pathetic doormat of a man, and saying she needed somebody who could take care of her (she hadn't specified financially, but George knew what she meant) he had gone back to it and with a bit of work and perseverance, he had discovered he quite enjoyed it. He had always loved music, and while he would have liked to be a guitar virtuoso, he was aware of his limits. He would never be much good at bass either, but he was fairly sure he could get away with being mediocre on an instrument nobody noticed.

'I'm finally trying to join a band Lin,' George shared, excitedly, 'I reckon I can play well enough now, and everyone says there's no point playing if you're not going to be in a band.'

'Everyone?' Linda wrinkled her nose, 'who is everyone?'

'Well,' George said, 'I've been posting on an online forum for bassists, and they are pretty certain on this one point. Bedroom warriors are not to be tolerated. It is apparently the trademark of the midlife crisis hobbyist, rather than the serious musician.'

'Well...' Linda began.

'Yes, I know what I am, you don't have to say it,' George cut her off before she could tell him he was a midlife crisis hobbyist.

'That wasn't what I was objecting to Dad, if you recall, I told you you should join a band ages ago, remember?' she smiled, sipping at her wine delicately.

'Oh, yes, well, I wasn't ready then, not good enough,' George flustered, 'it took seeing a few guys doing it for a living that were all worse than me to give me the confidence boost I needed.'

'As long as you remember whose idea it was in the first place.' Linda smiled smugly at him, ' I want my name in the sleeve notes on your first album.'

'Well, anyway,' he continued, 'it's not really been going that well. I've answered a few adverts from the music shop window in town.'

'And how did that go?' Linda asked enthusiastically.

'Well,' George sighed, 'I did not exactly cover myself in glory.'

'What happened?'

'It wasn't my fault,' he explained, 'I didn't really know much about how these things were done then. I took that with me,' he pointed at a 10 watt amplifier, about the size of a shoebox that he had tucked away under a bookshelf, 'it's only really meant for bedroom practice volumes. I mean, I've never been in a band before, I didn't know.'

'Did they laugh at you a lot Dad?' Linda tried to keep a straight face, without much success.

'Obviously they did, yes,' George replied, 'as did the queue of other hopefuls waiting outside the audition room with their massive amplifiers. The band let me play the songs they'd asked me to learn though, even though they couldn't hear me.'

'Well, that was nice of them wasn't it?' Linda couldn't have sounded more patronising if she had tried.

'Yes, I suppose it was,' George winced as he reminisced, 'did you know drums were that loud without being amplified?'

'Yes Dad.'

'Well, I didn't, but I have learned from my mistake.' He waved to indicate a large and expensive looking new Ampeg bass amplifier on the other side of the room, 'Happy birthday to me, from me.'

'Have you been out again then?' Linda asked.

'No, not yet,' George replied, 'I keep losing my nerve. I've tried going to play at those open mic nights in town, but I always bottle it at the last minute, and just watch instead.'

'Oh Dad,' Linda looked sympathetically at him, 'I've been to some of them, you are not as bad as a lot of the dross they allow up on the stage. You should get out there, it would be good for you, you might meet some new people, and it would be nice to come and see you play, point you out to my friends and say "that's my Dad up there."'

'Thanks love. But they are mostly a procession of waif-like girls with acoustic guitars singing pretty heart-felt ballads.'

'Yes, you do know all those heart-felt ballads are Laura Marling songs don't you Dad?' Linda said, a wry smile playing around her lips.

'I found that out after I congratulated one of them on her song writing, yes.' George confirmed, 'it turns out that all those earnest young men with beards are singing songs by some bloke called Bon Iver as well.'

'Did you find that out the same way?' Linda guffawed into her drink. George said nothing, but his face was all the reply she needed.

'Anyway, what about you?' George said, changing the subject, 'have you found a new job yet?'

'Yes!' Linda said, 'I have actually.'

'Brilliant, you're finally using that degree then?' George replied, 'What is it? How's the money? Do you think you'll stick at it?'

'Hold your horses there Dad,' Linda put her hands up, 'I'm afraid that this is just another opportunity for me to serve people drinks. It's a different place though, with nicer hours and a bit more money. Sorry to get your hopes up, it's not that easy to find jobs for psychologists down here in deepest, darkest Devon you know.'

'Well move away then!' George said, rather more loudly than he intended, 'Go to Bristol, or London, or Manchester or somewhere, there's nothing keeping you down here is there?'

'There's you Dad.' Linda said, all seriousness now, 'I worry about you being all on your own. You are lonely, and you need somebody, and in the absence of a real somebody, I am here for you.'

'Me?' George looked incredulously at her, 'Don't be ridiculous Lin,' George sputtered out, 'I'm forty two years old, and I'm your Dad, I managed a good two decades of life before you were ever even thought of. There's no need to worry about me, go, get on with your life, I will phone you, and visit and everything.'

'Oh, you know what I mean Dad, those friends of yours all mean well, but they seem to think another drink solves everything. Sometimes you need me to drag you back down to earth.' She grabbed his hand and looked into his eyes, 'And anyway, I'm a bit scared of the idea of leaving to tell you the truth. I don't really want to be too far away from my family just yet.'

George smiled back at her, and held her hand tightly, 'Don't worry, wherever you go I'm just a phone call away, you'll be fine.' It was understandable that she would be a little wary of big cities, having done her degree at the famously tiny Lampeter University in the deep, dark, depths of Wales. Rural living is very difficult to give up if it agrees with you.

'Of course!' Linda slapped her forehead, 'I should have thought of it before!' she exclaimed.

'What?' George looked at her, nonplussed, 'what are you talking about?'

'Your band,' she said, 'my friend Malcolm is always looking for people to start a band with. You should give him a ring, hang on, I've got his number here somewhere.'

The next day began, and there was the sound of fighting from the kitchen, apparently Danny had more cereal than Alice and this was not fair. Reluctantly George dragged himself down to sort them out. He began to wish that he didn't have the day off from work, as then he could have left them to Linda, who was mysteriously absent, or even better, have taken them back to their mother's the night before.

'But he's got more mallows in his than I have in mine!' Alice declared grimly, shoving her chocolatey, marshmallowy bowl across the table at her father. It appeared that the nub of the problem was even more specific than it had appeared. Her grim seven-year-old face told of a gross miscarriage of justice. While the smug face of youth looked across at her, and held the box away. At five years old, Danny had already managed to figure out which buttons to push.

'I haven't! Hers are just under the brown bits Dad, they're the same, she can't have any more, it wouldn't be fair then.' Big blue eyes looking out from under his blonde fringe made him look like it was him that was being cheated out of some wonderful prize. Kids do have the most amazing priorities sometimes, George sighed to himself, they'd forget all about it in ten minutes, and some other thing would then be of the utmost importance, perhaps a missing shoe.

'He may be right you know Alice, have a dig about under the flakes, there might be more marshmallows underneath,' George immediately regretted this mistake, and internally reprimanded himself, he knew better than to take sides normally, but tiredness had blurred his judgement.

'NOT!' countered Alice, folding her arms, and pouting like some kind of tiny super model. For kids with exactly the same parents they couldn't have looked more different, Alice had dark, near black hair, and piercing green eyes. The perfect features for making the terrifying expression of barely suppressed rage that was staring George in the face.

He considered just leaving her to starve, that's what his own parents would have done, but he'd never hear the end of it from Joan if he did that. So he stuck his hand down, grabbed the box from Danny, and pulled out a handful of marshmallow bits which were dutifully dropped into Alice's bowl. She grudgingly nodded, and accepted the breakfast gift. Danny just shrugged his shoulders, did a little 'win some, lose some' look to his father, and carried on eating. The kid knew exactly what he was doing. That was the sort of calculated wind-up technique that their mother, Joan, had spent years cultivating and testing on George until one day she had snapped at the total lack of reaction she got, and left him. Some people thrive on the drama and thrill of arguments, George was not one of them.

CHAPTER 3

'Get off me, are you pissed already?' George tried to extricate himself from Tim's one-armed bear hug, but Tim was a foot taller than George, and a good deal stronger.

'No my dear chap,' Tim grinned, his consummately coiffed quiff shaking with mirth as he released George, handing him a drink. He looked down to check his immaculate blue drape suit had not been creased, 'I'm just pleased to see you, Now drink this.'

Tim's cocktails were the stuff of legends, legends in which participants would end up playing Medusa to the cocktail's Perseus certainly, but legends nonetheless. George rolled his eyes at Tim, manfully had a sip of the 'started as some kind of daiquiri, but we're not sure any more' that had just been forced into his hand, and followed him into the house.

It was a Saturday night, a good six weeks after George's birthday celebrations, and George, Matt and Donna had all been invited round for an evening of drinks, food, fun and whatever else may occur (according to the text message invites). George and Tim had met Donna when she started working at Tim's Dad's hotel where the both of them worked as teenagers. Somehow they had managed to stay friends all this time, and Donna and Tim's marriages to Matt and Ant had not affected their group in the least, if anything it had strengthened it. In his more cynical moments George thought it might have been simply because they had never moved away from the small Devon town they all lived in that they were all still such good friends, unlike so many others.

As they passed the dining room, George couldn't help noticing that there were six places laid at the table.

'Not again!' He exclaimed, 'what are you bastards trying to do to me?'

His friends had, over the last couple of years, developed a terrible habit of inviting their single female friends over to 'make up the numbers'. George was none too keen on these unsubtle attempts at matchmaking, and had hoped that they might finally stop. He had been hoping for a relaxed evening with his dearest friends, free from having to make polite conversation with some crazy, middle-aged, cat-obsessed singleton.

'I don't know what you mean George,' Tim said, po-faced.

'Six places!' George replied as they came through the door into the kitchen, which was intended to be a beautiful clean lined piece of design, with it's copious escheresque ceiling racks filled with pans, a massive Belfast sink, and expanses of shining chrome and white. It had, however, been filled to overflowing with 1960s style bar stools, quirky jugs, novelty teapots and every kind of nostalgic paraphernalia, completely ruining the original architect's intent. 'Will you bastards stop trying to palm me off on your desperate old...'

'George,' Ant said, with deliberate calm, 'I believe you should remember Elaine,' he indicated a woman sat at their kitchen island looking distastefully down her nose at a strange pinkish drink with a cherry in. 'She popped into the hotel today and found Tim, she's just moved back from London, and wanted to meet up with you bunch of reprobates again.' Ant, Tim's husband, was ten years younger than everybody else, though his middle aged spread was just starting to really hit its stride. He had short, clipped, black hair and was wearing a comfortable jumper, jogging bottoms and big fluffy slippers, reasoning that since he was in his own home, he didn't need to dress up.

'Hi George,' said Elaine, with an embarrassed face, 'how have you been?'

George immediately turned a redder shade of beetroot. He did remember Elaine, Elaine had been his most useful ally when they were teenagers. Admittedly he had initially quite fancied her, but she had had a long term boyfriend and quickly friend-zoned him. He hadn't minded much, since they had turned out to be such good friends, and she was a very useful resource to call on when he was trying to worm his way into other girls' affections. She had moved away to London before even Linda had been born and George had completely lost contact with her since then.

'Bloody hell!' George said, open mouthed with surprise, it wasn't the most erudite greeting he could think of, but then since shortly after she had moved away his life had been utterly taken over by Linda, he had almost entirely forgotten that she existed.

'That bad eh?' she retorted, with a sly grin, 'I admit I might count as old now, but I like to think I'm not quite desperate yet.'

'Oh, god, no, I didn't mean...' George back-pedalled furiously.

'It's alright,' Elaine laughed, 'I'd have reacted the same if you'd turned up without any warning in London. Think nothing of it.' She patted him on the arm sympathetically, age had not treated her badly at all. Her hair was still short and spiky, as it always had been, but it was its own natural (well, probably not natural, George conceded) dark brown these days, and her smart casual orange shirt and black flared trousers were a far cry from the tie-dyed T-shirts and dungarees he remembered her for.

'Thank you, sorry, I mean, oh Christ, I don't know what I mean, it is good to see you though.' George stammered.

The sound of laughter from the other side of the kitchen broke the awkward silence, as Matt and Donna stood arm in arm and doubled over in hysterics. Matt in his rugby shirt and blue jeans, almost dwarfing Donna, her tiny elfin features hidden away inside her long brown cardigan.

'Oh you do know how to make an entrance don't you!' Donna's curtains of light brown hair swung wildly around her face as she laughed at him.

'Ha!' Matt added, his neck bulging with mirth where the thick, curling, black hairs of his body merged seamlessly into the thick, curling, black hairs of his head. George often wondered where exactly Matt decided to draw the line where he stopped shaving, and started washing instead, 'did you think my wife was trying to palm another one of her weird friends off on you?'

'Well, it wouldn't have been the first time would it?' George pronounced defiantly.

'Oh, I've stopped trying to matchmake you now darling,' Donna said to George, 'there's no point, you're too fussy.' She looked directly into his eyes, as if daring him to contradict her.

'So George,' Tim said, as they were all sat around the table, well filled by now, and sufficiently lubricated by the wine, 'have you found a band yet?' The dining room continued the same theme as the kitchen, a large glass table filling the centre of the spacious, well-lit room, surrounded by shelves and shelves of unnecessary nick-nacks and crockery.

'Oh, I remember you and Tim being in a band back at school,' Elaine said to George, 'I don't think I ever saw you play though.'

'You wouldn't have,' Tim said, 'we never played a note, we never even picked up any instruments. We spent one summer arguing over who was going to be the lead guitar player, and whether we were going to be rockabilly, psychobilly, trashabilly or punkabilly, and then kind of lost interest. We kept the story up though, George needed all the help he could get looking cool.'

'Well, you talked a good talk at the time, I believed you,' Elaine looked a little put out at the deception.

'Sorry,' George added, 'it was all Tim's fault.'

'Oh, as always,' Ant exclaimed, 'now enough about your dishonesty, what about now? Are you still trying to do something with this Malcolm bloke?'

George had, on Linda's advice, met up with her friend Malcolm, and the two of them had hit it off and agreed to try and put a band together.

'Yes, there's still only three of us at the moment, but we're still hopeful that somebody who isn't completely deluded might answer one of our adverts.' George replied.

'Colour me interested,' Elaine said, 'who is this Malcolm bloke you speak of, and why do you need more than three of you for a band?'

'You might have heard of Malcolm,' George said, puffing out his chest.

'I bet you haven't,' Tim interjected.

'Malcolm Devereaux?' George said, 'he played keyboards for Guacamole Window in the 80s?'

'Guacamole Window?' Elaine said, a smile spreading across her face.

'Yeah, do you remember them?' George said.

'No, sorry, it's just... well, Guacamole Window? What a name! Could they sound more 80s?' Elaine replied.

'Oh.' George looked a little put out, having mistaken her smile for one of recognition, 'anyway, he was, they were nearly very big. Malcolm was touted as the next Jean-Michele Jarre, and that wasn't an insult back then. They got swept up in the new romantic bandwagon, along with Spandau, Duran Duran, Visage, and all that. Unfortunately they were a bit too prog rock around the edges and all the predictions of greatness proved false. They drowned without trace after one album, but it was a corker, I've got it somewhere.'

'Very nice,' Elaine replied, nodding at George in encouragement.

'Anyhow, after that he was a session musician for years, played on loads of stuff from the 80s and the 90s that you've probably got.'

'So why's he down here starting a band with you?' Matt asked, slyly.

'Very good point,' George said, 'I don't know, to be completely honest.'

'And how did you meet him?' Matt continued to interrogate him, sounding like a concerned parent.

'Linda,' George replied, simply, 'she gave me his number. Apparently he was briefly living with one of her friends. She was using him to get at her parents, nothing like shacking up with a fifty year old "professional musician" to wind them up. It worked apparently, after a couple of weeks they caved in, bought her a car, payed the deposit on a very nice flat in the city, and off she flounced without a second thought. He didn't see it coming somehow, poor chap. Linda felt sorry for him and kept in contact, you know how she is with charity cases.'

'Sounds a bit seedy to me,' Donna said, 'how would you have felt if it had been Linda?'

'Wasn't though was it,' George said, stubbornly, 'she's not stupid enough to do anything like that, and I couldn't afford to buy her a car.'

'You couldn't, no,' Tim said, stirring the pot, 'but I bet her step-dad could couldn't he?'

'Well, yes, maybe,' George conceded, 'but Linda still isn't that stupid.'

George was saved from this line of argument by a whine of 'Daaaaaaaddddy!' from the door.

'I think he means you,' Tim and Ant both said in unison to each other, before rock, paper scissoring their way to a decision. Tim lost, so he went off to check on their son, Nicky.

'Sorry about this, you know what it's like with a four year old,' Ant explained, 'tiniest little excuse to come down and try and get a look at what's going on. I suppose you'll all need more wine?'

George, Donna and Elaine all nodded vigorously.

'I have been in rugby teams that drink less than you three when you get together,' Matt exclaimed, meaning George, Tim and Donna,

'I suppose you're the same then Elaine?'

Elaine merely smiled, winked, and drained her glass.

'Oh Christ, not another one,' Ant said, 'do you want a coffee Matt? We can be civilised, we don't need to bow to peer pressure.'

'No chance, you're on your own there I'm afraid,' Matt replied.

Ant went off to the kitchen and came back with two more bottles of wine, one of which he decanted into the glasses ranged around the table, and the other he kept in reserve, knowing full well that it would be needed quite soon. Then he went back to get his large mug of coffee.

'Are you still working for your Dad then Tim?' Elaine said, once they were all back around the table again.

'Certainly not,' Tim said, snootily, 'I run the hotel myself now. I am the boss.'

'Yeah, but your Dad does still own it, doesn't he?' Donna said, a sly grin taking over her features, 'so technically you do still work for him.'

'You were lucky to catch him in there this afternoon Elaine,' Ant added, 'he's got Roberto now, so he doesn't have to work evenings or weekends, or mornings, or any time he doesn't fancy going in really.'

'That's rich coming from you,' Tim fought back, 'at least I don't just sit in front of my laptop watching *Cbeebies* and pretending to work.'

'I get most of my work done in the mornings while Nicky is at playschool,' Ant sighed, 'you'd know that if you ever got up before midday.'

'Oh, what do you do then?' Elaine asked.

'I'm a graphic designer,' Ant replied, 'only part time from home now, since I'm far more qualified to look after Nicky than Tim is.'

'We did similar when Fiona was born,' Donna said, 'I gave up work, and Matt had finally finished his teacher training, so he could bring in some proper money. I only started working part time again when Willow started school.'

'So she could keep tabs on me,' Matt laughed, 'she's the Headmaster's secretary now, can't get away from her anywhere.'

'So you've just got the two girls then?' Elaine asked.

'Yes,' Donna replied, Fiona's nine now, and Willow's just a year younger.'

'Must be handy working at a school then, no need for child care in the holidays.' Elaine added. Donna and Matt nodded along.

'Yeah, and it's not like Matt even has any marking to do, since he's only a PE teacher,' Tim grinned, 'easiest job in the world.'

'Says the man who does nothing and still gets pocket money from his Dad,' Matt retorted.

'It's the family business, I am running it,' Tim shouted back.

'Calm down, both of you,' Ant said, pouring more wine into their glasses, 'there's nothing more dull than people getting all precious over their jobs.'

'No,' Donna added, 'true, but George will soon be able to tell people he is a rock star, that should go down well at parties.'

'Ha!' Matt said, 'he's not going to be a Rock Star. He's starting one of those god awful cover bands you get in the pub when you're least expecting it. Loud, out of tune, and oh so desperately sad groups of accountants and dentists living out their mediocre rock and roll fantasies in front of crowds of indifferent drunken divorcees on the hunt. No offence to anyone here obviously.'

'None taken,' Elaine said, smiling, 'I am neither drunk, nor on the hunt.'

'None taken here either,' George said, 'I'm a postman, as you well know, not a dentist.'

'Doesn't excuse any of it mate,' Matt smiled and shook his head, before taking a long drink from his wine glass, 'and you are lying on at least one point there Elaine.' She grinned back at him, and pointedly put her wineglass back down on the table.

'Oh, ignore my husband,' Donna said, 'how long before you and this Malcolm are out playing in public then George? I'd quite like to come and see you play.' Elaine nodded in agreement, arms folded across her chest now.

'Might be a while actually Don,' George had to admit, 'auditions are not going as well as we'd like.' This was true, most of the hopefuls that had turned out to join the band had made George look like an old seasoned professional.

'Tell them about that drummer George,' Tim laughed across the table, 'that was priceless.'

'Jesus! Which one?' George replied, 'I mean they're all terrible, I can't remember which one you laughed at most.'

'A couple of weeks ago,' Tim continued, 'you remember, you said he'd come into the rehearsal studio, unloaded and set up a brand new, terribly expensive-looking drum kit, tapped nervously here and there at it all the way through some dreadful old song or another, then when you lot asked him why he hadn't really joined in, he said it was a lot harder than he'd thought it would be, and admitted he'd never actually played the drums before.'

'Oh yes, him, well, that's pretty much the story right there Tim, thanks.' George confirmed.

'Sorry, didn't mean to steal your story,' Tim grinned.

'It's fine Tim,' George said, 'anyway, you'll like this one as well, last weekend we had a would-be vocalist who couldn't remember any lyrics. He wanted to do Nirvana's 'Smells like Teen Spirit', as he said it was the only song he'd prepared in advance, even though it wasn't on the list we emailed him. So we set off playing, all going very nicely, despite the drummer we had at this point playing some kind of free jazz behind it, and then he began. *Here we are now, entertain us.*'

'What's wrong with that? Those are the words aren't they?' Elaine asked.

'Well yes, but not for the entire of the first verse, and the chorus, and the second verse, and the rest of it as well. Admittedly, he did fit them into the entire song, and they did fit, but there should be other words. I remember them being in the song quite clearly.' George sighed, 'and that drummer asked us afterwards if we had a drum kit he could borrow for gigs, as he didn't own one. I've got another full day of it tomorrow, I really hope things improve.'

Much later on, Donna cornered George in the kitchen while he was fetching drinks, 'So, what about you and Elaine, hey?'

'What about me and Elaine Don?' George replied.

'You know, back in the day you guys spent so much time together, I was sure something was going on, and I still think there could be,' she smiled and nudged him in the ribs, 'maybe you could pick up where you left off?'

'Maybe we can Donna,' George explained, 'but we were like brother and sister back then, it would have been weird as anything else, and still would be.'

'Really?' Donna raised her eyebrows, 'because I've seen *When Harry Met Sally*, and I think you guys are fooling yourselves. I don't believe you were "just friends" then, and I don't believe you will carry on being "just friends" now either. And the sooner you realise it, the happier you will both be.'

'I will, once again,' George waved his arm expressively, 'have to respectfully disagree with you Donna. We were very good friends back then, and only friends, it would have felt incestuous to be anything else, I would be very happy if we were very good friends again, but it's been a long time, and even though we're different people now, I doubt enough has changed to make us fall madly in love with each other, so don't expect any wild romance any time soon, okay?'

'Whatever you say George,' Donna hugged him with one arm, almost impaling his foot with her kitten heel and nearly making him drop the bottles he was holding, 'I just want you to be happy.'

'I know Donna, but maybe you could let me have a go on my own once in a while?'

'Terrible idea George, you have awful judgement.' and they went back in to join the others.

CHAPTER 4

The rehearsal studio was a small low room with terrible acoustics. Calling it a studio was kind, since it was more of a shed, at best it could maybe have passed for a badly converted garage. The sound bounced from wall to wall creating unexpected harmonics that needled into George's head and made it feel like it was exploding. And that was without the hangover.

The shed was, as mentioned, small and dirty, and the cheap amplifiers that came with the room had clearly been used by those who followed the old rock and roll maxim 'turn it up and rip the knob off'. The sun beating down on the roof highlighted the lack of insulation in the ceilings, turning the room into not only a noise trap, but a furnace – which was exacerbating George's dehydrated discomfort even more. As was the fact that he was stationed next to the bin, filled to the brim with not-quite-empty cans of lager, cider, bitter and energy drinks and clearly not emptied for a long time. It had a very special kind of scent – especially in this heat – with no windows and a house rule about not opening the doors while playing.

This was where George found himself that glorious Sunday afternoon, with his Bass strapped round his shoulders and a full salsa drum section playing along behind his eyes. They hadn't even played a note yet and another day of auditions stretched out ahead of them. Malcolm was optimistic, but George was not so sure. Malcolm had already managed to persuade his friend Bill to join them on guitar. He was a little older than George, and like him, had taken it up to beat off the mid-life crisis and had been doing so relatively successfully for the last five or six years.

Bill was just setting up his guitar amps, and George wished he had followed internet forum advice and bought some earplugs, as the onslaught was going to be fairly painful today. Sure enough, a few minutes later, Bill fired out the opening chords to an AC/DC number, the latest drumming auditionee cracked out the snare drum (in completely the wrong place) and George decided he wanted to die.

The first vocalist that afternoon was screaming some lyrics, that may or may not have been correct, at the top of his voice. Sadly not in any key or rhythm that even vaguely approximated the song he was supposed to be singing, but he certainly had energy. As the final chords crashed through George's head, melting what few brain cells he had left in there, the vocalist shouted out '"Rebel Yell"! Come on, let's do it!' Bill launched into that Billy Idol intro, and off they went again, fingertip blisters were suddenly added to George's list of woes for the afternoon.

As the final notes rang out, the hopeful singer called out '"Wishing Well"! Lets go!' without giving them time to even have a slurp of water, or check their tuning. The drummer clicked them in (at a different tempo to the one he began the song in) and they all duly obliged, despite his tuning and timing not having got any better during the last attempt. This continued through six horrendous tracks, and a good half an hour's torture. With every enthusiastic shout to start another song, Bill and George shared a raised eyebrow, and an unspoken agreement that neither of them were going to stop this was instigated – they needed to see who broke first. Eventually Malcolm cut him off mid shout, told him that they had other people to see that afternoon, and they would definitely call him later on to let him know how he'd got on. That phone call never happened, and there were a lot of expectant emails to Malcolm's in-box for the next week, until Malcolm finally gave in and told the poor deluded chap that he was terribly sorry, but he hadn't quite made the final cut.

They took a break, and stood outside so that Bill and Malcolm could smoke. The atmosphere was grim, and it seemed that they would never get this band together.

'Maybe the world has moved on,' Bill said, 'perhaps we just aren't meant to be in bands any more, maybe all the good ones have been done?' Bill was tall and good looking, with a full head of short, dark hair and charisma to share. George would normally have hated him, but just couldn't do it as he was impossibly likeable. He was a very handy guitar player as well, which made George grateful that he could hide his fairly average bass playing under Bill's excellent guitar work.

'I've not even got my foot all the way in the door of the musical box yet guys,' George replied, 'I don't want to retire before I've even started!'

'Don't worry,' Malcolm said, trying to roll a large amount of what appeared to be dust into a rizla paper, 'we're not dead yet, there's two more guys to go today. It could still work out.' Malcolm was not a great deal taller than George, and his brown leather jacket, black raybans, stone washed jeans and silvering mullet hairstyle were reminders of his 80s heydey.

'Okay, but if they're as shocking as the rest can we give up and take up golf instead?' Bill joked. He got a lot of stick for being an accountant, and liked to get the golf jokes out of the way before somebody else did.

'Nobody is wearing those trousers any time soon Bill,' Malcolm joked, half choking on the dust coming out of his cigarette as he attempted to light it, 'by the way, is that another new guitar you're playing?'

'Yes,' Bill replied, 'I thought I should try a Gibson Les Paul custom instead, I never got on with that standard one I had. I think I might have found the one this time, it's a definite keeper.'

'You said that about that telecaster last week,' Malcolm rebutted, 'and I saw it on ebay yesterday.'

'Well, I was wrong, I went off it, and I had to sell it to fund this one, the wife's got me on a strict one-in one-out policy now, more's the pity.' Bill explained as a Porsche 911 pulled up in front of them.

'Is one of you guys Malcolm?' the driver asked, and after brief introductions, they took Chris (the driver) inside and showed him the drum kit he was going to play. In due course they were joined by the final vocalist of the day who nervously asked them if they would be okay going round the introduction parts a few times if he missed the odd cue, as sometimes he had a few problems remembering the line to get into each verse. They agreed that that wouldn't be a problem and once again Bill fired out the AC/DC introduction, Chris picked it up in exactly the right place, and the whole song began to fall together.

George looked across at Malcolm during Bill's blistering lead guitar solo, and saw an unmistakeable grin across his face, which he felt sure was mirroring his own. They caught the eyes of Chris and nodded approvingly at him, he also broke a smile, and put his head back down into the kit in concentration. Nobody could gain eye contact with the nervy vocalist as he hit every high screeching note of 'You Shook Me All Night Long' without missing a single cue, but he did it, and they noticed. As the song drew towards a close, Bill looked up from his fretboard at Malcolm and George, and nodded, grinning similarly. They turned to the vocalist who was looking at them nervously, waiting for some affirmation that it had been okay, seemingly unable to read the smiles across everybody's faces as the signs of approval they were, and Bill said, 'Perhaps another? Just to check?'

In case it had been a mistake, Malcolm forced this line up to run through 'Long Train Running' by the Doobie Brothers, Van Morrison's 'Moondance', 'Mr Brightside' by the Killers, 'Hard to Handle' (Black Crowes version, not Otis Redding) 'Brown Sugar' by the Rolling Stones and Deep Purple's 'Black Night'. Not a beat was dropped, not a cue was missed, and everyone was happy. They had a band, a slightly nervous singer apparently, but nevertheless – a band.

The singer, whose name was Steve, admitted that he had only really sung karaoke before, and, like George, was totally new to all of this, but really wanted to do it before he got too old. He was already the wrong side of fifty, and had the same haircut as George, though he was considerably taller at six foot one, and built like a builder. Because he was a builder.

Chris had just got back into it, having played drums in a band at school twenty years previously, he had had a go on a drumkit in a shop in front of his new, younger girlfriend, and she had talked him into buying it, and then into going out to join a band. He was younger than the rest of them at thirty five, and still had long rock and roll hair, drawn into a ponytail and contained underneath a baseball cap which George and Steve were as jealous of as they all were of his Porsche (the hair, not the baseball cap). They all shook hands, and agreed to meet again the next week.

CHAPTER 5

'Good day then kids?' George asked, as they trudged up the hill towards their mother's house from school, Alice with a downtrodden scowl on her face after realising they would have to walk the whole way home. He had received a panicked phone call from Joan earlier that day asking him to pick the kids up, and had agreed to it before remembering that his car was in the garage, and they would all have to walk. Luckily it was a nice day, and he had nothing better to do that afternoon.

'Yes, Paddy brought a frog in, and let it out in assembly this morning, and all the girls in the hall screamed and started running around, and we laughed and nobody found out that it was us who let it out until later when Wendy Jones told on us. But it was Paddy's fault, not mine, so I shouldn't have been told off as well as him, even though I was,' Danny said, hoping his father would see the funny side. He was in luck, as George couldn't hold in the guffaw the anecdote had brought on.

'Well, you should really have stopped him you know, and that makes you a willing accomplice, and you shouldn't do things like that should you?' George countered, trying to hold back the laughs. 'It's all very funny until someone gets hurt in the running around afterwards, isn't it?'

'I didn't run around, I'm not scared of frogs, it was very childish and irresponsible of them, and if I'd known it was them, I would have told on them as well.' Alice piped up, with huge emphasis on the first I, to ensure nobody thought she would be babyish enough to run from a frog. Although, truth be told, she had been screaming and running around with the best of them.

'Quite right Alice, good point well made, glad to hear you weren't upset by the frog.' George replied, with a conspiratorial look at

Danny, as if to say – *don't even think about contradicting your sister, if she says she didn't, then we agree* – as, after enough experiences with spiders, and moths, and other creepy crawly things, he found it difficult to believe that his daughter had sat still and retained her dignity in a room full of screaming girls.

'She was Dad, I saw her running and screaming as well, she was one of the loudest,' Danny helpfully corrected, having misunderstood George's look entirely. This did not go down well with Alice, but once everyone had calmed down a bit, George decided to change the subject, and told them about the band.

'Paddy's got an electric guitar, and his Dad's in a band, Paddy says they're on telly all the time, and they're the best band in the world.' Danny replied. Paddy was Danny's best friend ever, despite only having met him a few months ago when they both started school. Danny was utterly smitten with his new friend, who was clearly the coolest five year old ever to live – if you believed Danny. Pretty much every conversation with Danny at the moment would involve a 'Paddy said' or a 'Paddy's got' or 'Paddy did' at some point or another. George hoped it might pass soon, but he doubted it.

'That's nice, maybe we can meet up, I could use a few contacts.' George replied, hoping that it wouldn't prove to be another one of Paddy's tall tales as contacts would be useful.

'Are you going on *X-Factor* then Dad?' Alice asked, 'that would be awesome, everyone at school would be so jealous of us, with our Dad on the telly.' She beamed at the prospect of having such a good thing to hold over her friends.

'We'll see love, I doubt it very much, we're not really doing that sort of thing, but you never know, it might happen,' he tried hard to let her down gently, but the pout returned as quickly as it had disappeared.

They arrived at their mother's front door as Robin's shiny white Audi convertible pulled up. Robin was their Mum's new boyfriend, he seemed nice enough, but George thought that there was just something a little odd about him. He certainly seemed to like the kids on the surface, but the very fact that he had just pulled up as they finished school without having picked them up made George wonder why Joan had asked him to get them rather than Robin. Anyhow, at least it meant George didn't have to wait around for one of them to get back before he could leave, so he kissed his children goodbye, exchanged pleasantries with Robin and wandered home.

Sunday afternoon rolled back around very quickly, and the band were in the rehearsal studios. Chris had not let anybody have a go in his car, but he had explained that a year previously he had had a relatively modest win on the lottery. Enough to not have to work again, as long as he stuck to a very strict budget. The car, a fairly nice barn conversion and a very shiny new drum kit had been the only luxuries he had allowed himself, as the prospect of not having to drag himself in and out of a garage to fix other people's cars when he could be playing with his own every day was far too alluring. Everybody was suitably jealous of his lifestyle, but then cheered up when he suggested that they practice at his house in future, as it had no neighbours, and plenty of room. Despite their inherent awfulness, the rehearsal studios they were using were not cheap, so a nice room that cost nothing would be a considerable advantage.

Steve on the other hand was rather more down to earth. He was pretty happy working as a builder, but fancied a new hobby. He loved music, though not enough to go to all the trouble of learning an instrument, and had been a karaoke warrior for so long now that he had decided to take the leap into singing with a band proper. Not being able to rely on the words scrolling on the screen anymore was the thing that worried him.

They spent the day working through the set list George, Bill and Malcolm had agreed on a few weeks beforehand. It had taken hours of disagreements – and trashing of each other's music tastes - to finally agree on a fairly inoffensive list of twenty five songs that they were going to learn. Unfortunately, Chris and Steve were fighting them all the way through, everybody likes different songs, and everybody hates different songs, sometimes the middle ground is hard to negotiate.

'But I love that song!' Steve cried, 'everybody loves that song, it was the best song in *The Commitments* movie, "Mustang Sally" is a classic!'

George was in full agreement, but had already had this argument, and Bill and Malcolm weren't going to budge. They rolled their eyes as soon as it was mentioned, and pointed out that yes it was a classic, but every band who ever graced a pub stage had played it, and usually not very well. Both of them had played it more times than they cared to remember, and had absolutely no intention of ever playing it again, the same argument had been made for 'Brown Eyed

Girl', and no amount of arguing would bring them round. Chris had not helped by pointing out that the last band he had been in twenty years ago had played those very songs – and they had rolled their eyes about them back then. George was a bit miffed, as both of them had bass lines he loved, and he could play them quite well already.

'I don't mind throwing in a few crowd pleasers,' Malcolm had said, 'But a line has to be drawn, and that is where we are drawing it. If I have to play "Sex on Fire", then I have to play "Sex on Fire", it's fast overtaking "Mustang Sally" as the song I hate most in the universe, but the Kings of Leon have spent far less time sitting in the back of my subconscious laughing at me than Wilson Pickett has.'

Eventually they stopped arguing and ran through the few songs on the list they all knew already, and drew up a schedule of five song chunks for them all to learn between rehearsals. Sadly, at this point, somebody had to ask 'So, what are we going to call ourselves?' and the long, tortuous band-naming process began. Within days it became clear that if anyone really liked a name, everybody else hated it, and vice versa. While any name that they did all like would turn out to have already been used by somebody else. Lesser bands have never made it past this point and split up before ever playing a note, never speaking to one another again.

'What about Zebra Legs George? That'd be a great name for a band wouldn't it?' Donna shouted at him from the other side of the zebra enclosure. A grand day out had been planned, and George, Tim, Ant, Matt, Donna and all their associated children (except for Linda, who was excused on grounds of not being a child any more) were at the zoo, throwing over-priced, non-specific food pellets at bored-looking animals.

George had already had quite enough of people shouting random band name suggestions at him, his friends were in competition with each other to be the one who came up with the eventual winner. Not a day went by where he didn't receive a text with a random group of words like Tower of Wookies, Fatal Aura or Radioactive Flowerpots followed by 'what do you think?' from one of the band. His own suggestions, Spaced Invaders, Spudgun and Lean Against the Washing Machine had all been shot down in flames, and he now just sent the odd things that his friends (and kids, and random strangers in the pub who overheard the conversations) shouted at him constantly.

Danny could be heard shouting something very enthusiastically up ahead, George couldn't quite make it out, but either Nicky had jumped in with the Tigers, or Danny wanted him to. Nicky and Tigers were definitely mentioned in the same sentence. There was a sound of tutting and clucking, as can only be made by little girls of a certain age disagreeing with something that is happening, and then the shouting of small boys who do not agree with them. This was not going to end well, George looked around to see if anyone else was heading over to deal with it, and quickly realised that they weren't. Donna and Matt were nowhere to be seen, and Tim and Ant were looking fiercely at the Zebras, deliberately ignoring whatever was happening.

George rounded the side of the Tiger enclosure to see Fiona, Willow and Alice all lined up in order of age, height and level of outrage shouting at Danny and Nicky, who were red-faced and on the verge of tears.

'What's going on then?' he began, as quietly spoken as possible, hoping to defuse whatever it was before it started.

'Danny was trying to put Nicky in with the Tigers Dad, he wanted him to get ate!' Alice answered, with a look of utmost sincerity upon her features.

'How was he going to do that then?' George asked, 'there's a big fence here in front of us, and then there's a moat, and then there's another big wire fence after that. Doesn't seem a very simple thing to pull off to me.'

'He was giving him a leg up to the first fence!' Fiona said, indignant, in the way only nine year old girls really are, 'then he was going to jump the moat and put his hand through the other fence so the Tigers could bite it off!' Willow nodded along to this in an enthusiastic eight year old kind of way. Both of them were tiny miniature versions of Donna, but could pull off Matt's best menacing look perfectly, as they were doing now.

'Is this true Danny?' George turned to his son, 'did you try and get little Nicky to climb all the way over there, swim that moat, and stick his hand in the Tiger enclosure?'

To his absolute credit, Danny shuffled his feet a bit, shrugged, and admitted that yes, that had been his plan, but Nicky had loved the idea, and wanted to do it, he was just helping him. George reminded him that he was older than Nicky and he needed to set a better example. He also reminded him that Tigers are really quite dangerous, as are moats, and long sloping wet grassy banks that lead down to moats, that fences are usually there for a good reason, and that he would have to spend the rest of the day holding his sister's hand everywhere they went if he didn't manage to behave a little better. At no point did he mention that the first fence was twice the height of Danny and Nicky combined.

Danny and Nicky spent the rest of the day shadowing Tim and Ant, as they were usually the safest adults to be around on these kind of trips, being less inclined towards lectures, and more inclined towards buying ice-creams and making bad jokes about the animals. This proved to be very true shortly afterwards, and The Strawberry Mivvys was added to the list of band names that George was never going to use.

CHAPTER 6

The band had, for some reason, decided to test themselves out at the most terrifying open mic night in town. They had no name, and only a handful of songs that were working, but they went to play at the Palladium Club anyway. It was an intimidating venue from the off, you had to walk past the smokers hanging out in the porch (especially if it was raining) down a long passageway into a long narrow room with no windows. Back before the smoking ban it had been impossible to see from one side of the room to the other, but this had changed now. Unfortunately for the band, the clientèle had not (neither had the soggy, plastic-wrapped sandwiches for sale on the bar – the club's small nod to the licensing conditions that meant they had to serve food).

It was the local musos' hang out, and pretty much all of the grizzled-looking people that propped up its bar night after night played in bands, or had played in bands, or would in the future play in bands, and there is nothing more critical than a room full of musicians. Except perhaps for a room, like this one, full of bitter musicians who never quite 'made it', and still have to work crappy day jobs.

Malcolm cheerfully pointed out that if they went down all right in there, then they could go down well anywhere, so they had come down to play a slot. None of them had brought any friends with them: this was business, and they didn't want any witnesses if it all went pear-shaped. George had not taken his own bass with him – so that he could pretend to have come as a punter and run away if the opportunity presented itself. But sadly this didn't work, and the house bass player, a terrifying looking fellow with a purple mohican and matching forked beard, happily handed over his custom-painted five string bass. George had never played a five string before, and this did not help his nerves one bit, the dragon emblazoned over the front of the bass seemed to be mocking him before he had even played a note and he found himself dearly missing his beloved Candy Apple Red Fender Precision and its four strings, but it was too late now. Much too late, Chris had clicked them in, Bill had struck the first chord on his brand new Fender Stratocaster, and 'Dakota', 'Chasing Cars' and 'Bohemian Like You' later (the official limit on stage time was three songs, unless you were the 'house band' or one of the preferred locals, who seemed to just go on as long as they wanted to. There was also a ban on making those three songs 'Hotel California', 'Free Bird', and the half hour live version of 'Dazed and Confused'.) George's nerves had subsided enough for him to be able to see again, and breathe, and all the other things that people need to do to live.

It had been the most exhilarating ten minutes of George's life to date, as far as he was concerned. The audience had applauded, and even though he had sat at the bar and heard the vicious criticism that the regulars here levelled at anybody that got up to play before, he felt they had been accepted, imagining the bar props all nodding sagely and telling each other how much they liked it. He had been lost in the music for the entire performance, not least because he had to stare very hard at the extra string on the borrowed bass, and make sure he didn't play the wrong one. He had a feeling that that level of concentration was what had kept him from realising how terrified he should have been.

As he queued up at the bar for the free drink everybody who played was entitled to, the stoic-faced permanent citizens of the stools did indeed all nod sagely at him, a few of them gave him the thumbs up, and he even got a muttered, 'well done' and a pat on the back from the red-nosed, silver-mulleted landlord as he pushed past him to get his cigarettes from behind the bar. He felt like they actually meant it for once, even though he had seen them pull the exact same routine with a million other people they had just finished verbally crucifying while they played. He didn't care, he needed to do that again, and more often, the nerves might have been terrifying, but they were great nerves – like first driving lesson nerves, or new job nerves or even losing your virginity nerves – and three songs was not enough, not by a long way.

Two nights later George was sitting at the bar of the King's Arms, nearing the end of a pint of Lager that had the definite taste of not being his last drink of the day. It hadn't even been the drink he'd wanted, he had had a hankering for the rough cider he drank in his youth, as the triumph of the band's debut performance had made him feel like a teenager again briefly. Sadly, as he got to the bar, the barmaid had recognised him, and started pouring his usual lager. He was so happy to be recognised as a regular that he didn't feel right correcting the poor girl, and had meekly paid for the drink he didn't really want.

George had a long history with this pub, and had had his first illicit pint bought for him on the premises at the tender age of twelve by an errant youth club leader from the local church. He reflected on the changes that had happened in the last thirty years. Where there had once been nothing but cards of peanuts slowly uncovering pictures of topless girls on the wall behind the bar, there was now an extensive wine cooler, offering pink and white delights from South America. The overflowing ashtrays were long gone, and the windows no longer had the yellow skin of nicotine residue that he so fondly recalled.

Apparently the employment policy had not changed as much, for the girl behind the bar who had recognised him was young, relatively attractive and had little propensity for maths. At least George assumed that was the reason for having more change in his hand than should reasonably be expected from a five pound note, it was unlikely to be because she had a thing for him – she was younger than his daughter.

He looked out of the window, watching the rain as it poured down the glass and exploded in little atom-bomb puddles in the window boxes. Even if it had been a pleasant evening, any long term denizen of the town knew better than to sit on the tables outside, as the fumes from passing lorries had always rendered it a smokier place than inside even back in the days before extractor fans, let alone the smoking ban. Suddenly the door slammed, and a whirl of sparkly dress and raincoat jammed itself behind him and said, 'Don't move, please, I will buy you a drink for this, just hide me.' George twisted his head, and saw Elaine crouched behind his barstool with an expression like gone off cheese.

'Okay, mine's a pint of lager, this one's nearly done,' he said. It seemed foolish to switch to cider now, and he would still run the risk of offending the barmaid if it looked like he was correcting her. It wasn't as if he even fancied her, she was probably only eighteen, but she seemed like a nice kid, and had big, scared, on-the-verge-of-crying eyes most of the time.

'Thanks, I owe you, I really do – can you see the window from there?' came the voice from underneath his barstool.

'Yes.'

'Good, when you see a tall bloke with a multi-coloured umbrella walk past, let me know.' Elaine explained, 'if he sticks his head through the door, just agree with everything I say.'

George nodded, and kept an eye on the window. After a while, a man with a multi-coloured umbrella peered through, George raised his glass to him and grinned, startling him into walking briskly away.

'I think you're safe to come out now Elaine,' he said, 'your round.'

'Rude! Still, I'm certainly a little rounder than I used to be,' she grinned, and George shook his head as she staggered back to her feet awkwardly, 'two pints of your strongest lager and two whiskey chasers as well, please,' she said to the barmaid, who smiled sympathetically at Elaine and went away to fetch the drinks.

'Chasers? I'm not sure I'm up to chasers, but thanks anyway,' George interjected.

'Who says you're getting one? I need both of those after the evening I've been having.' She smiled a forced and terrifying rictus, as if having been attached to a mains cable.

'I see, in which case fill your boots.' George was feeling a little tired, and had been thinking of heading home. He was far too polite to just walk out on what was clearly a damsel in distress though. He raised his fresh pint to her, and took a long gulp. Elaine, true to her word, drank off half of the pint in her hand, and then drained the two whiskeys, one after the other – with barely a breath between the two.

'Good, that's better. I fully intend to give up on all this crap—' she indicated the flashy dress and shoes she was wearing, 'and buy myself a cat or twenty. I really don't know what I was thinking, I mean, me? In a fucking sparkly frock? Jesus!'

'Ah, I take it you are also suffering from your friends thinking they can find you the perfect partner to end your loneliness?' George was beginning to feel some empathy for the poor woman.

'Oh god, and how,' she blurted out, 'they have no fucking idea. How on earth could people who know me think I would enjoy spending an evening with a smug, self-satisfied, narcissistic twat like that? I have never heard so much gym talk in my life. The guy is obsessed with fitness, cycling, running, weights and something called spinning, which I assume is not just standing on the spot with your arms sticking out and whizzing around like a five year old. All kinds of crap, he kept wittering on about his BMI, it took me an hour to work out he wasn't talking about his car!'

'You have my deepest sympathy, I was set up with one like that a few months ago, they are awful aren't they?' George chuckled, remembering an evening at a restaurant with a fitness freak called Rebecca, who spent it tutting every time he had a drink. He had only managed to shake her off by scrounging a cigarette from a smoker outside – despite having given up a decade previously – causing her to sniff loudly and walk off in disgust.

'I wouldn't mind so much, but it's a bit rude really, I mean look at me,' she indicated her stature with a sweep of her hand, 'I'm nearly as wide as I am tall now – so I'm pretty glad about the fact I'm not very tall most days. I had thought that the sparkly dress might help, but looking in that mirror over there, I can't help feeling I look a bit like a disco ball.' She laughed infectiously, and George couldn't stifle his own amusement at the comparison. 'We'd just finished eating and were heading up into town for a few drinks when I just couldn't take it any more. I said I was busting for the toilet and that I'd meet him there and I ran off. I never said where,– which is why I ran straight in here to find a corner to hide in until he went somewhere else. Is that bad?'

'I've been out on a few dates where I would have liked to run away,' George began, empathising fully with her, 'but luckily, I am too much of a gentleman. Or rather this is a very small town, and if it got out that I was in the habit of abandoning ladies in the street of an evening I don't think my chances of not getting beaten up by some well-meaning relative would be very high.'

Elaine snorted with laughter and had a long swig of her drink, 'You could well be right, I seem to remember a lot of that happening round here.'

'Yes, it really hasn't changed I'm afraid,' George continued, 'you know, I can't stand the whole mating dance, where you fanny around people, pretending to be all interested in what they do, what they like, their family, their hair, everything except what you really want to know. It would be much easier if it were okay for the first thing you asked every girl you met to be, "is there any chance at all that you might sleep with me at some point?" and get a genuine yes or no straight away. You know, like monkeys, they just walk up to the lady monkey, slap it out and get a yes or a no at once. No wine bars, no shitty restaurants, no small talk, no false hope, no yearning whiny love songs, just either fuck, or fuck off.'

'Well, that's a charming image, if I ever had one,' Elaine grinned, 'I see your cynicism hasn't cleared up yet. In answer to your unspoken question, no, I do not want to sleep with you, and as you well know, have never had any intention of doing so.'

'Oh for Christ's sake, you know I don't mean you, we were always above all that animal stuff, and in answer to your unspoken question, I have no designs on sleeping with you either. I have given up on women now anyway, if it's meant to happen, it's meant to happen, and I am now fairly sure it isn't. The internet kept sending me crazy ladies who needed more babies, so I stopped using dating sites, nightclubs are the most horrendous places in the world now, and I have had enough of Tim, Ant, Matt and Donna trying to set me up with anyone and everyone.'

'Yes, I noticed that,' Elaine said, with a sly grin.

'Ah, yes, and I am still sorry about that.' George blustered.

'Well, in truth, they were trying to set me up with you, but, I'm pretty sure I can do better,' Elaine quipped.

'Oh, charming, thanks very much, kick a guy while he's down,' George riposted, 'but seriously, what happened to make you come all the way back down here again? Surely you were made for the big smoke, that's what you said when you left anyway.'

'Ah! The optimism of youth,' she gazed up at the ceiling wistfully, 'I thought I was, but once things went belly up I just wanted to come back home again.'

'What happened then?' George asked, earnestly, 'I haven't seen you since your Mum's funeral.' After her mother had died, Elaine had had a full re-evaluation of her life, realised she was going nowhere fast, and left on a bus to London the day after the funeral, having told everybody that that was what she had to do.

'Oh, you know, the usual, my Husband decided he could do better than me, he was probably right, so being considerably better connected – and richer – than I am he contrived to keep my Son living with him, and I had to leave,' she explained, 'after that kind of crap I decided I'd probably rather be back down here again. I needed decent, proper friends again, not the plastic people up there.'

'Can't have been all that bad can it?' George enquired.

'No, I'm still a bit raw and bitter over the whole thing to be honest,' she admitted, 'They weren't all bad, but everybody I still knew up there I mostly knew through Pete, that's my ex, and they were incredibly shallow, and, most importantly, his friends. Everybody I used to know up there when we were still young, wild-eyed and principled got to thirty, decided they were having babies, and that they didn't want to have them in London, or rather, couldn't afford to, and left. The only people still up there by the time we split up were the posh set, which I am still embarrassed to say includes my ex, he's old money, terribly wealthy family, you know the kind? So there was not much sympathy for me, sadly, he's that sort of guy, everyone loves him, and as he got to keep Jack they figured I was the bad guy. I just couldn't put up with it any more, so I came back.'

'Fair enough, how come you left Jack with his Dad then?' George was surprised.

'Are you kidding me? He's got money, he's got a support network – since his entire family are up there – Jack wants for absolutely nothing. I can't in all good conscience bring him back here to live with me in a damp rented flat on Nurse's money. I really would be the bad guy then, but I had to come back. It's funny, I left twenty odd years ago when Mum died because I couldn't take the slow pace of it any more, and now I've had to come back for exactly the opposite reason. Once I'm decently settled he'll have a neat place in the countryside to come to for holidays.'

'Countryside?' George indicated the lorries queued up outside the pub windows on their way to the industrial estate up the road, or one of the other four dotted around the town.

'Compared to what he's used to, yes,' Elaine replied, 'unless you count the many country piles his Grandfather owns, but that's all a bit tweedy and P.G. Wodehouse, not quite sure what I was doing being part of that set really.'

'It is surprising, I remember you as the anarchist girl with the Dr Martens boots and pretty strong views as to why the landed gentry should be unseated.' George reminded her.

'Yeah, I know, I think I was trying to fight them from the inside, Pete wasn't like them, or so I thought,' she explained, 'he wanted to change things, shake up the system – like I did. He said he hated all the wealth and privilege he was born into and wanted no part of it, and then it all just got a bit too easy and comfortable for both of us. I think he eventually regretted his rebellious youth, came to terms with being an awful toff, and finally embraced it.'

'Difficult to talk yourself out of comfortable though, even if it is against everything you ever stood for,' George winked at her.

'Exactly, but he gave me the push I needed, I am glad to be out of it and supporting myself again. I think the single life has a lot going for it, especially after tonight, I meant it about the cats earlier, but I would really love it if me and you could be mates again, you know, like we used to be? I'm so sorry I've ignored everybody down here for so long, especially you, we were good for each other back then. And you could do with some back up against those friends of yours.' Elaine said, and it was true, back before she had moved away, her and George had provided each other with valuable insights into the machinations of the opposite sex's mind.

'I have indeed missed having you around Elaine,' George admitted, 'it is good to know one female who has no agenda, no strings, no complications. You may have been the best mate I had back then, and I didn't really know that at the time. Every woman in my life is either trying to sort out my love life, or is a past or potential future part of it, Donna thinks I am the answer to all her single friends' problems, and my daughter is no better, she keeps trying to suggest things I can do to fill my long lonely evenings, and meet somebody nice. Technically it's her fault I got into this whole musical thing.'

'Ah yes, the erstwhile weekend warrior rockstar scene. I look forward to seeing the results, what do you think of calling the band Iron Spatula?'

'I don't think it's much worse than a lot of the suggestions we've had recently, but please can we not start on the band name game? It never ends, and I'm getting a bit sick of it.' George replied, and offered to get another round.

'No, let me, it's the least I can do for running away just as your life got interesting. Did you marry that pregnant girl in the end?' Elaine asked.

'Ah, now there's a story and a half, you get the drinks in and I'll tell you all about it.'

They spent a pleasant evening catching up on what they had both been up to for the last twenty two years. Later on George walked Elaine home without any expectations, it had been a long time since he had walked anybody he wasn't related to home, and even longer since he had done that without the hope of being asked in for coffee that wasn't coffee. They shook hands and parted ways, slightly wobbly from the drinks, but both eminently cheered from the evening's conversation.

CHAPTER 7

There was less than a week to go, nerves were starting to fray and George, Bill and Malcolm were in the pub again. It was Wednesday night, they had just got back from rehearsal, and their first actual gig was on Saturday night at the Blacksmith's Arms. Nobody was convinced that Bill's oft-quoted adage 'piss poor practice precedes perfect performance' was actually true. Even Bill was having trouble believing it at this point.

'I mean, it's not difficult to remember the words to "Louie Louie" and nobody understands them anyway. If he forgets them he should just make them up, or make gibbering noises.' Malcolm said, trying to think of ways to cheer them up after Steve's woeful vocal performance, 'It wouldn't matter so much if it had an interesting riff to run through. But it's just dadada da da, dadada da da, until he remembers his cue. Could you maybe do some bluesy lead stuff over the top Bill? Laid back enough so it won't sound like you've put your solo in the wrong place, but busy enough to keep people interested?'

'Yeah, no worries Malc,' Bill replied, 'we can cover for him there. I can do all kinds of interesting on this new Ibanez Iceman, it might be a keeper. Don't know what we're going to do with the rest of the set though. His timing goes all to crap on "Are You Gonna Be My Girl?" if we don't count in his ear until the drums come back in.'

George was quiet and worried, sipping at his pint, half glad that everyone was focusing on Steve's shortcomings rather than his, and half scared that the whole thing still might fall apart before it had even started. It had been an evening of dropped notes, missed cues, snapping strings and barely held tempers, and they had to go out there and play like rock stars in three days time. If they didn't improve they would be laughed out of the pub and never booked anywhere again.

'I've had an idea, and feel free to shout me down on this, because I like Steve as well he's a top bloke,' Malcolm began, tentatively, 'we could get a second vocalist in, a girl. I know one who's looking for a band, she's really good. She's pretty, she can sing, she'll pull the punters in, and her and Steve can share the vocals, we can get some decent harmonies at last, they can be like Stevie Nicks and Lindsey Buckingham in Fleetwood Mac – hell – we can do proper Mac songs, and Jefferson Airplane, this could be really good for us.'

'Well, I do like the Mac, and I do like Airplane, and having a pretty girl in the band never hurt anybody,' Bill said, spinning a beermat between his fingers and grinning lasciviously, 'and a little competition should make Steve try a little harder to get it right, I'm in.'

'Yeah,' George added, 'at the very least she can prompt him when he forgets the first line, this could work.'

'Well OK then,' Malcolm concluded, 'I'll give Verity a buzz later then, she can come and see us on Saturday. Hopefully she'll like it, we could even get her to come up and sing a couple of numbers if nobody objects.' Everybody nodded agreeably about this plan, and after reassuring each other that it really would be fine, piss poor practice would positively precede perfect performance, they went their separate ways to fret alone.

The night had arrived, it was make or break time, George felt sick as he parked up on the pavement outside the Blacksmith's. He dragged his equipment out of the boot of his Ford Focus, and carried it past a chalkboard proclaiming *The Artful Badgers, Live! Here! Tonight! 9:30 'til Late! Classic and Modern Covers for all Generations!* (They had finally settled on a name combining Malcolm's love of literary affectation with Chris's fondness for woodland animals: Chris had continually bombarded them with names such as Secret Squirrels, Like Rabbits and the not-as-subtle-as-he-thought-it-was Badger Fakir.) which did absolutely nothing for his nerves. He quickly piled all his stuff over in the stage area (a corner of the bar, near the corridor to the toilets which George would later have to keep moving the neck of his bass out of the way of, to let those in need pass) and ran back to his car to move it somewhere legal to park. The space he found, eventually, was nearly as far from the pub as his house was, but in the opposite direction. He looked at his watch: six o'clock, plenty of time, and trudged back.

When he returned, he found an unfamiliar orange van by the doors, with a leather jacketed woman passing drums out on to the pavement. Chris appeared from the doorway, and shook George violently by the hand.

'Exciting isn't it?' he said, 'Can't wait to get playing, by the way, have you met my roadie Bryony?' he indicated the woman unloading.

'Oi! Roadie? You cheeky git,' she smiled, and play slapped at him.

'Okay, she's my girlfriend, but a girlfriend with a van, which is incredibly useful when you play drums and drive a Porsche.' He made a shrugging gesture, and carried on lugging drums inside. Bryony grinned, and pushed yet another flight case up to the doors, she looked a good ten years younger than Chris, with long black wavy hair tied back from her slightly flushed, olive skinned face. George grabbed the flight case and followed Chris inside, shaking his head and wondering why on earth you wouldn't own a vehicle big enough to transport your own gear around. He had assumed Chris had another car somewhere, it wasn't like he couldn't afford one surely?

Inside they found Malcolm and Bill setting up the PA system and gaffa taping leads to the floor. George set up his amplifier, tuned up his bass, and looked about to see if anyone needed a hand. Nobody needed any help from George – his lack of expertise being exceptional – so he went to the bar and got the round in, then watched as Chris got Bryony to do most of the work in setting his drum kit up. Steve then finally wandered in with all the equipment he needed: a folder full of lyrics in case he forgot any words. George was fairly sure he was going to need it before the night was out.

'All right then George? How's your nerves?' Steve began, looking green around the edges, with a noticeable tremor in his hands.

'I'm fine Steve, a few butterflies, but nothing serious,' George lied, those were terrifying pterodactyl sized butterflies if there were only a few. 'Drink to steady them?'

'I won't mate no, not 'til after, strictly lemonade for now.' Steve looked like he might have been better off with a stiff whiskey or two, but would not be persuaded otherwise. 'I'm shitting bricks actually – literally if I'm honest – that's why I'm a bit late, stuck on the bog at home.' He shrugged and grinned at George.

'Sure you'll be ok?' George asked, genuinely concerned that the evening's entertainment would be interrupted as the lead singer ran around the bass player into the toilet, 'you'll not have to disappear mid-set or anything?'

'Yeah, I don't think there's anything left in there to come out now,' Steve clarified, unnecessarily, 'I made it through that jam night in one piece, I'm hoping it gets easier as it goes on.'

In fact, though George had not noticed it, Steve had not exactly covered himself in glory at their previous Palladium performance. It was because of this that the seed of hiring a second vocalist had been planted in Malcolm's head even before the recent terrible rehearsal. Steve had sung a lot of verses in the wrong order, or repeated them twice and it had taken some extra long introductions for him to begin singing the wrong words anyway. George did remember that Steve's face had looked even more terrified than his own, and his banter between songs was non-existent.

'Yeah, you were great, we were great, we will be great,' George reassured him, despite Steve's face being the colour of very badly made custard, 'it'll be fine.'

'Thanks George, I'll get there,' he indicated the folders full of lyrics in front of him, 'I won't need all these cheat sheets soon, they're just a crutch for now, 'til I get the hang of it, oh, shit, excuse me a second,' and he ran off to the toilets.

BOOM! Came the sound of the bass drum through a thousand watts of power, as the sound check began. Malcolm and Bill were shouting across the room at each other, Malcolm twiddling the thousands of knobs on the mixing desk and Bill using some strange sign language that only they understood, pointing at his ear, waggling his left hand up and down while spinning circles with the right and suchlike. George went to his bass, and made sure everything was ready.

What seemed like years later, Malcolm shouted, 'Right George, let's hear some of your bass then!' and George launched into Chic's "Good Times" for levels. Before he had even got through the opening riff, Malcolm stopped him, 'That'll do, cheers, right Bill, get your guitar out.' and Bill picked up his new Cherry Red Gibson SG and began playing through all his effect pedals while George went back to sit at the bar for another age. He was starting to get the picture of how important his role in the band was considered, and as he listened to the endless 'can I have a bit more treble, and some reverb as well please?' requests of Steve and Bill, he was feeling distinctly unprofessional. At least that was until he saw how Malcolm soundchecked his own keyboards. A brief five second noodle on each of his two synths, and then hitting them one after the other to check they were roughly the same level. Quick, and efficient, George allowed himself a smug little grin at the thought that maybe he was more of a pro than he had assumed.

Soundcheck was over and done with by seven-thirty, which left the band with two whole hours to sit and stew. Bill was sitting next to George and grinned widely as he said:

'That's the bit they don't ever tell you about being a musician; it's one percent playing music, and ninety nine percent driving around, setting up and waiting to play. Still, we've got the measure of how long it takes us now, so we should be a bit slicker next time, no need to roll up quite so early – although there are pretty much no venues left that want you sound checking in front of the evening punters, so you're usually still pretty early. And just you wait 'til we start doing weddings and corporate jobs. You can spend all day hanging around at them. It's enough to turn you into a full blown alcoholic some days. Speaking of which, I think it's your round again.' George shrugged, and got the round in.

Steve came back, looking a little less green, and could not be distracted from the football match on the TV above Chris's drum kit, along with most of the other men in the pub.

'We won't be able to play 'til the game's over, so let's hope it doesn't go to penalties mate,' Malcolm said to George, 'I wouldn't want to try anyway, the crowd get pretty nasty if you try and interrupt the football.'

'I've never really understood the attraction myself,' George said, 'I mean when you go and see a band or something, everyone there is going to have a good time, everyone playing enjoys themselves, everyone watching enjoys themselves, it is win–win and everyone leaves happy.'

Everyone was now looking at him as if he had grown horns, Chris said, 'what's your point?'

'Well, at a football game, only half of the people participating are going to go home happy, and about the same percentage of spectators. It's like taking all of your happiness chips to a roulette wheel once a week and sticking them on red, knowing full well that there is an exactly fifty per cent chance that the other people at the table will be getting them – as this roulette wheel has no numbers, it's just red or black. Seems a bit odd to me.'

'Were you any good at sports at school George?' Bill asked, with a smirk starting to crawl across his face.

'No, not really, I was short, a bit tubby, and not terribly well coordinated,' George replied.

'Thought so,' Bill said, mouthing, 'always picked last!' at the rest of the table who all laughed, 'the thing is George, and a lot of you anti-competition types seem to forget this, is that without competition, we'd all still be living in trees and eating bananas, natural selection, survival of the fittest, and all that stuff.'

'Yeah, alright, I suppose so, each to his own and all that,' George shruggingly agreed, while still secretly hating the whole thing, though realising that he probably was bitter from constantly being picked last for teams at school.

Nine-thirty rolled around, and George found himself staring across the top of a microphone at a not-entirely-empty room. He had spent the last half an hour alternating between going to the toilet (and smiling at Steve as they passed in the corridor) and wishing he hadn't steadied his nerves with quite so much lager. The Jurassic butterflies were churning around like they were trying to make alcoholic butter in there now. He peered nervously across the stage at Bill, and received a grin, a raised glass and a nod in return.

'Good evening folks, I think we're about ready to start now, are we ready lads?' Steve's opening speech left a bit to be desired, but it was better than nothing, and since he looked like he was about to be sick over the wedge shaped monitor speakers at the front of the 'stage' – which were all that separated it from being the bit of the pub next to the toilets – everyone was inclined to forgive him. Chris clicked his sticks together and they launched into that opening riff to the Spencer Davis Group's 'Gimme Some Lovin''. At which point the world dropped away, and all George knew for the next forty five minutes was a blur of blistering guitar riffs, shimmering keyboards, stratospheric vocals, bone crunching drums, and his own incredible trouser-flapping bass. It was, to put it mildly, amazing. A huge crowd of people were at the front – the ladies dancing provocatively at him. The sound, to George, was akin to the wall of energy that is the Who's *Live at Leeds* album. As the final crashing chords of Deep Purple's 'Hush' brought the first set to a close, and Steve said 'thanks very much, we'll be back in ten minutes, just having a quick break,'

George was puffed up like a very smug cat who has been given his own very large tub of cream.

He walked tall through his adoring fans to the bar, and got yet another pint of lager bought for him by an exotic siren in a leopard-print dress, who introduced herself as Kaye. George recognised her, she had been at the front for most of the gig so far, singing along and dancing, and just about staying inside that leopard-print dress. He spent the entire half an hour of their ten minute break listening to her tell him how great the band were, and how they were the best band she'd ever seen in here, maybe the best band she'd ever seen anywhere. He spotted Tim, Donna and Elaine across the bar and waved, but didn't manage to get away from Kaye before Bill tapped him on the shoulder and pointed at the stage, it was time to go back on, in truth he hadn't really tried very hard to get away.

The second set was every bit as enthralling to George as the first had been. He had found his raison d'etre, Kaye was in front of him for the whole thing, from 'Summer of Sixty Nine' right through to 'Born to be Wild', she was looking him right in the eye and singing every word, it was all he could do to concentrate on what he was playing rather than staring down the front of her dress.

As he reluctantly took his bass off, George felt cramp running through all of his fingers – making them into claws and leaving him unable to do anything useful for a good ten minutes, after which he discovered blisters on his fingertips that made touching anything impossible without extra pain. This didn't help much as he gingerly packed his things away.

Malcolm announced the good news that as the landlord was a mate of his, they could leave the gear there and pick it up the next day if they left it neatly in the skittle alley. They celebrated the good news with a round of tequilas, and congratulated themselves on their wonderful performance, surrounded by adoring fans. Eventually George left, accompanied by a beautiful lady in leopard print.

At least that was the way George remembered it.

CHAPTER 8

The morning was grey, the curtains were brown and the snoring was loud. George peered through the gloomy window and tried to work out where he was. The street outside was not one he immediately recognised, and last night's beautiful temptress had metamorphosed over night, as if she had unzipped a full skin suit and climbed out of it a different person. Sadly not one that George found remotely attractive, since she resembled the empty and discarded skin suit more than the temptress. He had woken from a very odd dream in which he was lying in a bag of satsumas, with their shiny orange skin rubbing against his face, into a very similar reality. It all came back to him now, she was awful: loud, brash, constantly swearing, never without a cigarette (in fact there was a burned out dog-end in her mouth even now, they were lucky to be alive) barely able to stand up and almost suffocating him by clinging on to him constantly.

As to exactly where he was, which was the immediate problem being directly related to how he was going to get home, he had absolutely no idea. In fact he had no memory of how he got here, or exactly what happened afterwards (which he was grateful for) but prayed his car was in walking distance. He was just going to have to risk it and get out now, hoping that it would become obvious once he got outside, before she woke up. It wasn't that George was a bad man. It was just that he was a coward, as he would be the first to admit. He scrawled a little note explaining that he'd had to get going early to pick up his gear (true) and that he didn't want to wake her as she looked so peaceful (not entirely true) and quietly let himself out, hoping that he had not given her his phone number.

He was lucky, he quickly realised that he was a mere skip and a jump from where he had parked his car. He went back to the

Blacksmith's, and knocked on the window to be let in. Bill and Malcolm were already there having coffee with the landlord.

'Morning,' intoned Malcolm, with a wry grin, 'and how was the fair maiden when you left her?'

Bill started softly singing '*did you ever go to sleep with Bo Derek, and wake up with Bo Diddley,*' from the NOFX song, 'Buggley Eyes'.

'Ah, yeah, well, you know how it is, I left her snoring into her bingo wings and tiptoed away.' George quickly realised he had said too much.

'Christ! You actually stayed all night?' Bill blurted out, 'an actual victim! She'll be very pleased with that. I wish you the best of luck together.'

'How do you mean?' George was a bit worried now.

'Kaye does this to all the bands, she gets right up in everyone's face while they're playing and then harangues them as soon as they come off. She really wants a boyfriend in a band, I tried to warn you last night, but Jesus Christ you were pissed. I mean steaming, you wouldn't have it. You said "we can't just ignore the fans, what sort of arsehole primadonnas would we be if we ignored the fans?" So I left you to it, probably shouldn't have, sorry mate.' Malcolm shrugged and drank his coffee, while George hurriedly took his things out to the car. When he came back they had made him coffee as well. He sat down at their table by the fireplace and tried to change the subject.

'We were great though weren't we? I mean really great, I didn't imagine that did I?' George's eyes were pleading with Malcolm not to disagree.

'I'm afraid you did a bit mate, but we should have been a lot worse,' Bill explained, 'you deserve an award for your services to drunken musicianship, considering how much you'd put away I'm surprised you could even hold the bloody thing. As it was you actually didn't miss any of the important notes, and there were no runaway train wrecks that could be laid at your door.'

'What Bill is trying to say, is well done George, you were ok,' Malcolm interpreted, 'but Steve was all over the place, Chris was trying to take out what's left of my hearing, and going faster than an amphetamine-fuelled intercity 125, and me and him,' he gestured at Bill with his thumb, 'have definitely played better. I would give it a solid rating of acceptably mediocre. But we have promise, and soon we'll have Verity – and pretty girls always beat talent every time. We will get better audiences even if we don't actually get any better.'

George slumped into his bar stool, and felt not a little bit stupid. The night before he had felt like he was living the dream: the band were a huge runaway success with a sound like Led Zeppelin while Jimmy Page was still sober, and he had a gorgeous groupie on his arm. All it would have taken was a private jet full of cocaine to make it any more rock and roll. And now it transpired that he had been dragged under a bridge by a cave troll, and had maybe played an alright gig with a mediocre band that some people had not entirely hated.

The Landlord said they could probably play there again sometime, he'd let them know what dates he had free.

Later that evening, George was sitting in his living room, nursing a large gin and tonic to take the edge off of his Sunday night fever. He was now feeling thoroughly ashamed of himself as, having been to see Linda that afternoon, she had told him a few more things he was not aware of.

'You know I came to see you last night don't you Dad?' she had told him. He had not noticed his own daughter being there. He felt a twinge of guilt as he stood in her doorway angling to get invited in for a cuppa. 'I went with my friend Verity, apparently Malcolm's asked her to join the band.'

'Oh, do you know her then?' George had asked, blissfully unaware of just how annoyed with him she was, 'what's she like? Any good at singing?'

'Yes I know her – she was at the same school as me, and she's pretty good, but that's neither here nor there – as I said, we came to watch you, we saw Tim and Donna there with a very pleasant woman called Elaine, they tried to catch your attention in the break, but you were apparently besotted with some awful skank at the bar. So much so that you didn't even spot me with them. Verity and I had a chat with Malc, she asked me some very difficult questions about you, and I tried to make excuses for you, you know: "it's his first gig"; "he's not normally like this"; "yes he really is my Dad"; stuff like that. Then we left before you finished, mostly to save me having to watch any more of you and that woman carrying on with each other.'

The guilt began to eat away at him, ignorance was no longer bliss.

'Sorry love, I didn't see you,' this at least was true, 'I think I had a few too many before we started – to try and settle the nerves, it wasn't my best idea. I'm truly very sorry, let me make it up to you, I'll make you dinner, come over to mine tonight and we can talk about it.'

'It's still a bit raw Dad, maybe another night, we'll just have a proper fight if I come over tonight, and I don't want to feel any worse than I do.' Linda scowled at him, 'you have no idea how embarrassing it is to go and see your Dad's band with your friend, who is going to join them, and have him completely blank you out because he is trying to cop off with some awful, orange, inflatable woman. Really Dad, it's going to take a bit more than dinner. I'll ring you in the week and let you know how the interview goes tomorrow.'

'Interview?' George looked puzzled.

'So you forgot that as well? So very wrapped up in your own shit today aren't you Dad?' Linda gave him a look – a very definite look – turned around, walked back into her flat, and closed the door on him. 'I'll ring you,' came a voice through the letter box, 'when I've calmed down.'

'I remember!' he shouted back through the letter box, 'I do, you told me you've got an interview for a private therapy practice tomorrow, you told me all about it last week, it's not exactly what you want, but its local, and the money's good. Sorry, hangover has eaten my manners, and my memory, ring me, I am sorry, really, I'll make it up to you.'

And that had been that, he had not managed to get a cup of tea, and he felt even worse. It also occurred to him that this particular bit of twattery could cost the band their new young singer, as her first impression of him would definitely not be a good one. Then he felt even worse that he was worrying about the band when his relationship with Linda was in tatters.

Equally, he was not a bad man, and he knew he was going to have to let Kaye down gently when he told her he didn't want to see her again. Bill had made it apparent that she would expect a relationship, and while George was almost at a stage where he might welcome a relationship, she would not be his first choice. It had been three years since he had split up with Joan, and he had had no significant female contact in all that time, he'd been on awful dates that Donna had set up, and lusted pointlessly after pretty girls clearly way out of his league, but none of it had ever come to anything. Which he had been fine with, at least nobody was getting hurt. And now he was going to have to either hurt somebody, fake his own death and start again somewhere else, or find himself stuck in a relationship that he really, really didn't want. He sighed, poured himself another large gin and was about to bury his face in a pillow when there was a knock on the door, and a shout of, 'Oi, twatypus, open up.'

It was Tim, with a bottle of rather nice Muscadet in his hand. 'Oh Bravo!' he said, spying the bottle of Hendrick's gin that him and Ant had given George for his birthday, 'stick this crap in your fridge, and pour me one of those – and you had better have some cucumber somewhere or somebody is going to get hurt.'

George grinned, took the muscadet, put it in the fridge and got Tim a glass. Thankfully he did have a cucumber, it was not terribly fresh, but since it was getting drowned in gin, he decided that Tim probably wouldn't mind and scraped the mould off. He poured off a very large measure of gin, waved the tonic bottle at it, and dumped in two slices of elderly cucumber and some ice cubes he had discovered hiding at the back of the freezer.

'Will that do you, you posh git?' George said, handing Tim the drink.

'I suppose it will have to, thank you dear boy,' Tim replied, taking a large swig and planting himself deeply into the corner of George's sofa, 'I have decided to deprive Anthony of my delightful company this evening, as you are probably in more need of me.'

'What did you do this time?' George knew Tim too well to imagine for one moment that this visit was entirely philanthropic.

'Me? Nothing,' Tim answered, 'it was entirely his own fault.'

'Not the squirty bottles of mayonnaise again?'

'Nothing so vulgar, he will never buy another one of those travesties,' Tim replied, 'I mean, why? After the first two squirts you have to wait at least ten minutes for anymore of the stuff to come out, you still need a knife to spread it, and you can't get a knife inside the fucking bottle to get it out either. A masterpiece of marketing ensuring that you have to buy more much sooner than you would normally, bastards the lot of them, and have you seen? Squirty bloody Marmite now! A liquid so unliquidy it will never ever get through the nozzles of a squirty bottle, the world is just wrong George, utterly wrong.'

George grinned, no matter how many times he heard Tim rant about something as inconsequential as squirty bottles it would never fail to make him laugh, the last time that he had found one in the fridge he had thrown it at Ant and slept in the spare room for a week.

'So how come you've stormed out this time then?' he asked.

'Still fridge related I'm afraid,' Tim replied, 'sadly I lost our latest round of fridge jenga, covered the floor in jam and discovered my birthday present that Ant had forgotten about.' Fridge jenga was how Tim liked to describe his and Ant's haphazard method of food shopping, whereby they just bought things they saw in the shop in case they didn't have any, and stacked it in the fridge without looking to check if they already had some. It generally resulted in there being multiple open tubs of butter, at least three jars of mango chutney, and several delicately balanced and cling-filmed plates of leftover stuff that would definitely be useful eventually, or, in truth, thrown away when somebody noticed that they had turned green. Sadly this meant that if you wanted to find something from the back you ran the risk of avalanching everything. Which would result in a shout of 'Jenga!' from any other members of the household there to witness it, little Nicky loved it.

'What was your present?' George asked.

'It was a very lovely Stilton,' Tim answered, 'or may well have been on my birthday, four months ago. It was hidden, right at the back, and explains the terrific stench that was assaulting my senses. I was just trying to round up all the ketchup into one place.'

'Still, that was a nice gift, shows that he cares doesn't it, you love Stilton,' George said.

'It would have if he had mentioned it on my birthday rather than hiding it in the back of the fridge and never getting round to telling me about it,' Tim nearly shouted this, 'as it is, I think it shows an aptitude for chemical warfare that I had never before noticed in him. I told him this, he told me to be more careful with the fridge, I told him to stop buying shit and building traps for unwitting fridge explorers, he said it was mostly my shit anyway, I found that unbroken bottle of white that is now resting in your kitchen, said that that most certainly was mine. He said I could have it as it looked pale, thin and posh, just like me, and I told him he was a common little tart and walked out, and so here I am. I am very much looking forward to making up later, but I will just have to wait, or it will not be the same. Quite the performance last night by the way.'

'Thanks Tim, though it has been brought to my attention that I may not have been as brilliant as I thought I was.'

'Oh, I don't mean the band, if you've seen one pub rock covers band you've seen them all, you're not the best, and you're not the worst I've seen, but you're not bad.' Tim backtracked, 'I mean your performance with that old fishwife, please tell me there wasn't a curtain call.'

'Very funny, you are not alone in your amusement, and I am very sorry to say that yes, there was a curtain call. I had to look through them to work out where I had woken up.' George knew Tim would get it out of him eventually, so he just told him what had happened, 'not my finest moment, but just a one off, never to be repeated performance. Feel free to make any more jokes you wish to now.'

'I'm not sure I need to, you appear to be humiliated enough all by yourself,' Tim grinned at him over his glass, 'Linda didn't seem terribly impressed by the way, you may want to go and see her sooner rather than later.'

'Good advice, a bit late, but good advice nonetheless mate, she made it abundantly clear this afternoon that later would be better than sooner sadly,' George shook his head.

'Sorry to hear that, I'm sure you'll get it sorted, she's a sound girl that one, just making you suffer a bit I'll wager,' Tim reassured George, 'on the upside, at least your dry spell is over. Now watch this.' Tim pulled out his phone, and pulled up a video in which you could clearly see George leaning over the monitors and grinning idiotically at a particularly wide lady, with very orange skin and pink hair, tightly wrapped in an indecently small leopard print dress. She reciprocated by wobbling all her wobbly bits (and she had a surprising amount of them) right at him, and touching him at every possible opportunity, while singing along loudly and badly, and pointing at everybody in the room while she 'danced' (for want of a better word), she was the centre of attention, though mostly because people were hoping to see her fall off of her improbably high and thin heels, which she did, several times. The camera panned across at one point revealing Elaine shaking her head grimly at Tim, who was grinning like a madman, and then further to show Linda and an extraordinarily pretty girl, with her arm around her. George felt another pang of guilt for noticing how attractive Linda's friend was before noticing the tear unmistakably rolling down Linda's cheek, he was going to have to come up with something fairly special to fix this one. Linda's friend Verity was incredibly good looking though. George was looking forward to band rehearsals now, as, after Steve's performance, they would have to bring her in.

CHAPTER 9

Tongue in George, tongue in, look straight ahead, try not to stare, try not to look like you are trying not to stare, shit, she said something to you, smile, answer politely, nod – Bollocks! did I say that out loud or just think it?

'Yeah,' he said, and nodded, hoping it was the correct response to whatever she had just said. She looked even better in the flesh, worryingly better. George kept having to remind himself to act like a normal human being, as he stood thumping out the bassline to Fleetwood Mac's 'Don't Stop' while Steve and Verity tried to get the harmonies right. Every thing about her captivated him, the way her androgynous black boiler suit wrinkled as it met her patent leather Dr Martens. The way she closed her eyes when she reached for those difficult high notes, the way she squished her face up every time she forgot a word, or hit the wrong note. As far as he was concerned she couldn't hit a wrong note. In truth however, she really could, but she looked good enough for it not to matter, especially to George.

Verity was twenty three, tall, thin and willowy, with a severe dark-brown bob cut. She was dressed all in black, with a red scarf on her head, making her look for all the world like a 1980s left wing political activist, or a party member from Orwell's *Nineteen Eighty Four*. While George was aware that it was almost certainly a midlife crisis he had looming, he no longer cared, and each time he looked at her, his head swam with elaborate fantasies of her without the boiler suit.

Steve, on the other hand, was looking more than a little put out that they had brought somebody else in to 'fill the sound out,' it didn't take a genius to figure out that this was a hint to either get his act together or get replaced. However, in the tried and tested mode of those who would rather avoid confrontation, he said nothing and got on with it, with a surly attitude towards everything she did. He kept stopping the whole band mid song to work on tiny scraps of harmony with Verity, trying to show up her lack of ability, and instead annoying everybody by dragging the rehearsal out for twice as long as it needed to be.

On the whole though, the experiment was proving to be a success as the new duets were sounding great, Steve was making more of an effort – because he was worried for his place in the band – and everyone was playing better in order to try and look professional in front of the new girl. Especially George.

'So was that alright then?' Verity turned round to Malcolm, as they were packing the gear away.

'Brilliant, just what we needed,' Malcolm replied, 'I knew you'd be able to do rock music if you tried.'

'Yeah, it's not what I normally do, but I like it, some of that Jefferson Airplane stuff you sent me wasn't that far away from the folk scene.' She flicked a stray hair away from her eye, and looked across the room at George as he coiled up his cables. He immediately felt terribly self conscious, trying his hardest not to turn a bright shade of red and staring very hard at the box he was putting leads into. He had always had problems communicating with attractive women, they intimidated him and fascinated him in equal measure, and he was torn between wanting to bow down and worship them and a strong desire to run away and hide. They were easiest to worship from a distance, however stalky that might sound.

'We could always throw in some Fairport Convention,' Bill chimed in, 'they've got some mean bass lines for George to get his head around, and Verity does a passable Sandy Denny impression.' Bill turned to George, as he put his new Epiphone Sheraton in its case, 'that's where we spotted her, down at the folk night in the Tavern on Sundays, torturing a guitar and wailing hey nonny nonny at the old beardy men in their fishermen's jumpers.'

Verity shot Bill a grin, and playfully smacked him on the head, 'Oi, you can't have hated it that much or I wouldn't be here would I?'

'Exactly,' Malcolm countered, 'any suggestions you have for the set will be duly noted, and most likely ignored by Bill and myself, I'm sure Chris, Steve, and George will let you do anything you like, as they don't really know any better. I, on the other hand, will take any requests for the Alannah Myles song "Black Velvet" as a personal insult and you will be asked to leave.'

'Wouldn't dream of it Malc, thanks for asking me in, I shall try and channel my inner Rock chick for you.' and with that she gave a little wave and left. George breathed out and let himself relax again.

Steve had left during the conversation without saying a word to anybody.

Two and a half weeks later, George was having a Monday morning reality check. The new line up of the Artful Badgers had played on both Friday and Saturday night, and had gone down a storm with Verity at the front. Her soaring vocals had carried them along and brought a new lift to the band. She could do between songs banter; she looked confident, strutting around the stage like she owned it, if George hadn't had to keep looking down at his left hand to make sure he was playing the right notes, he wouldn't have been able to take his eyes off of her – the audiences certainly couldn't.

Then he had spent Sunday with Danny and Alice in the park, where they met Linda. She was a little less cold with George now and it seemed that their relationship was on the mend. George had felt he was living the life, stomping across stages to adoring audiences by night and lazing in the sunshine with his adoring family by day. A Monday morning staggering through the rain delivering unwanted junk mail was a real jolt to the senses.

The peaks and troughs of George's life were becoming further and further apart now. The manic highs of playing with the band were utterly euphoric and he couldn't imagine any feeling better than the one he got when everyone was in time, in tune and in the zone. George neither knew nor cared if the audience were just there to gawp at Verity (and it seemed like a lot of the men were there for just that reason). It didn't change the fact that they were packing out venues, making everything feel worthwhile, whatever the reason.

But to drop from that back to the tedium of real life, pulling himself out of bed at half past four in the morning and trudging around town delivering final demands and glossy magazines to all and sundry, including those to whom the phrase 'no bills today please, postie!' is still the height of wit, and the lows can be strikingly low. Especially on mornings when the bag never seems to run out of letters and the clouds appear to be infinitely filled with rain. George occasionally thought it might just have been because he had been doing the job for twenty years now and familiarity had bred contempt, but mostly he just hated having to work for somebody else to make a living: particularly when it wasn't much of a living anymore, once all the bills had been paid.

There was now also the rather pressing matter of needing to go and see a Doctor soon. George was not one to go to the Doctors for every little problem, and tended to wait until there was definitely no way the thing was going to go away before he went. Nobody who knew him would have been surprised if he had tried to shrug off a severed arm, well, half shrug anyway, and claim that it would grow back in the morning. However, this was now the third morning in a row that he had expelled what seemed to be all the blood in the world from his rear end. It is the exact sort of thing that you are not supposed to shrug off and not even George could pretend it was just a stomach bug. Particularly when he had not been eating beetroot, or anything red at all. He was, naturally, a little worried about this.

The other problem was Kaye. Luckily she didn't have his phone number, or his address, but she turned up to every gig she could and managed to corner him at every opportunity. There had been no repeat performance of that first night, but George's mumbled explanations that he wasn't in the right place for a relationship right now – and his attempts to brush her off politely – were failing at every turn. She wouldn't take no for an answer, and kept telling George that she'd wait for him to be ready. He would never be ready, and would have to find a way to put her off for good soon, otherwise he would never get to spend any time with Verity outside rehearsals, not that he could ever manage to think of anything to say around her, the most he managed usually was to nod knowingly, and maybe say yes or no in the right places. If he couldn't shake Kaye off then he would have to give up on the idea of any kind of extra-curricular rock and roll activities with ladies, and that had been the whole reason he had joined a band in the first place.

CHAPTER 10

It was a beautiful Bank Holiday weekend. To the surprise of the entire country, it was sunny and there was absolutely no rain in the forecast. The Artful Badgers had managed to get themselves a Sunday afternoon slot at a local festival, and George was very much looking forward to playing in front of Danny and Alice. Everyone was there: Tim, Ant, Matt, Donna and all their various offspring, and Linda and some earnest, young, beardy, student bloke she had brought with her were keeping half an eye on Danny and Alice, while their Mum and Robin plundered the merchandise stalls.

Festivals were cool, and young and all that was current and hip, and George was aware that just using the words cool and hip at his age was an excellent short cut to not being either. However, Danny and Alice were young enough to be impressed by it, and Linda (and her beardy companion) appeared to be enjoying it as well. It would be good to play on a big outdoor stage to his kids, his friends, his friends' kids, and his kids' friends. It was like being a proper rock star, with ramps to load equipment onto the stage, big lighting rigs, enormous speaker stacks, and a proper sound engineer sitting out front behind a mixing desk the size of a dining room table.

As the soundcheck dragged its merry heels across the afternoon, it became apparent that George might have misjudged the properness of the aforementioned sound engineer. Malcolm and Bill certainly seemed unimpressed as the poor lad continued to twiddle knobs, and slide sliders fruitlessly, all the while telling Malcolm not to stop playing. They smirked at each other and Malcolm was about to offer to swap places with him when he finally gave a thumbs up and a grin, and moved on to Bill's guitar, which was a Gibson 335 today.

Verity grinned back towards George and mouthed, 'College students, got to learn somewhere,' and then went back to smiling and waving at her friends out in the audience before George had had time to think of a witty reply, or even the presence of mind to smile back at her. Of course she was right, George thought, how else could they have put all this on for next to nothing?

The local college had a performing arts course which included the technical aspects of the music industry. So they loaned out their big rigs to local events for very little money on the proviso that the acts had to put up with their students learning on the job. Given that most of the bands weren't being paid either, there was a lot to put up with. But it was good exposure, and a nice day out, and the kids could come, so not all bad.

There were no bad gigs for George, he loved playing in front of people, and that magic feeling he got when they were playing was the best feeling in the world. Malcolm and Bill were less happy about this particular gig, moaning that the guys selling the burgers were getting paid, the people selling tat to all and sundry were cleaning up, why should the guys providing the music be doing it just for the 'exposure?' Chris was coming round to this point of view, and was becoming unwilling to play just for the love of playing. It made George a bit sad that everything had to be commodified and make money, he just wanted to play, and feel like a rock star for a few hours.

So they played, and the sun came out, and the kids gazed adoringly up at him, and he was pretty sure Linda pointed at him and said 'That's my Dad up there!' like she had said she would, and he felt pretty cool for a middle aged guy in Bermuda shorts and a straw fedora. Verity stood at the front, swaying in time to the music in an unnervingly tiny dress, and shaking a tambourine in her left hand. She even managed to make a tambourine look cool. She looked back and smiled at him on at least seven separate occasions, he had counted them, it was becoming a more common occurrence which made him grin like a twelve year old. People sang along to all the songs they knew, some kids in the crowd climbed up to invade the stage and Verity let them sing along to the Katy Perry song, 'Firework'. People loved them, and they loved the people they played for. It was, all in all, a good show, maybe a great one.

The band had been so wrapped up in how well Verity had been working out that they had forgotten about Steve, and nobody had noticed his lack of enthusiasm that day. He dragged himself around the festival site like a sulking child. He had just gone through the motions on stage, not even trying to hide his lyric sheets and missing half his cues. He hadn't indulged in any of his usual pre-gig nervous ticks and none of them had noticed. It wasn't like they were all the oldest and best friends in the world. But they were a band, and had been for a decent length of time, and that brings its own special camaraderie between even the oddest of bedfellows. But they didn't expect what happened next at all. At least George didn't.

'I can't do this with you guys anymore, I just can't,' Steve began, while they loaded gear into Bryony's orange van behind the stage. He had finally broken his silence after Bill had asked him if he was alright, although Bill had only meant it as the usual English pleasantry.

'I know you wanted me out anyway, I knew it as soon as you brought in Verity as a replacement, just to force me out without having to fire me. No, hear me out,' He waved down an attempted apologetic outburst from Bill, 'I'm not that bothered, it's not like we've all been mates for years or anything, but it was a pretty shitty way to deal with it. I'm not the best singer in the world, and neither is she, but she's young and hot, and I'm an old bald guy, I can't possibly compete with that. So I'm out, to be fair, I'm not sure why I was ever in. I like karaoke, it's honest. Not like this, all of you pretending to be rock stars, and playing at these village fêtes that call themselves fucking festivals. I mean there's a lucky dip over there for fuck's sake, and some kids doing an egg and spoon race. An egg and spoon race. Wake up, you are on the back of a borrowed flat bed lorry with a know nothing kid pretending to be a sound engineer, and you are deluding yourselves, I am going back to reality, I can't do this fucked up fantasy anymore, I wish you luck, you underhanded narcissistic twats. Fuck you.' and with that, Steve raised a middle finger in salute and marched off across the park, past the hook-a-duck game.

'Well,' said Bill, 'he's right about the sound engineer anyway.' he took a swig from his can of lager, lit a cigarette, and carried on loading guitars into the van.

Malcolm shrugged similarly and made likewise with the stimulants, 'Easy come, easy go,' he said, 'I'll give him a ring later when he's calmed down, he might change his mind. Not that I really give a shit, but everyone deserves a chance to change their mind.'

'Really? Are we all going to stand here being calm about this?' Chris said, 'I don't usually take being called a cunt that well really, and I know he didn't say cunt, but he meant it, the cunt. Why aren't we all beating the shit out of him? We've been through all this shit, and it's just starting to work and he fucks off like that? Fuck him, we're better without some bastard like that, really. Wanker.' and he stomped off across the park, leaving Bryony to load his drums into the van. Verity was not privy to this conversation, having been out in the crowd being told how great she was, so Malcolm wandered off to find her and let her know what was happening.

George said nothing, just stared morosely into his lager and wanted everyone to be happy again, it had been a really great day until now. He mumbled some platitudes to Bill and Bryony and went in search of some friendly faces. He was starting to feel guilty that he had not noticed Steve's problems, he considered Steve a friend now, and he was worried that his new found obsession with Verity was preventing him from seeing things that were right in front of him. He would make a point of ringing Steve in the week, maybe they could go for a pint together (he never rang, and they never did).

He wandered aimlessly around the site, which was definitely a field next to a church, and browsed aimlessly at a stall selling bric-a-brac before buying a colourful shirt from a couple of ageing tie-dyed people sitting in the back of a ford transit. His eyes had sadly been opened by Steve a bit, this was a village fête, not Glastonbury. Oh well, he thought to himself, it was a good gig, the day is yet young, and the sun is high in the sky, I shall not let it get me down.

However, as he rounded the hog roast, George's eyes briefly locked with those of Kaye who was queueing in the beer tent, looking like she had spent a large part of the day sampling their wares. She waved at him as if to say: wait there, I'll be right over, and started talking urgently to the similarly staggering woman next to her in the queue. George realised he needed to hide, and quickly. He made a swift left turn behind a stall full of cheesecloth shirts and joss sticks. He came out next to a hat stand covered in flying goggles and horned helmets, and spotted Elaine nearby, she had one of those half tent sunshade things that you put children in to stop them burning in the sun. He leaped across the short distance, and after a quick, 'Hi, explain in a minute,' he turned the tent in Kaye's direction, and curled himself up inside it.

'In a bit of trouble George?' Elaine asked, innocently.

'Ha ha, very good, let me know when she's gone past will you?' George hissed through the tent, 'nice to see you by the way, how have you been?'

'I've been fine, thanks for asking, now who am I supposed to be looking out for?' Elaine replied, 'Ah, no I can see now, I take it it's the vision of orange in the Tiger print bikini top over there that you're avoiding?'

'Of course it is, I can hear your grin from down here you know. Is she gone yet?' George asked hopefully, cramp beginning to set in to his knees.

'She is peering around, coming this way, peering over the other way, I am waving at her to come over, and....' Elaine pulled the tent away revealing George to all and sundry. He let out a small terrified squeal, looked up at Elaine with a look of horror, and over her shoulder he saw...

Absolutely nothing, no sign of any highly-sexed ladies in tiger-print bikinis.

'Oh your face!' she cried, 'she squinted over this way a bit, then her friend brought her drink over, and they wandered away towards the crockery smashing stall.'

'Thanks for the shelter, no thanks for the heart attack,' George said, opening a can of lager he had stashed in his pocket for just such an occasion. 'I really can't seem to shake that woman off, I can't believe nobody warned me about her before I...' he tailed off without finishing.

'We tried George, everyone tried, you weren't having any of it, so we left you to it,' Elaine tried to sound sympathetic, but couldn't hide the laughter in her voice, 'Bill tried to tell you, and you wouldn't listen, so he spoke to Tim, who spoke to me, and you wouldn't listen to any of us, so we left you to carry on. Poor Linda, she was so embarrassed in front of her friend, didn't seem to put her off though, she has vastly improved your little band, you were lucky.'

'Yeah, we are lucky to have her, she is brilliant isn't she?' George perked up a bit at the change of topic back to Verity, 'I think we might be onto a good thing now we've got her with us.'

'Yes,' George's sudden enthusiasm at the mention of Verity did not go unnoticed by Elaine, 'I suspect you are. You certainly seem keen at any rate.' She grinned knowingly at him.

'What do you mean?' George blushed, 'it's purely a professional thing, she's not much older than Linda, and nobody like that would be interested in an old git like me anyway – would they?' he gave his intentions away.

'I knew it!' Elaine shrieked, 'you've got a little crush on her haven't you? That's why you're so desperate to keep away from that woman isn't it? You don't want Verity to think you're attached, do you? Oh poor, poor George, how very clichéd of you, a crush on a girl half your age.' she shook her head.

'Well, maybe a bit, ok?' George admitted defeat, 'what do you think? Do you think she might like me? Am I being a stupid old fool thinking I might have a shot with a young thing like her? Malcolm seems to get plenty of young ladies, and he's ten years older than me!' he regretted blurting this out, but suddenly it seemed that his and Elaine's rekindled friendship could be a mine of useful information about girls, just like it had been thirty years ago.

'Your best bet would be to forget all about it, it will not end well, even if it manages to ever begin dear,' Elaine began, with a concerned motherly look, 'however, if you ask me, she looks like she might well be interested in the older gentleman, and you fall wonderfully into the "nice bloke" template, which, if she's been through too many young dangerous types, she will want at some point. So yes, you might be in with a chance – but it's a really bad idea and at least one person will definitely get hurt badly, and that one person will most definitely be you.'

'Excellent news, cheers!' George clinked his lager against Elaine's pina colada in a can.

'You didn't hear a word I said other than "you might be in with a chance" did you?' she sighed.

'Nope, not a thing.'

'Ah, here comes my date.'

George swung his head around to see who it could be, as Linda, Danny and Alice swung into view round the corner.

'My kids are your date?' George asked.

'Yep. Thought I'd make up for twenty years of them not having a cool Aunty Elaine to hang out with,' she grinned, 'if only I were still cool, ah well.'

'That's very cool of you,' George replied, he understood why he had recognised the little tent thing now: it was Joan's and had come along with the kids plenty of times already this summer. Linda's earnest, beardy young man appeared to have vanished somewhere along the way, possibly exasperated by Danny's endless questions. He was currently interested in Jesus, thanks to a religious primary school teacher, which made any man with a beard fair game.

A shout of 'Oh my god it's only the badger bassist! We are not worthy!' announced the imminent arrival of Tim, Ant, Matt, Donna and all the associated kids. George smiled and settled in to try and enjoy the rest of the day.

CHAPTER 11

The posters on the notice board did not fill George with confidence. Large primary-coloured pictures of flowers bearing friendly-fonted messages such as 'Cancer is just a word, not a sentence,' and 'Early Detection saves lives' reminded him that this was not just a routine appointment. His GP had given him a concerned look when he told him about the blood, before sticking his finger up his bum and making concerned humming sounds. He then told him he definitely had haemorrhoids, and that could be all that it was, but he should still go and see a specialist who would look inside his bowel with a special camera in case there was anything more sinister going on. George was not looking forward to this, and hoped it would at least be relatively quick.

He was fairly sure he was the youngest in the room by a fairly wide margin, although he could just have been a terrible judge of age, the doddery old couples with the sad eyes – holding onto each other as if letting go would be a final goodbye – may not have been as old as he thought they were. Plenty of old duffers that he met these days turned out to be younger than him.

He was feeling ashamed of himself again having had his behaviour at the festival spelled out. As usual, he had drunk a great deal more than was good for him, and lost a portion of his memory. After not hearing from Tim, Linda, Elaine or anybody for a week, he had rung Tim to ask if he had done anything awful, and had once again been given a full, frank and graphic description of his behaviour.

While things had gone swimmingly for the afternoon, as the evening had drawn on George had spotted Verity, and being much the worse for drink, had decided to engage her in conversation, and possibly declare his undying love for her. He immediately walked off, without so much as an explanation to his friends and spent the next hour trying (and failing dismally) to chat up Verity, who was surrounded by her own entourage of young men desperately trying to win favour with her. The problem was that he still had no idea how to talk to women, and rather than helping the situation, alcohol tended to make it worse as the gate between brain and mouth was left wide open, so George spouted every little thing that came into his head.

'You're really pretty, you know?' had been one of his many brilliant opening gambits.

'Thanks, I do,' she had replied dismissively, but George was too far gone to recognise dismissiveness when he heard it.

'And talented, you can really sing, I think you're brilliant,' he blundered on, regardless of the sniggers of Verity's younger suitors around him.

'Thanks again, you're very sweet,' she smiled at him, that beautiful smile that eclipsed everything else in the immediate area making George feel like a hormonal teenager. He was drunk enough to think this was getting somewhere, unfortunately.

'You wanna go somewhere else? Me and you? Get to know each other,' and when he eventually recalled the lengthy, meaningful, and utterly cringeworthy pause that he had left here he wanted to die, 'a little better?'

He was then encouraged to leave by the other members of the entourage, luckily his self-preservation instinct was still very strong even when he was utterly sloshed, so he didn't put up a fight, just gave Verity what he thought was a meaningful look as he was escorted a respectful distance away by her self-appointed bodyguards.

Mercifully, Linda had not realised where George had gone, and so hadn't been part of Verity's little group. She was, however, part of the welcoming committee when he came back.

He had returned in full sulk mode, not engaging anybody in meaningful conversation, telling them to either 'shut up' or 'fuck off' depending on the nature of their enquiry. Thankfully, Danny and Alice had been taken home by Joan before George's sudden disappearance, and so weren't witness to their father's drunken moodswings. Linda, unfortunately, had been and was, understandably, very unhappy about it.

All this meant that George would need to repair his relationship with his daughter again, apologise to his friends for behaving like a tosser in front of their children, and, most importantly, try and ensure that his working relationship with Verity was not now irreparably damaged by his stupid libido. George didn't know what he would do without the band, it was becoming the most important and enjoyable thing in his life, and he was pretty sure that if there was a problem then he'd be out before Verity: she was their main selling point. He didn't really want to think about never seeing her again, as, even though he had barely said more than three words to her, he felt there was a connection between them.

As well as this, the band had been offered – on the back of their festival appearance – a fairly lucrative wedding booking. George was very excited at the prospect, as Malcolm had always told them that that was where the money was, and if they could break into that market then they'd be sorted. He had had the call that morning, this was that break, they would indeed be sorted, this would be great for the Artful Badgers. There was just one little problem, it was on Danny's sixth birthday, and it was a very long way away.

Normally this would be a no-brainer for George, his kids came first, always had done, always would do – but this was a big break for the band. And he loved the band, and since it was a Saturday, Danny would be having a huge party, as six year olds do, and almost certainly wouldn't be paying any attention to whether his Dad was there or not.

The reason the gig was such good money (and Malcolm and Bill assured him this was nearly always the case) was that they needed to get there and be set up and sound-checked before the reception began at lunchtime. They would then have to hang around most of the day doing nothing and waiting to play, then there would be another long gap between sets for yet more speeches and the like, and they would inevitably (apparently) be offered another pile of cash to play an extra hour or so of encores. It would be a long day, but they would be fed, plied with drinks and paid a great deal of money. George really wanted to do it, but it would mean only seeing Danny really quickly in the morning before he left. Without Linda to talk to about it George was having trouble making a decision, and he needed to let Malcolm know that evening if he could do it or not.

All of a sudden George's name was called, and he paraded down the corridor of sad, brown, faded-leatherette chairs, cheery posters and downcast faces to see what his fate would be.

Well, that didn't go as expected at all, George thought, as he drove the short distance from his house to Chris's later that day. There had been no cameras in sight, and he knew no more than he had before. He lived a good hour's drive away from the hospital, and the waiting time between seeing the triage nurse and the specialist – plus the ten minutes the two meetings lasted for – had managed to add up to a good two and a half hours. If you added the half an hour of driving around in circles, and trying to find a parking spot, plus the sprint across the car park to not miss the appointment time he had been given, then he'd lost five hours of his life.

Both nurse and Doctor had enjoyed the digital hospitality of George's rectum, and both said that he seemed to have haemorrhoids. Sadly, today was not the day for him to get a camera up there, but the Doctor said they should definitely do that and George would get a letter about how to make another appointment. So he had spent an entire afternoon of his life doing very little, only to be told exactly the same thing his GP had told him two months earlier. He realised that the fact that it was taking so long between appointments was probably a good reason not to worry, as, had it looked serious they would surely be rushing him around as fast as they could. He had seen that before when his Mum had died. Nobody was yet suggesting anything more serious than piles, but then they still wanted to look around up there, maybe there were just too many choices to narrow it down immediately? George decided not to worry about it for now, which meant that there was a little voice in the back of his head constantly singing 'bum cancer bum cancer bum cancer bum cancer bum cancer bum cancer...' and so on and so on.

And just to add to George's worries, tonight was the first band rehearsal since Steve's dramatic departure, and, more worryingly, George's unsuccessful attempt to woo Verity. He was more than a little concerned as to how it might go. The more pressing matter was brought to bear first as George pulled into the drive at almost the exact same moment as Verity did. He got out of his car and looked sheepishly at her as she slid her slim, sandalled foot from the footwell of her ford fiesta.

'Evening, look, about the other week...' he tried to begin, blustering and avoiding eye contact.

'No need to apologise Georgie,' she held up a hand to stop him, 'we'll say no more about it, ever. You were drunk, and I am irresistible,' and here she winked, 'and besides, it was quite flattering. Now lets go in and sort out what to do without Steve.'

George shouldered his bass, locked his car, and walked down Chris's driveway feeling like a man whose noose has snapped at the last moment, rolling under the gallows freed by an act of god.

'At least some good came of all this,' she added as she opened the door to let him through, 'you have finally managed to say more than three words to me, and you very nearly made eye contact back there. Perhaps we can manage an actual conversation sometime? I was starting to think you didn't like me.'

George struggled to think of some erudite and witty comeback to this, but as the seconds dragged past and he remained rooted in the doorway with his mouth open it became obvious that he was beginning to look a bit odd, so he quickly said, 'of course I like you, who wouldn't like you?'

'Well obviously,' Verity replied, and with a knowing wink, she rubbed George's bald head as if for luck, 'you are a sweetie you know.'

He grinned like a cat in a warm cardboard box and went in to set up his bass in the cavernous space of Chris's open plan ground floor. It had pillars dotted here and there to ensure the top floor did not come crashing down, and while the bathroom had walls, for modesty's sake, mostly it was just one huge space with as much glass as could possibly be afforded instead of wall. There were four seperate huge plasma screen TVs all showing the same thing, ensuring you were never out of sight of a screen, or out of earshot of his carefully hidden surround sound speakers. The walls that didn't have screens on them were adorned with formula one art prints and motoring memorabilia. One end of the room held a sparklingly clean kitchen area complete with barstools and an enormous wood and slate island. It did not look like it had had a lot of cooking done in it, but it would have been more than fit for purpose if somebody with a culinary inclination were to live there. By the largest end window Chris had set up his drumkit, a small PA system and some amplifiers. It was a truly lovely place to work in compared to the other rehearsal studios they had used.

'Right boys,' Verity announced as she swept through the door behind George, 'I trust none of you are going to let me down for this Wedding gig. I am very excited about it, a step in the right direction at last, no?'

'Seems like a hell of a long day to me,' Chris piped up, 'I mean the money's good and everything, but not when you count the hours we're putting into it. Surely we could just rock up and play like we normally do?'

'That's not how it works mate,' Bill sighed as he fiddled with the controls on his amplifier, 'you get the extra money because they know you'll act in a professional manner, turn up early, act invisible all day, and when the curtain goes up you play what they want when they want, grin like there's nowhere you'd rather be and play 'til they let you stop. Then you disappear invisibly with no fuss.'

'But we're the talent! That's what they're paying the money for,' Chris exclaimed, 'they should just be glad we accepted the gig and let us tell them how long we can play for and when.'

'Chris, Chris, Chris,' Malcolm chimed in, sitting back comfortably in one of the huge deep leather sofas that lined the room, 'if we were Led Zeppelin I would agree, if we were the Rolling Stones I would agree, but we are not. We are the Artful Badgers, a not too bad little cover band from the middle of nowhere. Even this gig is probably punching a fair bit above our weight, and if it goes right, then we go up a division. If you want to get to play the decent money gigs, you have to do what you're told. And you've been saying for ages that you want to do the weddings and corporate functions and get the big payouts. This is what they are like Chris, I've been doing this a long time, and this is how you make money from music if you're not Paul McCartney. You can like it or you can lump it I'm afraid. Now are you in, or are you with Steve?'

'Fuck off Malc!' Chris scowled, 'I know what you're saying, I just think it should be easier on the band. I'm not going to walk out on you, I'm in, ok, I'm in, but let it be noted that in future I would at least like these things to be closer – so I can go home between soundcheck and showtime.'

'Thank you Chris,' Verity said, turning her head and smiling at Malcolm, 'everyone else ok with it?'

'Of course,' George said, 'no problem at all.' he couldn't let Verity down now that their relationship was coming along so well. Danny would be fine, the gig would be good. Of course Danny would be fine, and Joan would probably be glad to have him out of the way of the Birthday organisation for once.

'Right then, down to business,' Verity stated matter of factly, 'let's see what we can do with this setlist, Bill, how's your voice doing?'

'Well, it could do with a little...' Bill tried to begin, as he tuned his new Rickenbacker 360.

'You'll be fantastic! We shall triumph over adversity, harmonise with me darling, it will be better than ever before.'

CHAPTER 12

It was a Sunday morning, well a gigging musician's Sunday morning, about noon, but George was only just awake – having not got home until three am – while the adrenalin had continued to keep him up until about four-thirty. The half a bottle of whiskey had helped a bit, but whiskey sleep is not as good as real sleep, ask anyone. Last night's gig had not been quite the triumph that Verity had hoped for, the dance floor had been empty for the first half, and then a Madness song had come on to the jukebox just after they had gone off for a break resulting in a dance floor filled with bald, middle-aged men in blue jeans doing that peculiar bent elbows and skipping kind of dancing that they are compelled to do to any Ska song that comes on. Needless to say, they had all sat down again when the band came back on and the Badgers didn't play any Ska songs. Not even 'Daydream Believer' had managed to pull them around, and that normally never failed. Whoever booked the band for that night had made a bad choice.

Just as George woke up his phone rang, and he had answered it, a thing he was now regretting. It had been Joan, asking about his plans for Danny's birthday, they had not gone down well. Joan was not pleased with him at all.

'What do you mean "you've got a gig"? Do you mean to tell me you're going off on a jolly with your mates all day and ignoring your only son's sixth birthday?' she screamed down the phone at him, after he quietly mumbled that he had to go and play at a wedding that day.

'Well, I have got a gig, it's a really important one for the band Joan,' he attempted to impress upon her just how much this one particular concert meant to him.

'Important for the band! You're a bunch of middle-aged fantasists,

not the next Arctic Monkeys, there are no important gigs for you.
There are, however, still important birthdays for your children, and
they should not be missed by their father – however deep his mid-
life crisis has become.' Her voice had taken on that icy cool tone that
George remembered from the less pleasant parts of their marriage.
His attempt had clearly failed.

'I know it's not ideal, but it's only one day, I can see him first
thing and I'll take him out for the whole of the next day. I can make
it up to him, and he'll be playing with his friends the entire time
anyway, he won't have any time for me as it is, he won't even notice
I'm not there, probably.' George argued his case, as much to himself
as to Joan.

'I know that he will be with his friends, and that it will appear as
if he doesn't give a shit who else is there. But you should know as
well as I do that he will be looking around every ten minutes to
check that both his Mum and Dad are there. The same as he will be
checking that Linda and Alice are there, and yes, of course I invited
Linda, she is his sister, even if she is a bloody know-it-all. He wants
her there, she understands it, and most importantly, she is coming.'

'There's nothing I can do love, it's all booked, I can't back out
now, they're counting on me, I'm sorry, it'll be ok, you'll see.' George
attempted once again to placate the angry beast.

'Well, you've always had a great deal of faults George, but I never
thought that selfishness would be one of them,' Joan calmed her
voice, speaking steadily, and trying to control her temper, 'it would
appear that I was wrong, I am sorry also, but not for you, for your
son. We'll see you next weekend anyway, don't forget you've got
them from Friday night, me and Robin are going away.' and she put
the phone down without even waiting for George's reply.

He was beginning to realise that this might not have been one of
his better life decisions. But he wasn't going to change his mind. He
couldn't even remember his own sixth birthday party and whether his
dad had been there or not. This was not going to scar Danny for life,
it was the right decision. Verity was counting on him. This was a
step up, they were going to the big time, not the Arctic Monkeys big
time, obviously, but decent money, a little respect on the local scene,
and hopefully bigger and better gigs. Last night had been in yet
another local toilet, which was exactly what the backstage changing
rooms had been. Chris had moaned about it, much as he was
moaning about everything at the moment: this gig is too small, this

gig is too big, Bill's guitar (a Fender Coronado on this occasion) was too loud, while simultaneously he was unable to hear it properly. George had a bad feeling about Chris.

He decided to start making some serious amends, and rang Linda to meet for lunch. Miraculously she agreed, so he hopped out of the door and went off down the road to the Joiners Arms, who always did a decent Sunday roast. Maybe she would be more understanding.

'You utter pillock Dad.' Linda's tongue was no kinder than Joan's, 'I can't believe you are shrugging Danny's birthday off.'

'I am not "shrugging him off!" by any measure, it's complicated, the band's the only thing I've got outside family at the moment that's keeping me going, and this gig is really big for us, it could be the break we need. I mean I love all you kids dearly, I do, but I've got nothing else in my life except work, kids, and wondering how to fill the hours in between the two. This band has given me a whole new outlook, I look forward to things instead of waiting for them to end so I can go home, people enjoy what we do enough to give us money for it. I'm completely and utterly knackered this morning, but I wouldn't change it for anything. And if it means missing the odd birthday party, then so be it – I never missed a single one of yours, and did you notice? Has it changed anything? You'd still be looking at me like I had just strangled your puppy right now whatever I had done fifteen years ago, right?'

'It's things like you never missing a birthday party that mean I am listening to you instead of hanging up the phone every time you ring.' Linda almost spat the words at him, 'I know you're lonely, and I know the band is important to you, but this isn't like you. You're normally the best dad in the world. I don't suppose I can change your mind can I?'

'Not really, I will still pop round and see him in the morning, hand over his presents and tell him I love him,' George ran over the same arguments again, 'it may be for less than half an hour, and it might have to be before eight o'clock, but it is something. He will be fine.'

'You had better make sure you do, Dad. You've never been good with early mornings, ever, despite your job.'

'Of course I will, you can count on me,' he gave his best winning smile as he leaned back to let the waitress put his dinner in front of him, 'more importantly, will you be alright there with Joan and Robin without me for buffering?'

'Oh I can cope with my former wicked stepmother and her

vacuous new lover just fine thank you. Despite appearances we do get on quite well these days. Well, compared to how it used to be, but I have grown up even if she hasn't,' Linda stuck out her tongue and chuckled, signifying that she was done telling him off, 'How's my future step mum doing anyway, the one with the animal skin wardrobe and the lovely tan?'

'Ha ha, very funny, not for me though, she still comes to every gig we do in town, it's making it a little difficult to bask in the post-gig glory,' George explained, 'I've been spending the breaks hiding in whatever room they've let us have as a changing room, it was a toilet last night – Bill thought I had a stomach bug.'

'I am sorry you can't shake her off Dad, but it really is all your own fault, you need to be a little more choosy about which groupies you go home with,' Linda shook her head, 'if you can call them that, I suppose that is still technically what they are right?'

'Search me love, anyhow, she won't let anyone get past her to talk to me now, so no choice really. That's one of the reasons I need to do this wedding gig, she can't come in to private functions so I might get to talk to some people, she growled at a lad with long hair that was asking me nerdy questions about my amp the other week, just because he looked a bit feminine. It's getting beyond a joke.'

'Well, you have reaped what you have sown,' Linda replied, through a mouthful of roast potatoes and gravy, 'I will urge Malcolm and Verity to book more gigs out of town for you when I next see either of them though. I can't imagine her taking a back seat in the business side of things, she's always been a bossy mare, even at school – head girl you know?'

'I forgot you were at the same school as her, cripes, I am very old aren't I?'

'Yes Dad, you are, and foolish, you should reconsider Danny's birthday, really.'

Hours later, George had paid the bill and said his goodbyes to Linda, who once again sternly warned him to change his mind. He was just finishing off his pint and was about to wander off home when the door opened, and a bedraggled Elaine stomped her way in.

'You'll do, buy me a drink before I kill somebody.' She declared loudly.

'Well, I was going to go home, but if you insist, what are you wanting?' George saw the look in her eyes, and decided that she

should not be left alone in a pub in her current mood, it might turn
out not to have been an idle threat. She declared a need for the
calming effects of Gin, and George obliged. There was tonic, but it
seemed to be more of a table decoration than a mixer.

'So, what's the problem today then Elaine?' George tentatively
asked once they were ensconced in a snug corner table.

'Oh the usual, my ex making my life difficult again,' she flustered,
'he's managed to persuade my son that he doesn't want to come down
and stay here with me over half term. So I've got to drag myself up
to London and find a place to stay if I want to see him at all. And as
you know, I cannot stand most of the people up there that I still
know, that's if they would even offer me so much as a sofa to crash
on. Also, it is raining, I had to get tea bags and milk, my car is not
starting, and I cannot afford to get it fixed until next week. I don't
desperately want to talk about any of it, I would like to get drunk
with an old friend and you are the closest thing here, ok?' she winked
at him and smiled a lop-sided smile.

'Ok, I agree to your plan – will I be enough for you or do I need to
ring around for some help?' George worried that he might have
exhausted his sociability quota for the day on Linda.

'If you are not man enough to cope with an angry drunk woman
on a Sunday afternoon, then you are not the same George I used to
get drunk with on Sunday afternoons.' She snapped, 'However, that
nice Tim always helps to defuse my temper, so by all means ring
him, as I am sure that's what you meant. By the way, if either of you
let me leave this bag here I will personally cut your balls off, I really
do need these tea bags and this milk, ok?'

'Ok then, I will see what he is up to, and I will take no
responsibility for your inability to remember your own shopping,'
George fumbled at his phone and managed to send a text message to
Tim, using their usual code, a picture of a pint glass drawn in
punctuation, thus, _/ with the word Joiners, to indicate where he
was, it saved a great deal of time fiddling with phone screens, and
was always understood. 'But I am more than capable of distracting
you with my own world of problems, would you like to hear some?'

'Oh yes please, how did you know?' Elaine waved her glass at the
barman on his way past, and, amazingly, it was refilled and brought
back. George sighed, gave him a good deal more money than the
drink cost and received no change at all, since that kind of service
deserves a healthy tip. Luckily there was still quite a lot of tonic on

the table from the last round.

'Well, I've got ex trouble myself as well,' George began, 'we've got a gig on Danny's birthday, so I can only pop round for a bit early in the morning before we leave, and I'm going to have to miss his big party. Joan has gone absolutely apeshit at me over it. Linda is no help either, she seems to be on Joan's side for the first time ever. I mean it's no big deal in the grand scheme of things is it?'

'You are a twat George, really,' was all the sympathy Elaine could muster, 'you know it's a total dick move that you are pulling and that that is, in fact, the organ you are thinking with. Your obsession with that girl is leading you to make bad decisions. I know nothing I or anybody else can say will change your mind, and yes, in the long term you are right, Danny will not be scarred for life over this. But in the short term, he will be pretty pissed off with you, and you know it.'

'You already know about this don't you?' George retorted, slightly blindsided by her reaction.

'Yep, ran into Linda in the Co-op, she's run out of teabags as well.' Elaine took a long swig of her drink, 'I was already going to the pub by that point, so it's not like she sent me in to spy on you and try to talk you round. Although she did, and I agreed, so at least we all know where we stand now. By the way, I did not tell her about your obsession with her friend, you're welcome.' she grinned impishly at George.

'Brilliant, everyone's out to get me,' George said, while nodding appreciatively at her for not giving his secrets away, 'I give up, there will be no backup, I have made a very bad decision, I will learn to live with it without changing my mind. The booking is made, the band are happy, well, mostly, if I pull out now I will probably be pretty much kicked out, and I don't want to have to find another band – it was a special kind of hell the first time.'

'Fine, let's not talk about it, I can see you have no inclination to upset the lovely Verity in case she finds you even less attractive than she does already.' Elaine winked at George as she said this. They both sat in silence for a bit and contemplated their drinks, their problems, and the general impossibility of just getting on through your life without upsetting the people you love.

'Did you ever see that TV series *Sliders*?' George began.

'No, what was it about? And would I have liked it?' Elaine countered.

'It was a science fiction show where all the main characters slid from one parallel universe to the next, each one slightly different from our own because of something that happened differently in the past. It is much underrated in my opinion.'

'Where on earth are you going with this George? I never did get all that nerdy sci-fi stuff you guys went on about, and I still don't.'

'Well, the theory goes that for every decision that is made, another universe branches off, and another and another for every slight difference, which creates an infinite number of parallel universes for them to travel in. In the series it was always the big stuff, like JFK not being shot, the Nazis winning the second world war, or dinosaurs not dying out, but if it were true, then there would literally be dozens of episodes in which they visited a world where a squirrel had gone up a different tree one morning and nothing else was different. Or one where Quinn's mum had put on yellow trousers last Wednesday rather than her blue jeans, or a leaf blew in a slightly different direction as it dropped from a tree one morning – but I digress.' George reined in his tangent as he could see Elaine's eyes starting to glaze over.

'Yes, you do,' Elaine added abruptly, 'get to the point. I neither know nor care who Quinn is, or why his or her Mum might wear yellow trousers.'

'I just wonder sometimes if somewhere out there, in a parallel universe, there's a George that is truly happy, and maybe doesn't get lambasted for every little mistake he makes. You know? One who paid attention in school and got qualifications. I left school at sixteen and I have done nothing but crappy jobs since – and do you know why?'

'If I remember rightly it was because all of us who went on to do A levels were, and I quote, "sucky tosspots" and you were better than all of us,' Elaine retorted, 'am I right?'

'Well, yes, that was what I said at the time, sorry, ok?' George waved his arms to emphasise his sorrow, and nearly sent his pint over the edge of the table, 'but I was pretty bright, they asked me to come back and do A levels. I could have done well. Remember that girl, Kelly McReever? She did A levels didn't she? Went on to uni, did really well for herself.'

'Yes, she was in my french A level class, I remember her well, all big hair and enormous boobs – and that frightfully posh accent.' Elaine mimicked the frightfully posh accent.

'Yeah, well she sent me a friend request on Facebook the other day, she runs a vineyard in the south of France and looks even better than she did twenty five years ago, if that's possible.' George continued.

'And now I am completely lost, what is your point?'

'I just like to think that in some other universe somewhere, there is a George who stayed on for the sixth form, who managed to get together with Kelly, and is now living happily in the south of France with his own vineyard, AND Kelly McReever. And yes I know it's stupid, but it makes me feel better if I think there's a me out there that's doing ok.'

'Kelly McReever!' came a voice from behind George's head, 'don't tell me he's doing that *Sliders* spiel again, I'll get the round in, clearly I have arrived not a moment too soon.'

'Tim!' cried Elaine, 'thank god you're here, this guy is completely failing to cheer me up. Speak no word of science fiction to me, and bring me gin.'

'I shall, and lest you have forgotten, it needs mentioning that George here probably only said five words to Kelly for the entire five years we were all at School together,' Tim added, 'unless you count the six years of primary school before that, in which case it might be a whole ten words, but it was ok, because back then girls were icky weren't they George,' George rolled his eyes at this bit, knowing what was coming next, 'they still are really, no offence Elaine.'

'None taken, fetch my gin,' she replied, and Tim wandered off towards the bar.

'George,' Elaine said beseechingly, 'you need to be happier for other people rather than jealous.'

'I'm not jealous, just sad,' He replied.

'I got a friend request on Facebook from Lindsay the other day, you remember Lindsay?' Lindsay had been the big love of Elaine's teenage life. When they had split up, Elaine had been devastated. George nodded in acknowledgement of this, 'well, it turns out that him and Diana, you remember the bitch he left me for?' George nodded again, 'well, they are still together, married, couple of kids, they look really well – and happy – and my immediate reaction was that I wanted them both to die in a plane crash on one of the endless tirade of expensive looking holiday photographs I saw on his wall.'

'Sensible reaction,' George agreed, 'that tosser screwed you up completely, you couldn't manage any kind of relationship for a good year after that, the girly-named bastard.' This was true, though it did mean that a lot of George and Elaine's best times together came from then, as while Lindsay had always accepted George as Elaine's friend, he had never really understood it, which had made for a difficult friendship at times.

'Yes, and I can't believe you are still so childish as to do the girly name joke, you do know you and Tim really messed him up with that right?'

George gave his best innocent look and pretended he didn't know anything about it, however, he and Tim had taken the kind of cruel pleasure that only teenage boys can when they heard about Lindsay's private therapist later on, apparently there were gender confusion issues.

'You do know that taking the piss out of somebody for having a stupid name doesn't actually have anything to do with genuine transgender issues don't you Elaine?'

'However, this is my point George,' Elaine waved away George's argument, 'after a minute or so I realised that I was really pleased for them.'

'Really? I mean, really?' George looked shocked at her, 'after all the heartache he put you through? All that pain and shit?'

'Yes, don't you see?' Elaine said, 'because he was meant to be with her – obviously – their Facebook walls are covered in soppy little messages to each other, which is both vomit-inducingly gross, and brilliant all at once. I didn't go through all that crap from catching them shagging in my mum's bed at my seventeenth birthday party just because he was a dick. It was fate, and I can't fight that, so I am very pleased to see that two people from the bad old days are still together.'

George nodded in grudging agreement, he much preferred to be bitter and resentful of people happier than him from the past, but accepted that he probably shouldn't be.

'The other thing about George's *Sliders* thing,' Tim said, oblivious to all that had been said in his absence as he placed fresh drinks in front of them, 'is that it is shit. He needs 'Time Slides' really.'

'"Time slides"?' Elaine queried, raising an eyebrow.

'Don't ask him to explain,' George sighed, 'we've been having this argument forever.'

'I'm glad you asked Elaine,' Tim said, ignoring George, 'it was an old episode of *Red Dwarf...*'

'More geeky TV shows then?' Elaine mimed banging her head against the table in exasperation.

'Yes, more geeky TV, but better, and with jokes,' Tim explained, brushing her concerns aside, 'in this episode, they found they could jump into old photographs and change the past, which led to all sorts of hilarity as they leaped into their own pasts and made themselves rich beyond their wildest dreams.'

'Ok, so how does that help George?' Elaine asked, regretting it instantly, as it would almost certainly mean that Tim and George would get into a nerdish argument like they always used to.

'Well, since George seems to live his entire life regretting his past decisions,' Tim said, 'he could jump into his old wedding photos and drag himself away, or leap into an old school picture and tell his teenage self not to be such a mopey twat when he grows up.'

'Yes, but you are forgetting something very important here Tim,' George piped up, Tim and Elaine both gave him a quizzical look, 'Teenagers never listen, ever. Even if I could go back and give that short, tubby, nerdy tosser a good kicking and a talking to, he wouldn't listen to me, even though I've lived his life for the last twenty five years. He was a stubborn git, and, and this is the crucial bit Timothy, you were right. Even if I could talk him into staying at school, he still wouldn't be able to talk to Kelly McReever, and he'd end up just as miserable as me, but slightly better educated. That's why it needs to be *Sliders* Tim, because the parallel universe George isn't so bloody awkward around pretty girls.' He folded his arms and stared down at his pint.

'I always quite liked the short, tubby, nerdy tosser really,' Elaine said, 'at least he always meant well, and it's entirely Kelly McReever's loss, I hope all her wine turns to vinegar.'

'Me too, hear hear,' Tim added, 'I'll drink to that.'

George raised his drink to the memory of Kelly McReever, and drank the last of it. The three of them spent the rest of the evening playing the 'what if' game, and Tim said that there was definitely a parallel universe in which George had not been born heterosexual, or so bloody ugly, or whiny, and they were together. He knew this because Ant kept telling him it was this universe, and he would definitely be told this again when he got home.

CHAPTER 13

'Hooray! Look who's finally awake,' Bill shouted from the passenger seat of the big borrowed Transit van, 'thought we might have to prop you up against a post and get Malc to cover the bass with his left hand tonight mate.'

George had woken up in the van, this was not a good thing. It meant that they were definitely on their way to the wedding gig: which meant he probably hadn't been home; which meant he definitely hadn't made it over to Joan's to see Danny; which meant he was in very, very, very deep shit when they got back. He fumbled for his phone and started dialling,

'Good luck with that George,' Verity said from behind him, 'none of us have had a signal for miles, not since we went over the Severn Bridge in fact, sorry.'

He put his face in his hands and silently screamed at himself. It had seemed like such a sensible idea at the time. They had had a gig the night before, so Malcolm had borrowed his mate Gavin's transit van for the whole weekend in order to leave all their gear in it overnight. As it had been a local gig, they had elected to leave the van in the pub car park, walk home, and meet back there in the morning. An excellent plan which couldn't possibly go wrong. George would walk back home, get up bright and early, nip over to Joan's to see Danny, give him his presents, and be back at the Van by eight-thirty in time to leave for the Welsh Wedding. Clearly something had gone wrong, but George's head was too fuzzy to work it out.

'Can anybody tell me how the hell I got into this van today?' he asked, fully prepared to be the butt of everybody's jokes all day long, but needing to know just what had happened in order to get his story straight for the lengthy apologies he was going to have to make later.

'Oh George, it was a night of nights even by your standards,' Malcolm chuckled from the drivers seat, 'as always it began at the bar mate.' He proceeded to tell George of how they had been having a few drinks after the gig while George desperately tried to avoid Kaye. This had led to some unpleasantness as George was seen talking to another girl at the bar. There had been nothing in it at all, she had just been saying that she liked the band and asking when they were next playing nearby. Unfortunately for the girl, Kaye had been drinking quite a lot, and was being even more unjustifiably protective than usual. So shortly afterwards – while the band were loading the gear into the van – Kaye had smashed a bottle over the girl's head.

There had been a great deal of excitement in the pub over this, but, it being the Friday after payday, the police were pretty busy elsewhere in town. The bottled girl was more upset than actually injured, the fight had been dragged apart fairly quickly by the locals, and Kaye was ejected from the premises. She was unwilling to leave the vicinity though and it began to feel a bit like a siege with her standing outside screaming for the girl to come out and face her and banging on the doors. The band had found themselves in an unexpected lock-in, and, as always, George was taking full advantage of the circumstances by pouring alcohol into his body in inadvisable quantities while eschewing any responsibility for the situation.

Eventually, as the night rolled inexorably towards morning, Kaye was persuaded by some friends of hers to leave it, as she (as in the bottled girl) was not worth it, and miraculously she had agreed, and gone home. After an advance search party to ensure that Kaye was not just hiding around a corner, some of the locals who had selflessly agreed to stay in the pub with them had escorted the bottled girl home and the siege party had broken up. Most of the band had then gone home, as in the original plan, though Bill had already planned to stay in the van to guard the equipment and George had elected to help – mostly because he could barely speak, let alone walk.

So when eight-thirty rolled around and Verity, Chris and Malcolm all turned up ready to go, they felt it would be rude to wake George, all squeezed in around him and set off for the gig. Bill was fine, having stayed relatively sober in case his nominal guarding of the equipment had had to become actual guarding.

George then explained to them all the terrible situation he now found himself in with regard to his son's birthday.

'Maybe you should have told us earlier George,' Verity said, with a stern look, 'I'm surprised you agreed to the gig in the first place to be honest, but if you'd told us we could have turned up earlier, woken you up and got you round to see him before we left.'

'Yeah you muppet, why on earth didn't you tell us?' Chris added, with no hint of sympathy, 'It's too late to turn around now.'

Malcolm and Bill agreed wholeheartedly that if he had told them, then they would have helped him – but he hadn't.

At ten-thirty on the dot (the very time they had been told to arrive) they rolled up to the venue, which seemed to be a holiday camp of some variety or another, but, this being October, it was not desperately busy. They enquired at reception as to whereabouts on the camp they needed to go, and followed a spotty youth down a dirt track at walking pace until they got to the entertainment centre. It was locked. The spotty youth apologised, said it was not his department he was just giving them directions, and wandered off promising to send somebody down whose problem it was, though not before pointing them at the restaurant and suggesting they go in there for something to eat while they were waiting. Malcolm and Bill leaned against the van, sighed, and lit cigarettes while George staggered off in search of a toilet to throw up in; Chris swore about how badly organised the whole thing must be and Verity walked around waving her phone in the air trying desperately to get a signal so she could ring her contact and find out what was happening.

George found a good old-fashioned payphone outside the toilet block which he had used to make himself slightly less disgusting (with the help of a vending machine he had found selling toothpaste, toothbrushes, deodorant and all the other things that people who go camping almost always forget). He dialled Joan's number and prepared himself for the attack. Luckily for him it went straight to answer-phone, so he left a wildly apologetic message with a tall tale about his car breaking down and having had no time to get round to see them as a result. He hoped it might work, noting that there was still no mobile phone reception here whatsoever.

They all went to the restaurant, in search of greasy food to kill George's hangover, except for Verity who stayed with the van in case anyone useful turned up. She was adamant that she had been told to be there by ten-thirty and that somebody would meet them and show them where to set up. She looked as if she might eat anybody who suggested otherwise. So they left her there.

They got to the restaurant, explained who they were and why they were there, and failed dismally to get even a slight discount on the incredibly mediocre, yet surprisingly expensive egg and bacon rolls and coffees that they bought. Sitting around a chipped formica table on chairs bolted firmly to the ground, George groaned all the way through his roll and coffee but forced it down while Bill talked at great length as loudly as he could about all the things that he used to do to breakfast buns when he worked in a place like this. George reminded him that he used to be a waiter, and nothing he said could shock him, or indeed make him feel any worse, so they left it at that and enjoyed listening to Chris swearing about 'what a fucking farce' this whole thing was. Malcolm then regaled them with tales of much worse organised functions he had played at, including one where they had had to stick nails in the fusebox to keep the power on; they all prayed that this would not be that bad and ordered more cripplingly expensive coffees.

An hour after they arrived a man in a tracksuit appeared with a bunch of keys, apologised profusely for the 'mix-up' and let them into the venue – reminding them at the same time that they needed to be set up and out of the way by twelve-thirty at the latest as the guests would begin arriving then. Everybody nodded and was polite and understanding about the whole thing– and then he left.

'Arsehole, we've got less than an hour now to get the whole rig set up, sound check it, move all the cases and get ourselves out of the way now,' Chris complained, 'and we've been fucking about here for an hour doing nothing, seriously, this is shit guys, we need more money for this crap.'

'True, this is shit,' Verity said, 'but we don't have time to complain about it now. We'll get the van emptied, you start setting your drums up straight away Chris, we will work around you and all your scaffolding, now, go go go!' and she waved her arms at them.

There was a general grunt of assent, and they went into overdrive, lugging gear from the van, through a narrow corridor with three separate doorways (all with self-closing fire doors, and not a door-stop in sight) into a big hall with a stage at the back. The stage was a great size, but had no steps leading up to it except by a door to the side, which was locked, and the guy with the keys had disappeared again. There was much clicking of knees, grinding of teeth and muttering about bad backs as heavy speakers were lifted up on to the front of the stage, followed by great attempts by people not to show their age or make wheezing noises as they hoisted themselves up afterwards. Verity spent a great deal of the time setting up trying not to laugh at her ageing bandmates.

At twelve-thirty exactly Malcolm announced that the sound was okay, and everything would be fine. They powered down the amps, jumped off the stage (since the man with the keys had still not turned up) and pulled the curtain over it to hide their presence. At that point the man with the keys reappeared, wearing a bow tie and looking a great deal more official, and pulled the shutters up to open the bar. The band immediately wandered over in his direction.

'So what time is our first set then Malc?' Chris enquired.

'If all goes to plan, we will be beginning our entertainment at about half past five, as the first evening guests start to arrive. Seems a bit mad and unlikely to me, but we'll see, might all be fine.' Malcolm explained.

'So that's five hours to kill now then?' Chris muttered morosely.

'Yep, tell you what, I'll get the first round in, particularly if we're on the free drinks,' Malcolm directed this last comment at the formerly be-tracksuited man with the keys, who shook his head, and gratefully took the drinks order before charging them all full price.

The next five hours were mostly spent either sitting in the public bar outside the large function room where the wedding party was taking place, or in the tiny backstage room (which was clearly a storage cupboard) that they had been given for a dressing room, though not all at once, as they would all have had to stand up to fit in and personal spaces would have been very much invaded. It was a fairly warm early Autumn day, so eventually Bill, Chris and George headed outside to have a look about.

'I don't believe it guys,' said Chris, 'look at that, fucking giant Chess, like some kind of movie set. Come on.' and he ran in the direction of the enormous lawn chess set that he had just spotted.

'I am very much up for that,' intoned Bill, and ran after Chris, clearly also glad of the distraction. They were just past the third round of drinks now, and it was not clear to George if a giant chess set would be a good distraction for them at this point. It was not even clear to him if the drinks were helping him to feel better, though he was going to keep trying. He dragged himself along to catch Bill and Chris up, nursing his drink so as not to spill any, and got there in time to witness two grown men trying to ride the big horsies.

'Look George! It's like Harry Potter!' Chris shouted as he slipped off backwards from his whitish knight in filthy mud.

There then followed a chess tournament like no other before it. Mainly because only Bill actually knew all the rules, and Chris was largely making lewd jokes about the bishop, and throwing pawns at George and Bill. George mostly just stood and watched the other two move chess pieces around in a thoroughly bemusing manner, due to the fact he did not know the rules and was still desperately trying to recover from the night before. Also it was not as warm as it looked, and he was feeling the cold and not enjoying the experience at all. After an hour or so nobody had brought them out any more drinks, so they declared Bill the winner, as the only player to have stuck to the rules, and went back into the bar in search of the next round.

'Where did you get that?' Chris's eyes went wide, as he saw the plate of yellow (scotch eggs, pasties, sandwiches, cheese, crisps, all running the spectrum of shades that can be described as yellow, and all standard buffet fare) wedding food in front of Malcolm.

'Buffet's open, and the bride says you can have as much as you like,' Verity explained, between mouthfuls of egg sandwich.

They ran into the reception room, and returned shortly after with plates piled as high as they dared, Bill was particularly proud of his mini scotch egg pyramid, while George felt his cheese straw buttresses were more efficient. As they were all silently munching away, the bride came in to the little corner of the public bar that they had made their home in for the afternoon to speak to them.

'Thanks so much for coming all this way you guys, I really wanted Verity here to sing for us, I've always loved her voice and I was made up when I saw she was in a band that could do a wedding at last,' she said. Bill, George and Chris all turned to look at Verity as one, Malcolm appeared unmoved by the revelation, 'anyhow, I'm really sorry about all the mix-up this morning, we've put a kitty in behind the bar for you now to say thanks, and we'll give you a shout about half an hour before we want you to go on, so you've got time to change and tune up and stuff, is that ok?'

They all nodded their assent, and muttered congratulations and thanks for the drinks and the food, while waiting for her to get out of the way so they could interrogate their vocalist.

'Okay, so we didn't exactly get the gig off the back of that performance at the festival,' Verity explained, 'Please don't freak out,

Shona's my cousin, it's her wedding, and I promised her I could sort out a band. It's still a good gig, and you're still getting paid standard wedding rate, so there's nothing for you guys to complain about. But I am sorry for the deception.'

'I'm not quite sure why you didn't tell us in the first place.' Bill said, 'we'd have been fine with it.'

'Would you though?' Verity replied, 'I mean, I'm trying to come across all professional here with you guys, and the first gig I bring you is my cousin's wedding in Wales. It looks like I'm just angling for favours for my family doesn't it? I'm not even taking my cut of the money today, just so that they can have mates rates.'

'Well that's your look out isn't it?' Chris chimed in, 'long as we get our money – as promised – and nobody takes the piss, I'm ok with it, I said I was in and I'm sticking by it.'

'You do know I'm missing my son's birthday party for this don't you?' George added, 'because it was important for the band, and would raise our profile, and so on and so on, and now it's just so your Uncle doesn't have to fork out for a proper band? I'm sure Danny will be understanding of your family's needs.'

'Oh, I will buy your kid a fucking present if that'll help,' Verity snapped, 'I knew somebody would react like that, that's why I didn't tell you until now. I didn't think it would be you though George.' her eyes started to well up, and George felt guilty for having a go.

'Sorry, it's been a long day already, especially with this hangover, you're right, it is still a good gig, and the money is good, it doesn't matter.' He apologised, he found it difficult to blame Verity for anything and could not hold grudges against her. It may have been that George's crush was impairing his judgement, or it could just have been that George was not the most assertive person in the world.

'You knew all about this didn't you, you sly old git,' Bill whispered to Malcolm, who nodded, 'probably your idea not to let us know as well wasn't it?' he nodded again, Bill grinned and went to get more drinks.

It was quarter to seven when the best man stuck his head round the door saying, 'when are you lot starting then?' resulting in a mad dash to change clothes and get on to the stage. Apparently, while they had decided that the band would be given a half hour reminder, nobody had decided who was going to do the reminding. Verity had been off with her family all afternoon, and Bill, George, Chris and Malcolm had spent the last hour drinking coffee to try and reverse the effects of an afternoon's drinking. Malcolm would continue with this as he would be driving home later. Bill, Chris and George were going to have a couple more while they played to 'keep their spirits up', besides, the drinks kitty was still holding up and somebody had to use it.

They managed to get themselves together enough to fire up the amps at dead on seven o'clock, and with a 'Good evening ladies and gentlemen, we are the Artful Badgers, congratulations to Shona and Alby, one, two, three, four,' from Verity, they launched into the opening chords of the Huey Lewis and the News classic, 'Power of Love'. Then a green light on the ceiling lit up in front of them, followed by an orange one, then a red one, and their power cut out.

'What the fuck Malc?' Verity shouted behind her, in the deafening silence of a disappointed crowd.

'Shit, volume limiter,' Malcolm muttered, 'nobody mentioned that earlier.'

A volume limiter is a very sensible invention, it ensures that all entertainments put on in a venue adhere to a strict volume limit, as proscribed by what level you set the machine to kick in at. Essentially, if you hit too high a volume for too long, the power is cut to your equipment. Eminently sensible, but, if you do happen to have one,and are intending to use it: it is even more sensible to turn it on and let the band know about it before they do all their sound checks. This had not happened here.

The power was duly switched back on and the man with the keys from earlier patiently told them about the limiter to sullen glares and sweary sarcasm. As the first chord from Bill's new Yamaha SG2000 guitar died away the crowd cheered. Unfortunately, the crowd managed to cheer loudly enough to trip the electrics again, which meant that once again they had to restart everything. Verity grinned at the audience, held her finger to her lips and said in a mock stage whisper, 'You're going to have to be very, very quiet, so take your shoes off girls,' to general merriment. There was a hurried fiddle with all the volume levels, a lot of one, one, two... one, two, check-check-checking and then they launched gingerly back into 'Power of Love'.

They limped through the first set, barely daring to play with any kind of vigour in case they excited the audience into shouting loudly enough for the limiter to kick in. Chris barely tickled his drums and Verity sounded more like a nervous child singing her first solo at a school concert, afraid to loose the full ferocity of her vocals. All eyes were on the traffic lights on the ceiling and the second it went from green to amber they all backed right off to make sure the power stayed on. It lacked the togetherness and vigour of their usual performance and the audience were mainly either sitting down chatting or had wandered off somewhere else.

At just after eight o'clock they came to the end of 'Proud Mary' and, after a polite smattering of applause, handed over to the best man, who was doing another speech for the benefit of those guests who had missed him at lunchtime – there were going to be a lot more speeches. The band were keen to avoid them, even Verity was keen to avoid them.

'What the hell man?' Chris shouted, once they were outside of the venue so that Bill and Malcolm could smoke, 'I could barely play at that volume, this is not Jazz for fuck's sake.'

'I did not know that would be there guys, I'm so sorry, I don't know what else to say,' Verity shook her head and waved her arms, 'we'll just get through the next set, take our money and go home. And remember to ask about this sort of thing in advance next time.'

'You weren't to know, that smug twat in the tracksuit should have told us when we came in,' Bill added, 'it's a pain, but we can get through it.' He smiled reassuringly at Verity.

'Honestly, they always set these things up for DJs and karaoke in these places. Nice overly-compressed uniform waves with no peaks, so it sounds good and loud with a lower decibel range,' Malcolm said, to blank looks, 'oh for gods sake, you lot call yourselves musicians? It's all about the dynamics, the peaks and troughs you get with a proper live band register more loudly on machines than on a human ear? No?' He looked at Bill for reassurance, who just shrugged, he continued in his best Tarzan impression, 'DJ sound loud no cut electric – band cut electric at surprisingly low volumes. As evidenced by the shouting of over-excited wedding guests setting it off. But, it only cuts *our* power out though right?' Malcolm continued, almost to himself, 'those plugs at the back of the stage, nowhere else, we all noticed that right? The lights stayed on.' They all nodded in agreement, 'Okay then, I'm just off to – err – check nothings broken – see you all in a bit.' and with that he went back inside. Chris wandered off moaning to himself about how shit it all was and Verity disappeared in the other direction.

'I like tonight's guitar Bill, are you thinking of keeping it?' George asked.

'No, it weighs too much man – hurts my back – I might get another hollow body instead, nice tone though isn't it?' Bill replied.

'Why do you go through so many of them?' George asked, genuinely interested.

'Bad case of GAS I think,' Bill said.

'GAS?' George asked.

'Sorry, Gear Acquisition Syndrome, very common among musicians. Means we are distracted by any and all new shiny instruments that we don't own. I'm surprised you aren't a fellow sufferer, it's very common amongst bassists.'

'Nah, I like my Fender,' George replied, 'it makes the noise I hear on all the records I like, and it feels right. I got scared playing that five string at the Palladium so I'm sticking with my Precision.'

'Fair enough mate, I'm just trying to find the ultimate tone, that one guitar that sounds exactly how I want it to.'

'And what is that sound Bill?' George asked, 'is it Jimmy Page on 'Stairway to Heaven'? Eddie Van Halen on 'Eruption'? Hendrix at Woodstock?'

'If only it were that simple George,' Bill replied, enigmatically, 'I'll let you know when I hear it.'

At ten o'clock they were finally back on for the final set, Verity reintroduced them to the audience, and they launched into Primal Scream's 'Rocks'. As the limiter lights (which could only be seen from on the stage) ramped back up towards the red, Malcolm played a throbbingly loud note which made it peak at red for a good five seconds, looking pointedly at Chris and nodding vigorously while the power stayed decidedly on. He grinned and gestured with his head down to the right, where George could see a power cable trailing out of the stage door to the main function room, Malcolm had bypassed the limiter. They relaxed and the second set was a whole lot better than the first had been.

If there had been any more encores, rounds of drinks for requests, or damp piles of money in pint glasses as bribes, then they would have finally run out of material. As it was, at half past midnight, as Wild

Cherry's 'Play That Funky Music' came to its climax, they were finally allowed to stop playing. It had been equal parts exhausting, exhilarating and exciting. George felt like a real professional at last. The second set had been perfect, nobody missed a note, Verity sang like a bird – strutting around the stage like Mick Jagger delivering off the cuff links and witty banter that would have made Wilde himself smile.

The whole crowd were on their feet and dancing, a far cry from the first set where they had been roundly ignored. Many of the bribes had been from people desperate to come up and sing with them. George was always happy to indulge this, as was Verity. Bill, Malcolm and Chris didn't like it though, and worried about having non-band members on the stage. However, you can't stop your singer from doing what they want to do when you're mid-set, and if the bride wants to sing, then you let her, so they did.

It was four in the morning when George finally fell through his front door, still buzzing. There were thirty seven missed calls on his mobile phone.

CHAPTER 14

This was not a quiet movie, and it seemed to consist entirely of strobe light effects, explosions and bright things moving very quickly. It had seemed like a really good idea to take Danny and Alice to the cinema to make up for missing the entire of Danny's birthday, especially since he hadn't turned up to see them until lunchtime. Joan had been terribly polite about the whole thing, but that was probably because the kids were there. It would not have gone so well had it just been the two of them. It certainly hadn't when she had phoned that morning to tell him to 'get his arse over there,' and that she didn't want to talk about his 'cowardly answerphone excuses'. It was better than a screaming match, but only just.

He had hoped that spending the afternoon in a dark cinema would give him a chance to pull his head back together, but these computer-generated bears, or whatever they were, wouldn't stop singing or being accompanied by what could only be nuclear explosions, or actual stars, given how bright they were. He accepted that relaxing was not an option, slurped at his overpriced coke, grabbed another handful of Danny's popcorn, and went back to reliving last night in his head instead. He had a constantly looping image in his head of Verity swaying in time to the music, the lights playing through her hair like a mini aurora borealis as she looked back at him and smiled that beatific smile.

Danny still hadn't thawed by the time they got back to George's house, even though they had stopped off for McDonalds on the way. He had bought both of them meals which came with toys of the very computer-generated bear things that they had just been watching at the cinema, and George had let them eat in for once. There are few worse places to be with a hangover than in a fast-food restaurant next to a multiplex cinema straight after the matinee showing of a much-hyped new movie. George was punishing himself, he hoped the kids appreciated it, his headache certainly didn't.

Nor did it appreciate the kids singing every song from the movie at the top of their voices all the way home. George cursed the day that the old fleapit cinema five minutes walk from his house had been turned into a nightclub. The walk would have tired the kids out, and helped to clear his head: unlike this car journey. Of course even the nightclub was gone now, it was sheltered housing for the elderly instead, such is progress, thought George as the concepts of sharing and togetherness were expressed in the most syrupy way possible into his ears.

We are better, when we work together, if we are apart then everything goes wrong,

If we are in harmony, we will get there faster, come on now and join our song

Over and over and over and over again, in the excited voices of children under ten. Thank you very much to the guys who wrote that one.

They spent the rest of the afternoon playing virtual tennis on the brand new Nintendo Wii that Danny had just got from his father. It had gone some little way to defrosting their relationship, but even the thank-you hug that George had received seemed to be more from a sense of duty than genuine affection. He was worried he may have seriously harmed his relationship with his son.

'What did you and Paddy get up to yesterday then?' George asked, by way of trying to start a conversation, while Alice had nipped upstairs to find the art set she had left there on their last visit as she needed it for school the next day.

'Didn't invite Paddy, don't like him anymore,' Danny replied, curtly, 'he's a liar.'

'Is he?' George asked, surprised since Danny had been so very taken with Paddy for so long, he had been starting to think they might have ended up like him and Tim, 'what did he lie about?'

'He's just a liar, s'all,' Danny shrugged, 'all that stuff he said he had, and that his Dad had done, all of it made up. Rowan went to his house for tea – it's smaller than yours – and Rowan said he doesn't even have a Dad.'

Poor kid, George thought, lied himself into a corner there, 'Maybe you could cut him a little slack? He might have just lied so you lot would like him? He might be alright really?'

Danny shrugged again, and carried on flicking through the piles of games that had been provided with his birthday present.

'You do know I would have been there all day if I could, don't you?' he said to Danny.

'Course,' Danny replied, shortly.

'My car broke down,' he had repeated the lie so many times now he almost believed it, and had a nagging feeling he needed to book his car into the garage the next day, 'and I had to go to Wales with the band, it was important. I know it wasn't as important as your birthday and I'm sorry. I will try and make sure it never happens again, ok?' Danny nodded vaguely, 'I would have been there if I could have, I love you, you know that don't you?' Danny nodded again, and mumbled something that sounded like it might have been affectionate. George decided it was probably the best he was going to get and went upstairs to give Alice the dress he had bought her so that she didn't feel left out. It had to be done secretly, so that Danny didn't think his birthday was being hijacked, George didn't want to risk making things even worse than they already were.

'He was really upset Daddy, you shouldn't have gone away,' she said, while giving her father a thank-you hug for the dress, 'I was upset too, I don't like it when he is upset. But don't tell him I said that.'

'I won't sweetheart, and I'm sorry for upsetting everyone,' George was starting to think he would spend the rest of his life apologising, 'now come downstairs and we'll have some tea before I take you back to Mum's.'

After they had all gone home, George was laid out on the sofa listening to Van Morrison's *Astral Weeks*, utterly shattered. As he mulled it all over in his head he came to a worrying realisation. If he had to do the weekend all over again, he would do exactly the same thing. He regretted nothing (well maybe drinking quite so much on Friday night and sleeping in the van) he wasn't sorry, he felt a bit guilty that he wasn't sorry but he really liked playing to happy drunk people, and they are never drunker or happier than when at a wedding.

He had spoken to Linda briefly on the phone, she was a little more sympathetic than expected having heard about the bottling incident in the pub on Friday night. She had told him that Robin hadn't been at Danny's birthday party either, but had just gone to the pub to watch the football with his mates, not making it home until much later on. George had the feeling that a lot of Joan's anger at him might have been projected.

He was also pretty sure he had fallen madly in love with Verity, I mean he already knew he fancied the pants off of her, who wouldn't? She was gorgeous to look at, entrancing to watch, enchanting to talk to and hypnotic to be around. But what he had assumed was a depressingly middle-aged crush on a pretty young girl was rapidly becoming a proper obsession: so he decided it must be love. He was realistic enough to accept that it would almost certainly remain completely unrequited – but he was prepared to accept that, and become her acolyte, worshipping her presence without physical contact.

CHAPTER 15

'Well we're going to need them doing and they're going to have to be paid for somehow – what do you suggest instead, Mr lottery-winner?' Verity fairly screamed at Chris. There was a discussion going on about publicity photographs, demo recordings and how to pay for them. Chris was unwilling to use the proceeds of the next big paying gig to pay for band-related things.

'I'm just saying we could take the pictures ourselves, Malc could probably do us an ok recording, and it wouldn't cost us anything,' Chris retorted, unusually calmly, 'I can't see why you're so willing to throw our money about on stuff we don't need.' This was a reference to the new stage lights that had been bought with the proceeds of an earlier gig. They now belonged to everybody, with the proviso that if anybody left, their share would be bought by the remaining members of the band – though none of that was in writing as it was an agreement between friends.

'And then we would be like all the other shitty little nothing bands trying desperately to claw their way into the big paying gigs without putting in the effort.' She folded her arms, tilted her head, and stared Chris down, daring him to challenge her, 'Tell him Malcolm.'

'She is right I'm afraid Chris,' Malcolm sighed, 'if you want to make the big money on the functions circuit then you need shiny glossy photos and a top-notch-sounding demo CD. The best we could come up with from my gear would be a slightly hissy, flat-sounding recording that you could clearly tell was done in a garage. Listen to the stuff on my website if you don't believe me.' Malcolm had a website on which he put his original material. It was a bit like Vangelis, only with either more or less of an edge, depending on your tastes. He was aware that it would never shake the music world, which was why he spent his time playing in bands like the Badgers.

'And no matter how nice your camera is, unless you know what you are doing with it and have proper lights and whatnot, all your promo pictures will look like your Mum took them for you, especially to promoters who see a hundred professional press packages every week.'

'Fine, ok, I guess I'm outvoted again then.' Chris grudgingly agreed.

'And don't forget the new look for you guys,' Verity added, 'black shirts – not T-shirts, proper shirts – black trousers, red ties, and no trainers: proper shoes. We want to at least look like we know what we're doing and this will really make us stand out from the crowd.'

They all mumbled and nodded their agreement, picked up the last of their gear and wandered off to their cars to go home, rehearsal was over.

'Pint George?' Malcolm suggested as they were about to drive off.

'Why not, see you in the New Inn in about ten minutes?' George agreed, after all, tomorrow was his day off and a drink or two might be nice.

Half an hour later the two of them were safely encamped in the corner window seat of the front bar with a pair of pints in front of them.

'Are you ok George?' Malcolm asked, concernedly, 'I mean, you're not used to all this, and when we started the band I didn't want to scare you off by warning you about it.'

'What do you mean Malc?' George looked perplexed, 'all what?'

'All the fucking arguing and craziness that's going on. All musicians are like this and I don't know why. It seems we are predispositioned to lie about everything for absolutely no reason whatsoever and take huge offence at every tiny little thing that comes our way. I don't even understand it when I find myself doing it, so Christ knows how it all comes across to you.'

'Malcolm,' George said with a wry grin, 'it's not just musicians you know. I've got three children, they are exactly the same.'

'I know what you mean mate, I've got a couple somewhere,' he swigged at his pint, sighed deeply and looked down at the table briefly. 'Actually no, I don't know what you mean, the ex won't let me anywhere near them – isn't that a cheery thought? Stay here, I'm going for a fag.' and with that Malcolm disappeared from view, only to reappear at the window gesticulating wildly at George to open it, which he did.

'So, anyway, I'm going to let Verity take charge of all the visual stuff, and not get in her way with that, and hopefully she'll give me free rein on the musical side of things again.' Malcolm quickly changed the subect, billowing smoke back inside the pub to mutters of consternation from the three other people there, 'what do you think?'

'I reckon that should be fine,' George replied, looking around worriedly at the barmaid, who was glaring at them with bad intent.

'Yeah, I mean she's a total control freak, but she can be played I reckon,' Malcolm looked across at the barmaid, and grinned his most winning of smiles, 'they can all be played usually.'

George was not happy at this slight against Verity's character, and was about to say something but bit his tongue in case Malcolm cottoned on to his burgeoning passion for her, instead replying, 'Yeah, course they can,' and taking a long gulp of his drink.

'I mean, take those stupid outfits she wants us all to wear,' he complained, not caring whether George was listening or not, 'I haven't the heart to tell her that every function band I've played with since I was a kid has worn black and red. Or that every single one of them has thought it would make them stand out. Next thing you know she'll be suggesting we take the promo photos all stood up against a brick wall, looking anywhere but into the camera. As if it is the most original idea under the sun,' he snorted.

George was now thoroughly lost, he assumed that Malcolm was feeling threatened by Verity's influence over the band and tried to make him feel better by getting the round in. This meant getting an earful from the barmaid over the clouds of smoke that Malcolm was infusing the pub with.

'Fight the power! Fuck the ban!' Malcolm shouted through the window, 'do you want a cigarette love?' She didn't, and George had to go and close the window, apologise for Malcolm's behaviour and promise that they'd be quiet and sit in the corner nicely for the rest of the evening. A hefty deposit in the tip jar ensured that they were allowed to remain there.

'Do you hate doing this Malcolm?' George asked, once they were settled down again, 'I understand that you wanted to be a proper musician, playing your own songs and stuff. But surely it's okay getting paid to play other people's stuff? I mean you don't even have to have a proper job on top of it like the rest of us do do you?'

'Well, I reckon teaching snotty kids the piano does count as a proper job actually, but yeah,' Malcolm answered, 'it could be a lot worse. I do hate doing these bloody interchangeable cover bands sometimes though, you're right, and any day now I'm going to let my guard down and she'll have us playing "Mustang Sally".'

'Is it really that bad?'

'Yes, it's a fucking terrible song George, nobody should ever play it,' Malcolm joked.

'You know what I mean Malcolm, selling out – playing other people's songs.'

'Ha! I may have sold out but I've not made any money you know, not real money.' Malcolm looked wistfully out of the window and started fiddling with the cigarettes in his inside jacket pocket. 'I'll let you in on a secret George, a few years back I was at my sister's fiftieth birthday party and they had a Duran Duran tribute band in. Now I absolutely detest tribute bands, they stand for all that is wrong and unholy about the music business, and before you ask, yes, I have played in more than a few. However, I did not want to listen, so I was outside smoking most of the night. But then I went in for a piss and I heard them. They were good – really good – and they were playing "Planet Earth", I fucking love that song – I cannot stress enough how it is possibly my favourite song of all time – and I had had quite a lot to drink by then, so I went to the front and I sang along, and I got in the band's face, and I was just like all those twats we get at our gigs who desperately want to sing along to "Hi Ho Silver Lining".'

George looked shocked, 'That does seem a little out of character for you Malc, you're normally a little cooler than that. I would have you down as the guy standing at the back nodding sagely.'

'Yes mate, so would I, in fact I normally am, so far to the back that I am outside, smoking a fag and not listening,' Malcolm laughed enthusiastically, 'but it turns out nobody is immune. When you hear your favourite song, played really loud, on real instruments, and done properly, there is no better fucking feeling in the world, I would rather listen to "Planet Earth" in a shitty pub at full volume, played by those guys – who were proper awesome by the way – than the crap version the real Duran Duran are doing these days. I'd rather do that than have my dick sucked off by a super model while I drink Veuve-Clicquot out of her twin sister's cleavage, that's how great music is when it's right. And that's why I still do this. We have purpose my friend, real purpose. We make people happy: stupid people mostly, but we do make them happy.'

'I do love it Malcolm, when they are all singing along and dancing,' George admitted, 'it's a real rush.'

'And that's why the covers scene is so much nicer than trying to play your own stuff these days man, I mean it all sounds brilliant doesn't it?' Malcolm continued, 'the internet and cheap recording software means that anybody can put out a record, and the choice available to the listener is very near infinite. The trouble is that, without people to sort through the chaff, the average consumer gets very bored and just buys what they hear on the radio, the same as it ever was.' George nodded along, sensing there was more to this rant.

'Back when I first started doing this, I'd knock up a tape, and I'd give copies to some of my mates, maybe optimistically chuck some in the local record shop. People would tell me they liked it, and I would feel sated, I mean they were probably lying, and hadn't even listened to it, but there was no way I could know that. Nowadays though, you stick it up online, paste it all over your social media feeds in the hopes that somebody listens, and, bear in mind, this is a little piece of your soul that you've probably spent months, maybe even years struggling with until it's the best it can possibly be – the pinnacle of your artistic achievement – and you just want to share that with your friends.'

'I get that, I mean I've never done it, but I think I understand what you're getting at,' George said, almost as punctuation.

'Yeah, but then nowadays, while people still lie to you and tell you they listened to it and enjoyed it, you can go and look at the listening stats on your website that show that six people have listened to it this week and all of them skipped it after less than thirty seconds and probably went back to watching fucking kittens jumping out of boxes on youtube instead,' Malcolm sighed, 'anyhow, that's why it's a lot more fun to go and play other people's songs in pubs to drunk people who will love you like you're the fucking Beatles.' He raised his glass at this and grinned maniacally at George.

They spent the next hour or so talking about how and where to record the demo CD – to which George contributed absolutely nothing since he knew nothing about the process – and which songs to put on it – to which George contributed plenty of ideas all of which were shot down by Malcolm as being utterly wrong. When he finally got home George was not really any the wiser as to what was going to happen with the recordings than he was before.

CHAPTER 16

'Honestly guys, it is not in the least bit glamorous,' George began to explain. They were all round at Matt and Donna's for the evening: Elaine now having been fully adopted as the other sad single friend that they have to invite to all occasions. This particular occasion was a bring all the kids for a sleepover, get thoroughly legless, and test drive (well, sleep in) the holiday chalets that Matt had been building in the garden to make a few extra pennies party. This ensured that nobody needed a babysitter and nobody had to drive, or wake up a grumpy child to take it home, a total win-win party idea, hopefully. It had been one of Tim's, so nobody had the time to disagree, and certainly not to suggest that they could do the same thing in his hotel and not even have to clean up after themselves.

'We spent the whole weekend in a freezing cold shed out on a disused airfield. I was not needed for very much of it at all if I'm honest, but as we were all there together with only the one vehicle, there was no escape. And it was an airfield, there was nowhere else in walking distance to go to.' He was trying to explain that spending the previous weekend in a recording studio trying to record a demo CD for the band had not been as glamorous as his friends believed it to be.

Just as he had said, they had all gone a good seventy miles away to a recording studio which was owned by Bob, a mate of Bill's. They had had to borrow Malcolm's friend Gavin's van again, as Bryony had no intention of spending a whole weekend in the middle of nowhere just to drive Chris around and nobody had a car big enough to fit his Drums in. It also worked out slightly cheaper in fuel than it would have otherwise – even with the van hire fee.

'Surely one of you should just buy a bloody van now?' Matt cut in, 'it would make your lives much easier than borrowing one all the time, or all turning up in a fleet of cars with nowhere to park? What sort of twat plays the drums and doesn't have a car big enough to put them in?' George admitted he made a rather good point, but he had neither the funds or the desire for a van, so it was really up to everyone else – none of them could understand Chris and they had stopped trying to.

It had, as previously stated, turned out to be an old hangar in the middle of a disused airfield with limited facilities. Really limited in fact: there was the remains of an outside toilet, with a tap which spat cold water occasionally, that had left Verity mortally afraid of her own bodily functions. Inside, Bob, the owner, had made sure there was a big fridge in the control room filled with beers to aid the creativity of the clients, as well as lightening their pockets, since he was selling them to his clients at four times what they had cost him. There was also a kettle and a surfeit of ashtrays, as this was the business that the smoking ban forgot.

'You could sue over that you know,' Ant cut in, 'it's thoroughly illegal now, you were paying him to be there, and therefore he was obliged to not fill your lungs with cancer.'

'True Ant,' George replied, 'but given that a great deal of that cancer was coming from our keyboard player and guitarist, I don't think I'd really have had a leg to stand on.'

'I'm just trying to help you fund this van you so clearly need, and a nice compensation payout would go some way towards it,' Ant grinned.

They had got there at eight-thirty on the Saturday morning, and then waited an hour and a half in the freezing cold for Bob to turn up. There had been many attempts to ring him, but, as with pretty much every venue they had ever played at outside of town, there was absolutely no mobile reception. When he finally turned up, and they loaded all of their gear in, there was an immediate tea break before they started to set up.

By one o'clock they were pretty happy with the drums, and George, Bill and Malcolm went into the live room to set up their equipment. At quarter past one Bob said that George's bass was fine, and he was ready to go, so he went back into the control room and sat back down. At half past two everything was set up and they were ready to go for a take – so into the live room they marched.

'Sorry,' interjected Tim, 'but you were there for four and a half hours before you actually did anything yourself? And you were happy about that?'

'Well, not exactly happy,' George shrugged, 'but entirely without choice in the matter I think you'll find.'

'And then they spent another hour and a half with the other guys, after you only got ten minutes of their time to get things right?' Tim continued, 'giving you a total of six hours of your day, and I'm not including time spent sat on your arse in a van here, completely wasted.'

'Not entirely wasted,' George refuted, 'I only had three beers – badoom-tish.' George mimed the rimshot.

'Oh very good,' Tim applauded him.

Five long hours of missed notes, forgotten cues, and people being 'not entirely happy with that take, can we do another please Bob?' and they had managed to get the basics of their three songs recorded. At this point George was horrified to find out that all the vocals had just been guides for them while they were playing and they were going to have to record all of those separately as well. So the men returned to the control room, which had become a fog of smoke by this point as Bob was rarely without a roll-up hanging from the corner of his mouth, and listened while Verity overdubbed her vocal parts, take, after take, after take. At nine o'clock she was pretty happy with what she had put down and they all trooped back in to put the backing vocals over the top. At half past ten they sat in the control room and listened back to what they had done. It took eight minutes and thirty six seconds.

'Still, it must have felt pretty good to hear it all back mustn't it?' Ant interjected.

'No, not really, it didn't sound good at all in fact,' George replied, and went on to explain the next painstaking process they had to go through. They had gone back again the next day for the mixdown process. This is where all the individual parts which have been recorded onto their own seperate tracks are blended together, and all the exciting whooshy noises that make it sound like a proper record are stuck on. George had expected it to maybe take an hour or so out of his morning.

However, it had taken two hours of listening to each individual drum to get the sound of the kit balanced before anything else could be done. Then George's bass sound had been the focus of attention. Five minutes later they had begun intertwining the guitar and keyboard tracks, and eventually they managed to blend all the vocals in to make a recognisable and pleasant sounding recording. Then they moved onto the next song.

George had foolishly assumed that they would just leave all the settings as they were and run the other two songs really quickly. He had not counted on Bill's ability to say things like 'can you make that lead solo a little more crunchy?' or Verity's squinty face as she declared herself 'not happy, can you make it float more?' and other vague requests that made no sense at all to George, who felt that his bass parts sounded nice and low and thumpy just as Bob had mixed them, and that everything else was alright anyway. He was pretty sure that every time somebody made a special request to Bob to change something, then by the time he had finished doing what they asked him and it sounded how they wanted, it had gone all the way round the houses to be exactly the same as it had been in the first place. He mentioned this to Bob when they were briefly alone together, and got a knowing wink and an 'I couldn't possibly comment on that mate,' in return.

Eventually, they had done another twelve hour day but had now got a CD with three songs on it to send to prospective punters. Now they just needed to get some photos done so they had the full press pack. Verity was talking about holiday camps and cruise ships as well as the corporate function circuit, and George was happy to do whatever she said.

'Again, stop me if I'm wrong George,' Tim cut in, 'but you spent a whole day listening to the same three songs – which we have already established only last for eight minutes and thirty six seconds in total – over and over again, with incredibly subtle tonal differences in the individual instruments and voices, until you thought it couldn't sound any better?'

'Pretty much mate yeah,' George agreed.

'And now, and I apologise for this,' Tim steepled his fingers and looked down at the table, 'may I point out that you have pretty much got cloth ears when it comes to precise tonal differences. You told me that my gold plated speaker cables were a waste of money, along with my two thousand pound Linn turntable – in fact all my hifi gear, you have unequivocally said was no better sounding than your old transistor radio. I put it to you that you had no idea what was going on for the entire of that day.'

'I had an idea, the different sounds did sound different, I'll admit I wasn't sure what made them better, but everyone else seemed to

know what they wanted, and it did sound much better at the end.'
George flailed his hands in the air as he spoke.

'Thought so, so they probably could have mixed it without you if
you'd had the balls to admit it and just stayed at home.' Tim slammed
his hand on the table as he triumphantly pronounced this. George
nodded sadly and admitted it was true.

'So then George,' Donna sidetracked, playfully, 'when and where
is this photoshoot taking place? And will you be on the cover of
Smash Hits next month?'

'It's next weekend, and I don't know where yet,' George replied,
'and even if I did, I am not sure I'd tell you in case you showed up
and tried to do your stylist impression.' He mimed a hair flick and
grinned at Donna, who responded with an actual hair flick.

'And *Smash Hits* Donna?' Ant interjected, 'I'm pretty sure that
hasn't been around for a very long time, stop living in the eighties
and get with the program, nobody reads print magazines anymore.'

'Well, I for one am now bored shitless of hearing about it,' Tim
declared, 'put the fucking CD on so we can all say how lovely it is,
and maybe then we can talk about something else!'

George obliged, and they all left the dinner table and sat in the
large, empty spacious lounge with its infeasibly uncomfortable
white-leather sofas that looked so very nice. They listened patiently,
singing along with the bits they knew, all the while smiling
encouragingly at George.

'That was pretty good George, well done,' Elaine said.

'Yeah, very nice, pour us another glass of that blue stuff Tim,'
Donna added.

'I liked it, it's pretty good, but I can't see the point of it really,'
Matt said, running a hand across his hair and slamming his pint of
lager on the table, 'I mean if I wanted to hear "Strange Brew", I'd
stick on a Cream album, if I wanted to hear "Sex on Fire", and I
admit that is very unlikely, but if I did, I would put on a Kings of
Leon album, and if I ever want to hear anything by Fleetwood
fucking Mac then you can shoot me squarely between the eyes but
the same point stands, why does this exist?'

'In our defence, and I really do get your point mate,' George
retorted, 'it's not for selling to the general public. It's so that people
who want to book the band for weddings, christenings, bar mitzvahs
and the like can hear what we sound like.'

'Yeah, were you not listening earlier when George went on and on about it for ages, and I fell asleep and stopped listening?' Tim grinned fiendishly, pouring out another glass of 'possibly a Margarita, but I got a little carried away with the curaçao'.

CHAPTER 17

'So how come you owe Malcolm a drink then George?' Bill asked, settling in for the long wait between sound check and show, 'some ridiculous bet I assume?'

'Yeah,' George replied, 'something like that. You know the photos we did last week?'

'Yes mate, a masterwork of moody-looking rock and roll documentation I think you'll find,' Bill grinned.

'Well, Malcolm successfully predicted what they would look like a full month in advance of them being taken, and I, sadly, took him up on the bet.' George explained.

'Ah, and you have never come across the "mean-and-moody-leaning-on-the-wall" photo shoot before now then?' Bill chuckled, 'I forget that you haven't been doing this for long, he definitely saw you coming.'

'Yeah, I suppose so,' George sighed, absent-mindedly. He was unwilling to admit that Malcolm had told him all about the phenomenon of the band brick wall photo shoot.

It is a truth universally acknowledged that for some reason, most bands tend to think that having their photograph taken in front of a brick wall lends them some kind of an edgy image. And even if this is not really the case – there are more band promo shots taken in front of brick walls than not, possibly because of their availability as a back drop, and aesthetic advantage over your mum's living room wall, complete with your old school photos. George had refuted the very idea that Verity would plan such an unoriginal idea for them, even after Malcolm had done a bit of googling and shown George no less than twenty five separate band websites that featured a band in black shirts and red ties standing in front of a brick wall on their front page.

It had been with heavy heart that George had turned up to the Gannet for the photo shoot, only to head out into the beer garden to stand in front of its old, crumbling brick wall. Both George and Malcolm had decided not to intervene with Verity's vision – so as to keep their bet untampered with. The photographer had been Verity's former art teacher from sixth form college (and Linda's, George realised after he had asked after her) and was an older gentleman who spouted forth about his artistic vision, and the juxtaposition of their clean, crisp, black and red outfits against the old crumbling wall, with its webs of ivy and missing bricks. Verity hung on his every word and the rest of the band just went along with it, gawping at his red paisley cravat and British racing green velvet jacket. George had been given a particularly knowing look from Malcolm when the old chap had told them all to look 'anywhere but into the camera'. The bet was well and truly lost, but at least they now had all the promotional material they needed.

This evening's gig was also in the Gannet – since the landlord had let them use his garden for the photoshoot in return for them playing at his wife's birthday do. They had agreed to the deal as the photographer had cost them enough without having to hire a photographic studio for the day as well; also the landlord was throwing in a load of free drinks for the band along with inviting them to enjoy the buffet he had laid on. George had been going there for long enough to know that a night like this would be pretty good for some after hours drinks – so he, at least, didn't mind doing the gig for nothing.

George's luck had turned a little towards the better, losing bets notwithstanding, in that Kaye had managed to latch herself onto the lead guitar player of a local Bon Jovi tribute band (Bovey Jovey, you really have to know the westcountry to appreciate the name) and was now finally leaving him alone. He could, at last, go out in town without looking behind him every two minutes, and relax after gigs and talk to people without fear of them being assaulted by a wailing banshee in leopardskin.

'Still, thirtieth Birthday party eh?' Bill said, changing the subject, 'should be a cracking view from on that stage mate!' Bill was always fondest of the female members of the audience when they were scantily clad and dancing at a lower level than his eyes. Looking was not cheating, he said, and anybody who said otherwise was under strict orders never to speak to Bill's wife. Although since none of the band had ever met Bill's wife, it was suspected that she might be a figment of Bill's imagination. He just said that she didn't like loud music, and left him to do his thing – while she went to her book club, which held no interest for Bill.

'Yeah, cracking view Bill,' George agreed, he was actually rather looking forward to tonight's gig, since it was local, there was a guaranteed audience, and Kaye would be somewhere else, attacking someone else's female acquaintances. Although his eyes would, as always, be fixed on the cracking view at the front of the stage, where Verity stood.

'Any luck finding out why everybody's in such a shitty mood tonight by the way?' Bill enquired.

'Not a clue mate, seems it's only me and you that look forward to a room full of drunk women that don't get out enough,' George replied, 'though I have a feeling that Chris turning up in the passenger seat of his dad's Volvo tonight might have something to do with it. No idea about Verity's sour face, and Malcolm is always like that.'

Bill nodded in agreement, 'I might have a clue about Malcolm actually, you know he was in that almost famous band back in the eighties?'

'Yeah, Guacamole Window, I've got the record,' George said.

'Yeah, that was them, very arty, very clever, on the verge of being huge when the whole baggy scene came along and shafted them. The NME stopped writing about them, the Stone Roses became everybody's darlings, despite being even more arty than Malc's proggy noodlings, then along comes the nineties and Nirvana, and being a bit classical and clever goes entirely out of the window so they quietly disbanded and disappeared without trace. Leaving Malc doing session gigs, and eventually leading to this kind of thing,' Bill waved his hand around to indicate the band and the scene they were part of, 'that's why he's usually grumpy anyway. The thing is, I was googling them the other day, and it turns out they have hit the comeback trail, nostalgia is all the rage and they are going to try and cash in.'

'Well that's great for Malcolm surely?' George cut in.

'It would be if they'd asked him, but the website says that they've got a new keys player. The bio kind of glosses over why, but it seems to suggest that they can't find him.'

'So surely he could just email them, or get in contact some other way then?' George added, 'I mean he'll want to be in on this? He could make some cash, and play his own music again, that's what he always wanted right?'

'Right, only I happen to know that they know exactly where he is, they've never not known, they have his mobile numbers, email addresses, hell, it doesn't take a lot of googling to find his website,' Bill continued, 'but they haven't. They don't want him, I don't know exactly why, but that's more than likely why he has an even more miserable face than usual on this evening.'

'Blimey! I expect he's proper pissed off about that, I wonder what happened?' George exclaimed.

'Search me, but I am going to try and find out, I'll keep you posted,' Bill smiled and sat back in his chair as they settled in for the long wait.

A little later on they took to the stage. It was a show like no other they had ever done before. Chris's anger was all channelled into beating his drums relentlessly in perfect time, whatever was upsetting Verity was all coming out in her voice, Robbie Williams' 'Angels' was a heart wrenching tour de force, their *Grease* Medley had the whole room singing along, *ooh ooh ooh honey*, and every single note of every single song seemed to wrench at the audience's very soul. Verity had them in the palm of her hand, literally at times, as she merely had to wave at a section of crowd and they would sing the backing for Donna Summer's 'Hot Stuff', or whatever they were playing, for her. All of this pushed the band into that mythical, magical place where nothing goes wrong – they missed no notes, no lines were fluffed, nobody had to go around the intro riffs again to find their place; even Bill and Malcolm's reluctant backing vocals sounded good, hell, even George's occasional vocal was passable.

The crowd were on their feet from the beginning, there is nothing like a full dance floor to give a band confidence in what they are doing. And there is nothing like confidence to make anybody perform better, and when everyone feels confident, then the unit sticks together better – and they really stuck together. That night they were a real, untouchable, class act.

During the break George asked Verity what had got her so upset, 'Because it's really working for you! You sound fantastic!'

'Well thanks George,' she replied, still a little breathless, 'I'll try and get dumped more often then shall I?'

'Oh Christ! I'm so sorry, are you ok?' he backtracked, trying to sound concerned, but every little part of him was incredibly happy that she was single now, despite the fact he had never realised that she wasn't single anyway, 'do you have somewhere to stay? Do you need somebody to talk to?'

'I'm fine, Mike was a dick anyway, I don't really know why I was still with him,' she explained, 'I think it was because it was easier than having to split up, and work out who was going to keep the flat, and all the crap that goes with breaking up – which ironically I've got to do now anyway – and he's gone to stay with his parents for the weekend while I get my crap together and leave. So I'm ok for now, thanks.'

'Ok, do you need somebody to hit then? I've had a lot of practise, and enough padding for it not to matter.' George grinned, offering his ample stomach.

'Very funny, I'm more upset with myself than him to be honest, I should have broken up with him ages ago, I could have moved away, done all kinds of wonderful things, and now I'm kind of locked into a load of stuff down here, so I still can't move away, and it's my own fault, and I am not entirely sure what to do about it all – or why I am telling you this.' she broke a smile, slowing her words considerably, 'Though he did also fuck my hairdresser last week, so not entirely my own fault.' she drank off the last of her vodka and lime, and walked off.

'That explains that then,' Bill said, appearing behind George's shoulder with an amused expression on his face, 'seems to be the night for it.'

'What do you mean?' George asked.

'Same thing happened to Chris, I just found out,' Bill explained, 'seems he bought himself a new car last week, and it didn't go down too well with Bryony.'

'What's it got to do with her?'

'Well,' Bill continued, 'he'd always fancied an old Lotus, so he traded in the Porsche and got one. She suggested that maybe he should have bought a bigger car that he could fit his drums in so that she didn't have to drive him to every gig anymore, he felt that he could drive whatever he wanted, and it kind of escalated from there. Looks like you were right about him turning up with his Dad.'

'So they split up over a car?' George said.

'It certainly looks that way, and if there's any more to it then he's not letting on, at least, that's what Malc says – can't get a word out of

Chris myself. Frankly I'm amazed she lasted as long as she did driving him around everywhere like a doormat, any normal girl would have chucked him straight away. I can only assume he has a massive cock.' Bill smiled impishly, 'Come on, time for the second set George, lets go.'

They went back on, Bill launching into the intro riff to 'Lady Marmalade' on his new Gibson Firebird. If anything the second half was even more exciting than the first – clearly the mix of anger and alcohol was exactly what Verity needed for a stellar vocal performance. They all grinned intensely at each other between every song, and every climactic ending was greeted with rapturous applause, and whoops of appreciation. As the final crashing chords of The Who's 'Won't Get Fooled Again' died away, and Verity said the fateful words, 'We've been the Artful Badgers, and you have been awesome, thank you and good night!' an absolute maelstrom of shouts, clapping and stamping of feet assailed their ears, and the words 'More, More, More' echoed around the room. A genuine, heartfelt, and very much wanted encore, rather than the usual half-hearted cries of more, given by an audience who know that the band will come back on at the least provocation anyway. They did four encores in the end, and then decided to leave them still wanting more.

The landlord had agreed to let them leave all the gear there overnight, as long as they left the PA set up so he could play music through it all night. They were happy with the agreement, and after changing out of their stage clothes, and packing away the breakables, they joined the party. Well, except Chris, he had packed his drums away and phoned his Dad for a lift home: slipping out without so much as a goodbye, which seemed fair enough, given the circumstances. George briefly felt bad for Chris, then figured he had probably brought it upon himself, realised he had enough problems of his own to deal with thanks and went off to see how many free drinks he could get.

It turned out he could get quite a lot of free drinks, and, after a few of them, he found himself alone at a corner table with Verity, since Bill and Malcolm had abandoned them for a group of young, giggling women in gravity-defyingly low-cut dresses. George was trying to cheer Verity up by telling her about his own wonderfully failed marriages – it seemed to be working.

'Oh George, how could anybody leave you?' she said, grasping his hand, 'you're so sweet. I don't think you'd fuck anybody's hairdresser.'

'Chance'd be a fine thing,' he joked, 'ever since that awful Kaye woman, I've had all female attention chased, screamed, or bottled away from me, I'd fuck anybody's hairdresser right now, even Malcolm's, and I'm pretty sure his Mum does his.'

Verity threw her head back and shook with laughter, the vodka she had been drinking now coursing through her veins, 'I'm glad she's gone away now though – it means I can talk to you at shows without fear of being glassed.' She smiled, 'And I do like talking to you George, you feel safe – and right now I think I need safe.' She squeezed his hand again, and went to get more free drinks.

George was having the night of his life, the drinks were free, Kaye was nowhere to be seen, they had played the most incredible show, and now he had Verity all to himself. He pinched his hand to check he was awake, accidentally drew blood and decided he was definitely awake. He looked around and couldn't see Bill or Malcolm anywhere, he assumed they had either managed to persuade a couple of the girls they had been talking to to go somewhere else with them, or given up trying and gone home. He didn't really care either way.

Verity returned, and wobbled into her seat, 'Where are the drinks?' George asked.

'Oh fuck, I forgot the drinks,' she said, 'oh well, never mind, I think I have a better idea anyway – come with me,' and she stood up, and beckoned to George to follow her.

She walked through the people on the dance floor, their smoke-silhouetted arms waving eerily in time to that Celine Dion song from *Titanic*. The lights played gently across her face, making her eyes glint and sparkle with magic, the mirror ball threw it's multi-coloured rays to reflect from her shining hair and she appeared as some kind of hallucinogenic vision, looking over her shoulder to check George was still following.

'Where are we going?' George mouthed, getting nothing but a mischievous smile for his trouble. She pushed through the doors of the bottle store that was serving as equipment storage and dressing room for the evening, and pulled George through.

'I meant it when I said I needed safe at the moment George,' she whispered in his ear, 'I think it might be time for us to get to know each other...' and here she left a deliberately long pause between words in echo of his earlier drunken proposition, 'a little better.'

She pulled him towards her and kissed him passionately, he was too surprised to even think about trying to push her off, and by the time it had occurred to him that she was drunk and vulnerable – and that he should at least check she knew what she was doing – she had ripped the buttons from his flies and curled her fingers around the very thing he had always wanted her to curl her fingers around. He managed to break his mouth away from hers for long enough to ask if she was sure, she just pulled back slightly, smiled devilishly at him, and sank down to the floor before he felt her tongue go to work where her fingers had been but a moment before. He decided that definitely counted as a yes, and inadvertently exacted revenge for his lost trouser buttons on her tiny tartan skirt before they did the inevitable on top of George's speaker cabinets, amidst a pile of ripped and discarded clothing.

Later on, George carried her back to her flat and put her into bed, where she passed out, having been copiously sick three times on the way. George was now sure he was dreaming, and, despite having mixed feelings as to whether he had taken advantage of her or not, he had decided to be a gentleman and sleep on the sofa rather than continue to take advantage. He would have gone home, but it would be beyond callous to have left her on her own; finding out that the love of your life choked to death because you were trying to seem chivalrous is not a thing anybody wants. He really hoped that she both remembered what had happened, and didn't regret it in the morning. It seemed a shame to fall asleep, since his dreams could surely not match up to his new reality.

CHAPTER 18

'So you're living with my Dad now then,' Linda stated matter-of-factly as she stared amusedly over the top of her cup of tea. It was a week later now, and Linda had come round to find out what was going on with George's new living arrangements. They were all sitting in his living room drinking tea while *The Antiques Roadshow* chattered away to itself on the television in the background.

'Well, when you put it like that it sounds a little odd, but yes, I suppose I am,' Verity replied, turning a little red round the edges if you looked carefully.

'It's only while she finds somewhere else love,' George added, 'she's staying in your room while she gets herself together again. Mike was having no arguments – it's his flat, he's keeping it.'

'Thanks George, I can speak for myself you know,' Verity cut in, 'I know it seems a bit odd Lin, me staying with your Dad, but he was kind enough to offer – and I need all the help I can get at the moment.'

'Well,' Linda chuckled, 'I'd make sure the bathroom door's locked if I was you, Mum always reckons that Dad's quite the old perv after he's had a drink or two, but he's mostly a decent bloke if you don't let him cook.'

Verity and George shared an awkward look, 'Thanks Lin, make sure the poor kid feels safe why don't you?' George said.

'Look, Verity, my room mate is moving out in a few weeks and I need somebody to help pay the rent. Maybe you could move in with me?' Linda put on her best businesslike face, 'seriously, I need a room-mate, you need a room, we should do this.'

'Sounds like a plan,' Verity replied, 'if my money problems ever manage to sort themselves out, the whole reason I'm here is because I can't afford rent anywhere at the moment – and your Dad can't say no to a damsel in distress.' She gave George a knowing wink, which Linda missed, thankfully.

'Excellent, I will hold off advertising for a replacement then.' Linda took another biscuit and dunked it in her tea victoriously.

Later that night, George was sitting at the bar of the Custom House talking to Elaine. It had been a very odd week, he needed to talk to somebody about it and Elaine was currently the only one of his friends he trusted enough not to go blabbing all of his secrets. Also, she had rung him and asked if he wanted a drink, and George had never before knowingly refused an offer of a drink.

'So nobody knows?' She furrowed her eyebrows in disapproval.

'No, we are keeping the whole thing secret for now.'

'Even though she is living with you already?'

'Yes – although that's more to do with convenience than anything else,' George explained, 'she really doesn't have anywhere else to go at the moment. I'd have offered her the room even if we weren't sleeping together.'

'Only because you would have wanted to be sleeping with her,' Elaine snapped, 'would you have done the same for your drummer? Would you do the same for Malcolm? Would you do the same for that leery bloke on the guitar?'

'Of course I would,' George lied, there was no way he would want Chris living in his house, or Malcolm really, but that was more to do with his special aroma than his personality. Bill he might have been able to put up with for a while, although given recent events, he would probably say no to him, even if he was desperate, 'I would offer that room to anybody in need if they asked me.'

'And did she ask you?'

'Well, no, I offered, once it became apparent that she wasn't going to be able to fund a new place, and that her old place was clearly Mike's,' George spluttered, 'He owned it outright – I'm not sure what made her think there might even have been a question of her staying there. Bit odd really, but I suppose she is a creative type, and not so clued up on stuff like property law.'

'Yeah right, I would watch your wallet George,' Elaine warned, 'I mean, I am glad you're happy and everything, but she might not be everything you wanted. It all seems a little convenient to me,' George shot her a look like fire, 'I am just looking at all the angles for you George!' she defended herself, 'she could be totally into you, and this could all be fate. I am your friend, I am just looking out for you. Especially since nobody else knows about it – so nobody else can look out for you.'

'Okay, sorry, thank you, you are a good friend, I can take care of myself though,' George waved at the barman to get another round of drinks in, 'it would be nice if I could tell people though.'

'So why is it all such a secret?' Elaine tried to hide her scepticism, she clearly felt that secrecy was another bad omen for the relationship, 'if that's not also a secret, that is.'

'Oh, very good,' George complimented her little dig, 'no – no secret to that, it is to prevent tension in the band. Verity's been in bands with couples before, and she says it inevitably leads to all kinds of problems if they weren't a couple before the band started. And hey, even if they were it's not always good news – look at Fleetwood Mac.'

'You are not Fleetwood Mac George, and anyway, all the trouble led to *Rumours*, and everybody loves that album,' Elaine joked.

'Yes, but after that it led to *Tusk* and *Tango in the Night*, so it's a fine line really isn't it?' George retorted, 'We've got enough trouble anyway at the moment without this adding to it.'

'Why, what else has happened in your wondrous rock 'n' roll dream?' Elaine raised one eyebrow and failed to hide her amusement at George's attempt to change the subject. She also diplomatically avoided letting him turn this into an argument about her taste in music. She liked *Tango in the Night* very much, as George well knew.

'Bill quit, just like that – no warning, no notice – he just sent Malcolm a text message at five o'clock on Friday night,' George sounded exasperated at the weight of all his problems, 'said he wasn't coming to do the gig. Luckily Malcolm's mate Gavin was available, so we paid him his huge dep fee...'

'Dep fee?' Elaine quizzed.

'Sorry, yeah a dep is what we call a guy who stands in for a band member that can't make it for whatever reason, deputy if you like. They are usually booked weeks in advance, and all neatly organised for a cut of the regular fee. Sadly, due to the lateness of the request – and just how desperate we were – we paid him pretty much everything we were making that night.'

'Tough break, so more auditions then I suppose?' Elaine asked.

'Yeah, I suppose so,' George fiddled with a beer mat nervously as he spoke, 'be nice to see just how many more nutters can crawl out of the woodwork. Shame though, cos me and Bill were really starting to gel as a unit, I mean the other night, the night everything happened – we were great, we were such a good band, and Gavin – I mean he's good, all the right bits are mostly in all the right places – but he doesn't have the same attention to detail as Bill, it's just close enough to make almost no difference, but it does to me – you know what I mean?'

'No, I don't really, and I think you might be focusing in all the wrong places George, I wouldn't worry so much about the band, I would worry about your daughter,' Elaine pointed at him with her drink, 'Linda has never liked it when you lie to her, and this one is a pretty big one. She and Verity are friends for god's sake, it would not occur to her that you would be romantically involved. This relationship will end badly for you in at least that one respect.'

'I know,' George sighed, 'and it's the worst thing about it. I hate lying to Linda, but there's no way she wouldn't say anything to Verity if I told her. And Verity was very explicit that she did not want to tell Linda yet – I have to respect that. I know it's going to be difficult when it does all come out, but I am hoping it might be worth all the trouble.'

'Well, I for one hope it is George, I really do,' Elaine clinked her glass against his and took a drink, 'you deserve a little happiness, and I hope this is what you want – and what she wants – and that it all works out for you, here's to fairytale endings, bagsy I get the next pretty young thing that comes along.'

It was true, George thought to himself later on as he walked home. Things were a bit odd, he and Verity hadn't actually had 'the talk' after what had happened. The next morning he had checked she was still alive, made her a cup of tea and respectfully gone home (holding his trousers closed with one hand as discreetly as possible all the way due to the lack of buttons) without pressing any issues – like a proper gentleman. She already had his number, so there was no awkward leaving of hopeful telephone-numbered notes anywhere. Even so, that very evening he had got a call from her asking if he had meant it when he had asked her if she wanted a place to stay.

Obviously he had, and said so, and she had turned up half an hour later on his doorstep with a couple of bags and a battered acoustic guitar. He had fed her and listened to her complain about Mike's incredible selfishness in not letting her have his flat, how she was having trouble selling any songs, pictures or poems at the moment (she was a freelance artist, poet and songwriter for a living, apparently) and how she really appreciated him letting her stay with him for nothing. Eventually she had talked so much that George opened one of his good bottles of wine (the ones that cost slightly over a fiver, rather than slightly under) and another, then another, and they had ended up in his bed together without once having spoken about their earlier encounter.

He had now assumed that they were an item, although the only discussion that they had had on the subject was the one in which she had told him that under no circumstances was he allowed to tell the band, his friends, or his family about her. Ostensibly it was to protect her from accusations of gold-digging and to ensure the smooth running of the band, which all made sense to George. Once she had found another place to live the situation would look a lot less suspicious, and they would be able to come clean. Though George was not so sure that Verity and Linda would have such a nice time living together if this came out, and he was going to have to try and talk Verity out of it.

When he got home he found Verity sitting on his sofa, in his blue-striped pyjamas, picking at a posh box of chocolates he had been given for his birthday.

'I bought this CD today in Oxfam,' she almost shouted, waving her arm excitedly, 'it's amazing! You have to hear it!'

She was listening to *Faith,* by George Michael, as if it had only just been released. George grinned at her and walked over to the stack of old vinyl records he had on a shelf by the stereo. He pulled out a very old, well-played copy of *Faith* and waved it at her.

'Do you know, I bought this the week it came out for a girl who dumped me before I had a chance to give it to her – so I've heard it plenty of times already,' he said, barely hiding his amusement.

'We should do some of this stuff in the band,' she said, oblivious to George laughing at her, 'do you think the audience will know it?'

'I forget how young you are,' George chuckled, 'yeah they'll know it, good idea.'

'I got some other stuff too,' she added, 'have you heard of a band called the Happy Mondays?'

'Yes, I have,' he said, shuffling through his records again and waving his *Madchester Rave On* EP at her.

'Do you want one of these then?' she asked, proffering the chocolates at him, with a pouty face in mock hurt at his condescending attitude to her new musical discoveries.

'Yes I do,' he replied, took one, turned off the stereo and cuddled up next to her on the sofa to watch the late movie. It was *The Breakfast Club*, and George was amazed to find that Verity had not heard of that either, let alone seen it. It was years since he had met a woman who hadn't told him how much she loved it before making him watch it over and over again, so the irony of watching it voluntarily was not lost on him.

Yeah, we're a couple, he thought as they snuggled in together, there's no way we're not a couple now. And when they went to bed together later, he was even more sure of that. Things were definitely looking up.

CHAPTER 19

'It's not so bad mate, Gav says he'll take any gigs we can throw his way until we find a permanent replacement. And he'll do it for whatever cut Bill would have got anyway.' Malcolm reassured George as they waited for the barstaff to let them load their gear into tonight's venue, The Terminus, a popular gastropub. They would be playing in the restaurant area, and had to wait for a large group to finish their meal before they could move the tables out of the way to set up. They had been waiting for a while now, and there was no other space inside to pile things up, so everything was still outside in the cars.

'And how many people are we auditioning tomorrow?' George wanted to know how long a day it would be, as he rather wanted to spend his weekends alone with Verity now, rather than with the entire band.

'Three lined up so far, all answered the ad in the guitar shop in town, no response from the online ads yet – but I only put them up this morning, so we'll see. Tomorrow shouldn't take longer than a couple of hours mate.' Malcolm sounded confident, so George assumed it would all be in hand and things would be back to normal soon.

It had transpired that Bill's departure had not been entirely his own fault, from a certain perspective. Unfortunately, his wife had found some terribly skimpy underwear in one of Bill's jacket pockets, put two and two together, and worked out that he had been getting a bit more out of gig nights than he let on. Admittedly, it was true – he had been enjoying the extra female attention and partaking in readily offered pleasures from ladies of questionable virtue. He hadn't reckoned on one of them leaving a souvenir in his pocket though. She had given him the ultimatum, her or the band, and he had had to say that he would give them his notice and leave at the earliest opportunity. He may have enjoyed his extra-curricular activities, but he loved his wife.

This had been at five o'clock on gig night, the car was loaded and Bill was ready to go. Unfortunately, so was Mrs Bill, and she said that if he went, then so did she: and that was why he had left with no notice. Malcolm had seen him since then, and had been given a drinks kitty for the whole band by way of apology from Bill – who would not be out to see them any time soon. It was surprisingly generous, so they felt a little less angry towards him for leaving them in the lurch. It had come in particularly handy this evening; since they had been there for two hours now without being allowed to unload.

There was a bit of an argument going on by the doors – Chris had brought in his entire kit and left it in the middle of the bar, rather than waiting for the diners to finish. He had spent most of the time that they had been waiting muttering about 'not fucking hanging around here doing nothing', and referring to the diners as 'a bunch of posh twats'.

'I was at a gig years back, and Chris Wolstenhome was throwing a similar sort of paddy you know,' Gavin said to George in a not-quite-whisper.

'Chris who?' George asked back.

'Wolstenhome?' Gavin said, incredulous, 'You know? From Muse? We were on the same bill as them back in the day, before they made it, right diva he was – they supported us by the way, funny how it works out isn't it?'

'Umm yeah?' George wasn't sure how impressed he was supposed to be by this, or even if he was supposed to be impressed. He briefly considered trawling out an anecdote about how he once met Rolf Harris when he was at Primary School, but thought better of it.

'I told you, my Dad can't hang around, he's got to get back, especially since he's got to be back later to pick me up, so I can't wait.' Chris was saying, George, Verity, Gavin and Malcolm all exchanged a look of astonishment that Chris's Dad had been waiting outside in the car for all that time. In fact he hadn't been – he had driven round the corner and gone to visit a friend of his. But he had just got back, and Chris was impatient to load in.

'I don't care, you can't leave all that in the way there, it's a fire hazard,' the Barmaid countered, 'what kind of grown-up gets their

Dad to drive them around anyway? Can't you drive?'

'Of course I can drive, it's just that my car isn't big enough to fit my drums in, and Dad only lives round the corner and has a nice big Volvo.'

'So why don't you just borrow it for the night and leave the poor old man at home?' she countered.

Chris stopped at this, and, as he was considering his response, a voice came from over his shoulder, 'Because I wouldn't trust the little tosser with my beautiful car my dear, that's why. I have had that car longer than I have had him, and I think I know which one I prefer,' Chris's Dad had come in to see what was keeping him and was making his feelings known about his classic Volvo 140.

'Brian Thomson, pleased to make your acquaintance,' he stuck his hand out in greeting to the barmaid, who took it, smiling at Brian's terribly home counties accent and Navy Blue double-breasted blazer, 'I am awfully sorry about my son, but I do have to get off you see, we could leave all this stuff in the car park – that was my suggestion – but he wouldn't hear of it, said he didn't want to sit outside guarding it while he was waiting. Now, what say me and you take it out now, and then I can hop off? I'm sure I can persuade him to sit out there for a bit if I try,' he grinned a terrifying leer at his son.

'No, it can stay for now, thanks for the offer – but if he plays here again, I suggest you ensure he sorts out better transport,' the barmaid relented in the face of Brian's charm offensive.

'Nothing I can do about it dear, he's thirty five years old and considerably better off than I am, but charmed to have met you, and I do hope to see you again later, goodbye.' and with that, he went out, leaving the barmaid with a knowing wink, and Chris staring at the back of a closing door.

The barmaid took up a whole new argument with Chris at this point, asking why couldn't he be as polite and charming as his father, while Chris tried to defend himself against a girl not much more than half his age who was verbally outwitting him at every stroke. Luckily, at this point, the table of diners lurched across the bar, thanked the barmaid and handed her a pint glass stuffed with notes that they assured her would more than cover the cost of their meal.

'Right then, you can load your stuff in now if one of you gives me a hand with these tables,' the barmaid shouted. Gavin jumped straight in to help her, not to save Chris from the argument, but because he was impressed by her arguing skills.

'I like a girl with a bit of fight in her – like Gina G when she slapped me backstage at Butlins – I reckon I might help this one out.' he whispered to George,

George sighed, hoped that Gavin wasn't married – or that tomorrow would find them a new guitar player – and started lugging gear in.

CHAPTER 20

'What do you think then?' Verity asked George, 'my money is on
him being about thirty six, still living at his parents house – possibly
in an attic– and running some kind of online business – maybe
selling small models of dragons.'

George nodded sagely, they were looking out of Chris's
conservatory window, watching the second guitar-playing hopeful
struggle up the drive underneath an enormous speaker cabinet. It had
been Verity's idea that they should try and guess what each candidate
would be like entirely on first appearances and so far it had proved
to be a good game. George had correctly guessed that the first
auditionee had been over fifty, recently had his children move out,
and was trying to rediscover his lost youth when he had yearned to
play in rock bands. He had given up this dream and spent the last
thirty years dedicating his life to dentistry and paying for his
children's education (George hadn't guessed quite this much, they
found this out by talking to him). Malcolm thought it might have
been better spent learning to play the guitar properly. George
couldn't help sympathising with the guy as a bit of a kindred spirit –
except for the dentistry.

The person that they were currently observing still had some of
his long, thinning black hair left, carefully combed to cover the bits
where it wasn't. Had he not been struggling with the speaker cabinet
he would have gotten away with it. Unfortunately he was in a state
of dishevelment, and the gaps were clearly visible at the crown and
the receding sides of his hairline. George felt a little sympathy,
though not enough to stop the game.

'You may be correct,' George countered, 'but I would venture that
he actually lives in a small one bed flat, or a bedsit, no more than
five minutes walk away from those parents you thought he was still

living with. I also suspect that our hard won tax money is subsidising his current lifestyle – which may or may not include models of dragons holding crystals and recreational drugs.'

'Oh very good, lets see what you've won!' she intoned, in an unconvincing Bruce Forsythe impersonation, leading George back inside. George had to keep reminding himself not to touch her. They had been pretty good at hiding their relationship at gigs, but the relaxed atmosphere of a rehearsal made it easier to slip up. They hoped their extended visits to the conservatory didn't look too suspicious, and ensured that they invited Malcolm and Chris to play the guessing game as well. Luckily they had both declined, giving them a chance to spend some time alone.

Verity had suggested to him on the way there that once they sorted this niggling guitar-player problem, then they could go all out for the big gigs and go professional. He was not sure if the maths added up, and was reluctant to leave his job just yet, but the idea of playing music and spending every day with Verity instead of delivering letters was enticingly seductive.

Since the first hopeful had been a total disaster – with the poor chap tickling the strings of his custom made PRS guitar (which cost more than George's car) like he was scared he might hurt it and having only the vaguest idea how to play the three songs they had asked him to learn – they had high hopes for this next guy.

'Where's he gone?' George asked, as they came in to the big television-lined living room expecting the scraggy-haired one to be there already.

'He's gone for "the other one", apparently,' Malcolm indicated the ominous looking 4x12 Marshall speaker cabinet to his left, 'I do hope we all brought ear plugs?'

'Jesus, two of them?' George whistled, 'for a rehearsal?'

Malcolm and Chris both nodded in tandem, and then shook their heads in unison.

Twenty minutes later the rig of doom was set up, and all looked up at it in awe, as Dave (the axe-wielder in charge of it) fiddled with the knobs on the front of the 100 watt Marshall JCM800 amplifier head perched atop it (which to Verity's absolute delight had a large dragon sticker on its side) and, to everyone's amazement, proceeded to put a pair of ear plugs in.

'Ready to go then Dave?' Malcolm enquired, he received a curt nod, and passed it on to Chris, who counted them in. The opening riff of Lynyrd Skynyrd's 'Sweet Home Alabama' corkscrewed its way into their ears threatening to pop out their eyeballs. A little over eight bars in, just before the vocal was supposed to begin, Verity waved them all to a sudden stop.

'Seriously? Can you please turn that thing down? If you can't hear yourself, you might want to take out the earplugs – it will help.'

'But it's my sound, you can't get it at lower volumes, the valves don't break up as nicely down there,' Dave explained, shouting a bit so that he could hear himself through his earplugs, 'and all musicians should wear earplugs when they're playing – otherwise you'll damage your hearing permanently.'

'We've been using the not-playing-so-loud-as-to-cause-permanent-damage approach instead, this is the first time we've been afraid for it really,' Verity countered, getting an incredulous look from Dave.

'Maybe you could try it with just one speaker cab?' George intervened, trying to help.

'Nah mate, you got to shift the air to get the sound, otherwise it just ain't rock and roll is it?' Dave continued.

'Or you could use a smaller amp, I think Chris has got a small one around here somewhere – in fact I think we suggested that people used it today.' Verity said, looking pointedly at an amplifier, all set up and ready to go having been used by the previous hopeful.

'But it's my sound, it's what people expect to hear when they see me, I've been doing this a long time round here – people expect it.'

'Maybe just for now, you could play this one song at a sensible volume – and if you seem to fit with us, we might think about buying earplugs so we can work with you,' George said, diplomatically, 'just for now?'

'Do you know how loud Ed King had his amps turned up when he recorded this song?' Dave shouted, mostly because he couldn't hear anything, 'really fucking loud, that's why that intro sounds so good, he had to play the guitar in a different room from the speakers to stop it feeding back. I'm not as loud as that am I?'

'I don't know, I wasn't there Dave, now can we have a go at a normal volume, or are we going to have to call it a day already?' Verity folded her arms and looked askance at him.

'Fuck this, I don't need some skinny bitch telling me to turn down,' Dave muttered, 'I'm out of here, I turned down four gigs this week to prepare for this audition, I heard you guys were good.'

'We are thanks, and I think this audition is over,' George tried to stick up for Verity.

'Too fucking right it is,' Dave unplugged his old, abused-looking black Fender Stratocaster, and tried to walk out in a hurry. It became more and more embarrassing for all concerned as he took three separate trips to the car to get his gear packed away, carefully coiling up all his connecting cables between journeys. Chris's offer of a cup of tea did not go down well, and the whole thing was topped off by Verity (half an hour later) saying to George, 'Oh, I forgot to find out if he lived with his Mum, damn it,' before shouting across the driveway, 'Oi, Dave – do you still live with your Mum?' which was greeted with a perfunctory 'Fuck off,' and a raised middle finger as he drove away.

'Well, I guess we'll never know about his living arrangements,' she shrugged.

'At least we know we were probably right about the Dragons though,' he replied, desperately wanting to put his arm around her in camaraderie, but worrying that it might seem too familiar. She elbowed him in the ribs and grinned widely at him, he figured it was the best he would get and took it gladly. They all went back in and made yet another pot of tea, since they had a good half an hour before the next victim was due.

He proved to be all of seventeen years old, and turned up on a pushbike with his guitar strapped to his back. George and Verity realised that the guessing game would be too easy and gave up. It was immediately obvious, however, that were he to be good enough for the position one of the band would have to pick him up and drive him around for every gig. Or at the very least his amplifier – should he actually own one. Luckily, or unluckily depending on your perspective, he also turned out to be of little use. He would come to a grinding halt every time he made a mistake or lost his way, and rather than fluffing through and trying to pick up in the same place as everybody else was, he would start again from where he had gone wrong – blithely ignoring everybody else. This resulted in his playing the verse riff of Neil Young's 'Rocking in the Free World' over the chorus, and blasting out a blistering solo all over the quiet bit where it should just have been Verity singing over a stripped back drum and bass section.

'Well, that was a total fucking waste of time,' Malcolm declared, cracking open a can of lager and sinking back into one of Chris's very comfy chairs. Having called it a day, they were having a few drinks and trying to figure out what to do next.

'Not a total waste of time,' Chris replied, 'we have managed to identify three total jokers to avoid in the future. We ought to put their names on a list somewhere, to warn others about them, save people time.'

'Ironically, I already knew about that Dave bloke,' Malcolm admitted, 'he's pretty well known around here, he wasn't wrong about that – but Anna, out of the Funked Up All Stars, told me he auditioned for them, and it was exactly the same. I didn't believe her, I really should have listened, sorry all.'

'Not your fault Malc, you weren't to know,' George said, supportively.

'Ah, but I should have believed her, it just sounded proper crazy. Besides – Anna told Gav that he was too loud as well when he depped for them.'

'Gav is too loud,' Verity said, 'but we need him at the moment, and so I haven't said anything.'

'Really?' Malcolm replied, 'I thought he was alright really.'

'That's because he's always set up on your deaf side,' Chris said, 'same as I am, and everyone else. I know exactly why you always go all the way over on stage right. So you don't get any noise in your good ear.'

Malcolm grinned sheepishly and admitted it was true. They carried on trying to think of other guitar players that might be able to fit in. Sadly, nice guys who didn't overplay, play too loud, or who actually knew how to play were few and far between. Eventually they just decided to wait and see what the internet adverts brought.

CHAPTER 21

'Still no decent bites then?' George asked Malcolm. They were out for a sneaky Sunday lunchtime pint and discussing the difficulty of finding a replacement for Bill. Verity was off doing something, George hadn't pried too much as he didn't want to scare her off, so he had accepted her explanation of, 'you know, things to do, people to see' as a perfectly decent one.

'No, nothing mate, it's lucky we've got Gav on standby,' Malcolm replied, 'he gets pretty busy sometimes. Well – he says he does, but then Gav says a lot of things.'

'Yeah,' George shrugged non-committally, he was glad they had somebody to fill in, but he missed Bill. Gav could play, he just didn't seem to think it was important. It was as if he had phoned his parts in, which was probably fair enough, seeing as he wasn't technically in the band. He had even told George that he felt the whole thing was beneath him. He played in another band that wrote their own material, they had done quite a few big shows around the country and, more importantly, in London – with some fairly well-known bands. George was hoping they could find somebody more committed soon so they could find a way to make it all pull back together.

'Do you reckon I might be able to go professional with this then Malc?' George asked tentatively – he was seriously considering Verity's suggestion that he do this full time.

'Well mate, it is looking profitable, I haven't been behind on my rent in a long time, and I've not got many students at the minute either,' Malcolm answered, 'it's not a reliable income, I won't lie, but if you do a bit of teaching on the side, maybe run an open mic night or two, yeah, you could live on it. Maybe even without claiming jobseekers.' he winked.

That was what George had wanted to hear, he wanted this life, not the usual drudge of working for somebody else. Maybe he could back Verity playing her own songs somewhere, maybe they could make it properly.

'Have you seen Gav's proper band then Malc?' George asked, trying to find out if they were as good as Gav claimed.

'I have, they're alright,' Malcolm shrugged, 'nothing special – vaguely retro glam rock. Think bastard child of Mötley Crüe and Bowie before all the synths and you won't be far off the mark.'

'Ah, riding the nostalgia waves then?' George said, 'they must be pretty good though, if they're doing all these gigs in London?'

'Hah!' Malcolm spat, 'that does always make a band sound very cool doesn't it? A London gig, getting in amongst all those bands scrummaging for room up there. Well, let me tell you something,' he gestured with his pint, 'any tosser with an instrument can get a gig up there. There's a million venues – trying to fill seven nights a week with music. If you want to impress me then tell me you got a headline gig up there on a Saturday night and you got paid enough to make a decent profit playing your own songs. Seriously, the guys who live up there are always looking for fall-guy support acts, and the wide-eyed bumpkins from the shires, like us, are exactly the stooges they need. I saw Gav's band up there last time they played – it was half past seven on a Wednesday night in Fulham. There were five of us watching them, one of them was the barman, and one was the soundman. The other acts had gone off somewhere else, and I'm pretty sure the other two guys were mates of the singer. Don't be so easily impressed George, there's a lot of bullshitters out there, Gav is by no means the worst of them – but he is prone to make himself sound more important than he is.'

'Ok,' George said, 'but he did support the Undertones yeah?'

'He told you that one as well did he?' Malcolm chuckled, 'again, bit of an exaggeration, Gav's band were at a pretty nice mellow festival out in Hampshire somewhere. They played in a very small tent on the way from the campsite to the main arena on the Friday afternoon – it was a good gig by all accounts. Even though the Friday afternoon slots are always a curse, they got a few people in and dancing. The Undertones headlined the main stage on the Saturday night, so it's hardly a support slot; and Feargal Sharkey isn't with them any more, so it's hardly the Undertones either.' Malcolm reached into his pocket for his cigarettes and George got up to follow him outside.

'Oh,' he said, slightly disappointed that he was not really rubbing shoulders with someone who rubbed shoulders with the stars.

'Don't take it all to heart though mate,' Malcolm shook out his match, and threw it across the beer garden, 'they are pretty good. In fact... we've got nothing on Saturday night after next, and they're playing out at the Golden Lion – we should go. It would be a good night.'

'Oh, I don't know,' George stalled, 'I was going to have a night in with V...' he tried to stop himself from letting Malcolm find out what was going on, but the damage was done.

'With Verity?' Malcolm grinned, 'You still a bit sweet on her are you?'

George shrugged, non-committally again, 'don't know what you mean Malc, I was going to say a night in with.... *vin rouge*, yeah, the red stuff, that's it.'

'Jesus, I knew she was staying with you for a bit, but you're not shagging her as well are you?' Malcolm exclaimed.

'It's not like that Malc, we didn't want to keep it a secret but, hang on, what do you mean "as well"?' George's ears suddenly caught up with his mouth.

'Oh come on, she's not pure as the driven snow is she? Why do you think Bryony dumped Chris?'

'She was sick of driving him around wasn't she?' George replied, all innocence.

'Nope, he fucked Verity, and Bryony said it was the band or her – he chose the band.'

'Really? I don't believe you – and even if I did, that's in the past, it's got nothing to do with me and her.' George went into some form of shock, reeling from this revelation – could his beloved Verity have had a thing with Chris as well? He found it hard to believe, but was willing to forget about things that had happened before. Then he remembered something, 'What about Mike though? I thought she was with him?'

'Yeah – the thing about Verity is she expects her long term partners to be loyally monogamous, and yet refuses to adhere to such a strict code herself – she's got a very different set of ethics to most people George. I think she'd have a male harem if she could.' Malcolm explained.

'No, I think you're wrong Malcolm,' George denied emphatically.

'Did you ever meet Mike?' Malcolm asked, 'at all? He never came to a single gig, hell, I don't remember her so much as mentioning him. Probably just used him as a meal ticket.'

'Well, maybe she did cheat on him as much as he cheated on her, but it must have been an unhappy relationship – it doesn't matter that she slept with Chris, these things happen.' George convinced himself more than Malcolm.

'Bill too, mind you, everybody fucks Bill – I'm surprised you haven't really,' Malcolm joked, 'but he chose his wife over the band, weirdo.'

Bang, another punch in the metaphorical guts for George, he quickly weighed it all up, realised that it must have happened before them, and, from what he knew of Bill, he couldn't blame Verity. No, he was still sure of their relationship, really, he was – honest.

'It doesn't matter.' George lied, of course it mattered, 'we're fine, I'm really happy – please don't tell her you know about us.'

'Ah, so you're in love, and happy, but you can't tell anyone about it? Is that it?' Malcolm asked.

'Yeah, because it's always difficult being in a band with two people in a burgeoning relationship, and it will screw up the dynamic.'

'That what she told you yeah? Because I know two other people with a similar story – they both confided in me as well,' Malcolm intoned.

'No, it was a joint decision, I agreed with her. Besides, she's friends with my daughter, and it looks weird, her living with me, but once she's got her own place again we'll tell Linda, and it will all be in the open and fine.'

'Yeah, it'll be just like a movie,' Malcolm said, drily, 'wake up George, I know you've not had the best time of it the last few years, but she's just using you to get a free place to stay mate. I dare say she's skinning you for all the cash she can while she's at it.'

'No, not at all,' George lied again – only this morning he had given her, not loaned, given, another hundred pounds to "tide her over 'til a cheque clears".

'I believe you George,' Malcolm shook his head.

'You haven't....?' George's words faded away, unable to ask the question he so desperately wanted the answer to.

'Me? Christ no, well, not for a long time anyway,' Malcolm answered, not quite removing all George's fears.

'Not for a long time?' George asked, indignantly.

'Not for a few years now – we had a bit of a thing once, a long time ago, but I realised she just wanted money, and an easy in to the local music scene – so I got rid.' Malcolm answered, quietly, with his eyes closed, lighting another cigarette, 'you should do the same, seriously.'

'Thanks for being honest Malc, but she's changed, I'm sure of it,' George stated.

'You should still watch yourself mate, I don't entirely believe it. Stop it now, before it destroys your professional relationship, we have a good band, I don't want to lose another member when it all goes wrong.'

'It wasn't her that left the underwear in Bill's coat surely?' George said.

'Heh, no, that was not her fault for once.' Malcolm recovered his good humour chuckling at the memory of Bill's downfall.

George was visibly relieved that she had not engineered Bill's problems, but he was still unwilling to think ill of Verity. He was happy – didn't Malcolm understand that? Didn't he want him to be happy? Maybe he was jealous.

'Anyway, now I know, maybe we can all go to see Gav's band together,' Malcolm suggested, 'I can find a date probably, and maybe Chris can bring his Dad along or something,' he cracked a grin, and they headed back to the bar.

As he walked home George's mind was spinning around from all this new information. What should he do about it? Should he have it out with her and discuss his fears? Was this the time to have their first big stand-up row? Was any of it actually that important? After all, it had happened before they got together, and it wasn't like he didn't have any skeletons. Besides, this proved that if they did ever split up – and he really hoped that that wasn't going to happen – then they would still be able to play in the band together. She and Bill and Chris and Malcolm had had no major professional problems as a result of their dalliances, so the band would be fine – no matter what.

He decided that it would be best not to bring it up, it would only cause trouble. He stopped off to buy them both Chinese takeaway and a bottle of something nice on the way; then they could get past this, without her ever knowing there was an it to get past.

CHAPTER 22

'Really?' Tim said, incredulous, 'they are actually called Carnal Interest?'

'Yes Tim, Carnal Interest,' George repeated, trying not to smirk.

'And with no trace of irony at all in that?' His mouth was wide with a mixture of glee and surprise, 'Oh I do hope they have leather trousers, and waistcoats without shirts, maybe cowboy boots? Red cowboy boots? And much less hair than they used to have, but, a cavalier attitude to keeping what hair they have left as long as they possibly can. Like nineties Michael Bolton – or you last year.'

'You may or may not be disappointed mate,' George replied, 'however, I take it that you are in?'

'Wouldn't miss it for the world, I will get my coat.' and he disappeared inside to fetch it, and check with Ant that it was ok for him to go out, well, tell him that he was going out, same as usual.

George was meeting Verity in the Golden Lion, as she had some business out that way, and would already be over there. As she had moved in with Linda last weekend – having sorted out her finances to some extent, and despite George's misgivings about his daughter and girlfriend sharing a flat – George had decided it was time to tell his oldest and dearest friend about his new and exciting relationship, so had stopped off on the way to invite Tim along. He was quite looking forward to a Saturday night out without gigging. They walked the short distance to George's car and headed off.

George was also excited to see Verity again, as they hadn't managed to find the time to see each other since he dropped off the last of her stuff at Linda's place last Sunday afternoon. Of course, he had been at work, and she had been busy with moving stuff – and whatever she was doing to earn the money to pay for it. Also it was a little difficult now, George couldn't just go around to see Verity without Linda asking awkward questions, and equally, Verity would have had to come up with a cover story to come and see George. He would be glad when everything was out in the open.

'But you can't tell Linda any of this yet, in fact keep it under your hat until I tell you otherwise,' George said to Tim after briefly outlining his new relationship, 'it could get a bit dangerous what with them flat-sharing now, I don't want anything getting back to her before I've spoken to her myself.'

'And when are you planning on doing that?' Tim asked, still a little surprised at George's uncharacteristic good luck.

'I'm taking her for lunch tomorrow actually, so I'll probably tell her then, as long as Verity agrees, I'll check with her later. I'll probably tell Lin that I'm jacking my job in next week as well, let her try and talk me out of it.'

'Are you really making enough out of the band then?' Tim asked, concernedly.

'Verity reckons we will be soon, there's a lot of weddings and corporate functions coming up, all good payers, plus some holiday camp residencies over the summer – I've done the maths, and I've got enough savings to cope for a bit if it does all go wrong.'

'Well, I can only wish you luck, even if you are clearly under her thumb already, you poor thing. Never does take you long to get henpecked does it? I shall endeavour to keep it utterly secret for at least the next twenty four hours. Even I should be able to manage that– although I must warn you, Ant will know about it already.' Tim said.

'What? I mean, I know you'll tell him, you tell him everything, but how would he know about it already?' George looked confused as he navigated the terrifying one way system.

'I texted him while you were talking, sorry.' Tim confessed.

George threw his head back and laughed, a full-throated belly laugh, he was glad he could share his happiness with Tim.

'Oh, you're in a covers band then,' the impeccably dishevelled bassist of Carnal Interest said, as if there was actual human faeces held under his nose, 'I suppose the money must be pretty good, but isn't it a bit, you know, shit?'

George was slightly taken aback at this, he hadn't really encountered this attitude before in real life. He had seen plenty of it on internet forums, where there are literally enough words to fill every copy of the bible ever printed twice over devoted to the never-ending conflict between covers and originals bands, and there was always Malcolm's morose attitude towards it. He had decided to be friendly, and go over and have a word with the bass player – since they were both friends of Gavin, and he wanted a look at his gear. It looked old and tatty, or vintage as they call it nowadays, he had to remind himself, and therefore probably interesting, valuable, or both. Graham, for that was his name, had been aloof for the entire conversation, and George was already looking for a way out.

'Well, it's not bad, but I don't do it for the money, I do it for the pure pleasure of playing,' George replied, fully aware that this was just asking for a contemptuous response from the black-suited, cowboy-booted, open-shirted, snake-necklace-wearing ball of barely concealed malice that he was trying to get away from.

'Huh, if you're going to sell out you should at least be well paid,' Graham adjusted his huge black cowboy hat, pushed his sunglasses back up his nose (despite being indoors, and it being night time) and continued tuning up his ancient-looking Gibson Thunderbird bass. 'You lot are the enemy anyway, I was telling Gav the other day – the reason we all end up having to charge on the door and play to nobody is because every other pub now has a shitty cover band in it every weekend. It's always free to get in, and the punters already know the songs – who's going to take a punt on paying to see a band they've never heard of playing songs they don't know when you can go to that instead? That's why there's no good new music on the radio: no investment in it from the public. It's your fault, all your fault.'

'Well, I sympathise with you, but I think you may be exaggerating,' George hadn't been expecting this assault and tried to stick up for himself.

'Not really, any twat can pick up a guitar and play somebody else's songs can't they? Shouldn't mean that they get to hog all the decent venues of a weekend and steal our audience should it?'

'I think we're going to have to agree to disagree about this – anyway, nice to meet you, I'll let you get on.' George resisted the urge to tell Graham that Gav and the lead singer wrote all of his band's songs, so technically he was no different and was playing other people's music as well, and went back to the table where Malcolm and Tim were chuckling at him before the argument developed any further. Graham clearly had some major issues and Verity still hadn't arrived.

'Jesus, will you look at these lot?' Tim exclaimed, once George had sat down, 'I mean, I thought you looked a bit like a time warp Malcolm, no offence, but these guys look like the seventies never ended.'

He was right, there was Graham's black suit and hat look, Gav in a floor length Leopardskin coat, the drummer in frilly cuffs and silk drape jacket, and the piece de resistance for Tim, who had never been so happy to see anything else, was the lead singer in a black leather waistcoat and matching trousers, with no shirt underneath, two fading sleeves of tattoos and yes – red cowboy boots. His greying lions mane of hair was in no danger of disappearing, but Tim was happy enough with its silvery hue, he didn't need balding as well.

'None taken Timothy, though it is definitely your round next.' Malcolm grinned, waving an empty pint glass at him.

'Fair enough, another lovely lemonade for you George?' Tim grinned, 'I'll get a slice of lemon as well so you can pretend it's a gin and tonic.'

'Thanks Tim, but I think I will let you buy me my one pint of the night, since you find my driving sobriety so amusing, I'll have a Carlsberg please.'

'Ah! Cooking lager, how lovely, as you wish,' Tim wandered off to the bar to get the drinks in.

'Wait 'til he sees the other bands, he'll have a field day,' Malcolm grinned.

'Other bands?' George asked.

'Yeah, there's always at least three bands on at original music nights,' Malcolm explained, 'it's about the only way that they can get a big enough audience for it to be worthwhile. Sometimes you get people that aren't actually in the bands turning up, like us, although they are almost inevitably, like us, mates of one of the bands.'

Just then, Verity appeared through the doors, walking with her usual assured poise, her hair tied back severely from her face, wearing black and white striped leggings and a short cut leather jacket, utterly un-phased by walking into a pub full of people alone. She spotted them, waved and made her way over. Time slowed for George as he watched her strut across the room, his heart leaped a little bit as she caught his eye and gave a little smile of recognition, the orchestra in his head rising to a crescendo as she passed a mirror and pushed her hand up to her hair, checking it was all still as it should be. Then she arrived at the table and time came rushing back with a jolt.

'What are you drinking babe?' he asked, suddenly realising he was back in the real world, 'and be quick, Tim's at the bar already.'

'Erm, I don't know, shit, under pressure – what's everybody else drinking?' Her question was met with blank stares and shrugs as she flailed her arms, 'fuck it, vodka and tonic, that'll do for starters.'

'Oi! Tim!' George shouted, 'stick a vodka and tonic onto that round will you?' He saw Tim's hand appear above the queue at the bar, thumb raised aloft.

'Ok, but I'll need more hands, get over here.' His disembodied voice called back.

George got up, excused himself, kissed Verity awkwardly on the cheek (and received a hard warning look in return, apparently public displays of affection were out still – he immediately regretted calling her babe) and went over to help Tim. When he returned, he found that Chris had also turned up, with Bryony, much to everyone's surprise.

'Alright George?' she said, 'how've you been?' and she leaned over, hugged him and gave him a kiss on the cheek, which he reciprocated in kind, blushing right down to his feet. He mumbled something along the lines of not-so-bad-how-about-you and sat himself down on the other side of Malcolm from Verity – taking the hint about acting like a couple. He wondered briefly if the night could get any more awkward when all tension was broken up by Tim's raucous laughter.

Tim was standing next to the sound desk, chatting to a group of very young people who could only have been a band. They were all in black, with the occasional purple stripe, and heavily made up with white faces, eyeliner and Edward-Scissorhands-style, back-combed black hair. They were so androgynous that George could not tell boy from girl. Tim appeared to have immediately insinuated himself into their group, and was holding court as usual – probably with one of his stock of unutterably filthy stories.

'Goths!' he exclaimed, as he made it back to the table, 'actual goths! I had no idea they were still around, and their bass player is a spit for a young Ant. He was a goth when we met you know, it's a shame that Andrea is a girl, but you can't have everything I suppose.

Oh, hello, by the way,' he waved vaguely at the table as a whole, which had grown by three since he had left for the bar.

Pleasantries and introductions were exchanged between Tim and those he did not know, or remember, and he gave Verity one of his special knowing winks, which left her thinking he might have some kind of eye problem.

'Are they actually old enough to be in here?' Chris asked, referring to the goth band that Tim was now so fond of.

'Maybe, maybe not, as long as they say they are, then that's ok by me,' Malcolm answered, 'I remember years back we were on the same bill as a band who weren't. They kept the bar closed until after their set, and nobody could get a drink because of the underage band. I have never seen a more hostile crowd in my life, or more people offer to help a band pack up after they'd finished.'

'Christ, sober musicians, how did they cope?' Bryony said, with a grin firmly aimed at Chris.

'Badly,' Malcolm said, 'most of us had bottles stashed somewhere in our gear cases, but you have never seen such relief as when the bar finally opened. A guy out of one of the other bands tried to walk back in with a beer he'd bought in the other bar, same pub mark you, but different bar – the bouncers beat him up so hard he ended up in the hospital. Luckily he was only the bass player so nobody noticed that he wasn't there,' he nudged George, and they all laughed.

Gavin's band, Carnal Interest, were first on the bill, and at eight o'clock on the dot, a brainsmashingly loud guitar chord from Gav's shocking pink Kramer Baretta announced their arrival, and all conversation ceased for a bit. It was impossible to stop Tim from laughing hysterically at every ancient rock and roll cliché that they pulled off, and his laughter was almost louder than the thundering, relentless rumble of Graham's bass.

In Tim's defence it was pretty funny: the lead singer had screamed 'Hello Golden Lion! How you doing tonight?' as the dying chords of the opening song faded away in a manner reminiscent of Paul Stanley in Kiss's heyday, at an audience not more than four feet away from him – and not through anticipation and trying to get to the front, it just wasn't a very big room. Even George felt this was a little over the top. Particularly since there was just their table, the other bands, and a few people on the other side of the room who were clearly trying to drink up and leave. Graham putting his boot up on the monitor speaker and aiming his bass like a machine gun at the audience during Gavin's five thousand note a second guitar solos was good too. George wasn't sure if he'd been guilty of this himself or not, as he often forgot himself while he was playing, he was pretty sure he hadn't though. And when the singer was on his knees licking Gav's guitar strings during yet another endless guitar solo, Tim actually fell off of his chair laughing, while Malcolm just shook his head knowingly.

The band weren't bad, and, were this 1982 they might have managed a support slot with Whitesnake – but it was not 1982, they were not as young as they had been in 1982, and this was not Wembley so the whole thing felt a little embarrassing. George was pleased to note that Gavin's ability to hit bum notes and forget where he was mid song was not restricted to his performances with the Artful Badgers. After their set George prayed that Gavin wouldn't come over and ask them what they thought, at least, not if Tim was there – he really hoped Gav hadn't seen Tim, or heard Tim, or been aware of him at all.

Luckily, Gavin had a quick word with Malcolm, waved at them all and then him and the rest of Carnal Interest packed up their gear and disappeared, claiming that they had another gig to get to. Gavin admitted it was a lie, but it made them look in demand – apparently they did it a lot to improve their image. He actually did have another gig as it happened, playing acoustic backup to a young female singer songwriter at an open mic night across town. It was only three songs, but he had promised her he'd do it, and she was, apparently, related to some folk musician from the seventies that none of them had ever heard of, but Gavin clearly felt that they should have, and going to be the next big thing. Since they were there, the whole table elected to stay and watch the other bands, as they hadn't had a Saturday night out without gigging in as long as they could remember, and it was nice to hang out without doing band things for once.

A good deal later on, everybody was pretty drunk except for George and Bryony who were both driving. Tim was back talking to his new favourite band who he had dubbed the Gothingtons – despite their name actually being We Are Your Pain. Chris was arguing about drums with another drummer. Verity was talking to a group of girls by the bar, and Malcolm was doubtless outside smoking.

'Tell me again, why are you two back together?' George asked, as bemused as ever as to why a seemingly intelligent, good-looking and funny girl like Bryony would find herself with such an uptight ball of crazy as Chris, 'I mean, I'm pleased and everything, I just didn't think you were the forgiving type.'

'It turned out that I actually love him, despite his inherent twatness,' Bryony replied, stirring the ice cubes in her diet coke with a straw, 'I mean I was really unhappy without him. I tried to be happy, I tried going out with other people: really clever, good-looking people of exactly the type my mother would approve of – she doesn't approve of Chris one bit by the way – but I missed him. I missed the way he gets so frustrated at every tiny little obstacle that gets in his way, I missed the way he counts every last penny of his precious lottery winnings just so that he doesn't ever have to do a proper job again – and there was good stuff I missed as well.' She grinned from ear to ear, and flushed red.

'I know what you mean, I had a similar problem after my second wife left me,' George said, 'only she still thought I was useless, and there was no talking her round. Turned out I was wrong, she is awful, and I am better off without her.'

'Yeah, I understand that point of view, but me and Chris have a really good time most of the time. I know he's older than me, and that he lacks ambition, but I love him, pure and simple, just that. It doesn't matter that he shagged that tart, he won't do it again, and if he does, it's just sex, not love. I've been thinking we could start swinging or something.' George nearly spat his lemonade out, 'or not, either way I'm not letting conventionality get in the way of my happiness. So I told him: "I'm putting you on the van insurance, you can drive yourself to gigs from now on, and I want to move in with you," and he was actually lost for words. It was kind of sweet.'

'So you're going to live together now, and invite people round for dirty sex parties?' George enquired, with a raised eyebrow.

'Why? D'you want to come?' she grinned mischievously at him.

'No – god no – no offence you understand,' George flushed bright red, 'I was just wondering if you were serious about all the *Eyes Wide Shut* stuff, I have enough trouble keeping just one woman happy, let alone a whole group of them.'

'Don't know, maybe,' she gave George a coquettish look, 'anyway, he rang me up to see if I wanted to talk, and when I met up with him he looked so sad, and he told me there hadn't been anybody since we'd split up, and as far as he was concerned there never would be anybody else. I mean, I knew it was bollocks, I know it is bollocks, as soon as a pretty girl looks at him twice he's hopeless – no idea how to say no. So it's lucky he's so ugly really. Anyhow, I knew we had to get back together again. I reckon if I suggested that we went dogging tonight, he wouldn't be able to say no, even if he wanted to – excuse me a minute,' and she wandered off in the direction of the toilets.

George sat and listened to the band that were playing, they were some kind of folky thing, with a banjo and a ukulele and plenty of tweed and waistcoats. It seemed to show a lack of foresight from the organisers, as the only people who had stayed for the whole thing were the staff and George's table. Even the other bands had just played their set and then run off somewhere else, apart from the Gothingtons, and they were trying very hard to politely get rid of Tim so that they could leave as well. There had been the unbridled cock rock of Carnal Interest, then a thin quirky-looking girl with a keyboard who sang sad, wistful songs about boys, then the Gothingtons, who fitted quite well with the sad thin girl he supposed, and now these folky types, George wondered vaguely if the evening might end with some death metal, and looking at the last band wandering in now, he thought he might well get exactly that. There was a lot of hair, black t-shirts and piercings in evidence.

'I see the tart's got her hooks into another one of you lot now then,' Bryony said, easing herself back into her chair opposite George.

'Jesus Tim's got a big mouth,' George replied, 'I told him not to tell anybody about me and Verity, I assume that's who you mean by "the tart", no offence taken by the way, but I suppose he must have thought you knew about it already.'

'You? And Verity?' Bryony's face went white, 'oh shit, you might want to go and see what's happening in the ladies then.'

CHAPTER 23

George leaped up and walked as gracefully as he could across the bar, and, amid a few cries of consternation from a group of young girls giggling outside, he crashed through the door of the ladies to see Verity on her knees in front of Malcolm, fully engaged in the fine art of fellatio. George's mouth dropped open, and he could find nothing to say.

'Told you,' Malcolm mouthed towards him, pointing downwards at Verity's bobbing head, as George just stood, open mouthed, the entire world crashing down around his ears. He had really thought Malcolm was his friend, and he had really thought him and Verity had something good, and worth holding onto, and none of it was true, and he could think of nothing to say to make them understand the betrayal he was feeling. He could see his reflection in the mirror behind Malcolm, it was in a gilt frame above the marbled sinks, he wondered if it was actual marble, or some kind of plastic coating put on to make it look like marble, he looked pale, in fact his pasty visage brought that *Scream* painting to mind, who did that? Was it Munch? He wished he had paid more attention in art classes at school, well at school full stop really, then he wondered why he was thinking about paintings and school at a time like this, and how long exactly he had been stood there staring and saying nothing.

'You pair of unutterable cunts!' shrieked a voice from over George's shoulder, and a pint of something flew at them, bouncing off Malcolm's chest and covering the pair of them in sticky drink, 'Come on Georgie, we are getting the fuck away from here,' and George felt himself being steered away from the horrendous sight, before even finding out if the glass had bounced or broken, wondering vaguely to himself if she would finish off the job or not. He looked over his shoulder to see Tim, looking angrier than he had ever seen him, and smiled vaguely at his friend as he was pushed past Chris and Bryony – waving at them on the way past as if in a dream.

A few minutes later they were at the bar of the Tavern in the Town, and George had a line of vodka shots in front of him. The Tavern was best known for its cheap alcohol, and regularly did deals such as buy six shots and get the seventh free: it looked as if Tim had gone for bulk discount tonight.

'You ok yet?' Tim said. George looked down to see that four of the shots in front of him were empty, and realised he must have drunk them without really paying attention.

'Fuck, I've got to drive us home you tosser, what did you give me these for?' he punched his friend in the arm.

'You are driving nowhere dear boy,' Tim replied, sounding terribly serious, 'remember back in the days when we used to miss the last bus home?'

'Yes Tim, of course I do, we used to walk back along that bike trail, but surely you're not suggesting...'

'Yes I am, it will be utterly brilliant, I'll give you a lift back to get your car tomorrow, don't worry, now get those shots down you, and I'll get you another pint,' George noticed an empty pint glass next to the line of shots that he must have downed as well. They got through a great deal more of them before they left – which they wouldn't have done had the pub not been closing.

'Now here's a thing that has changed for the better,' Tim exclaimed as he came out of the twenty four hour garage with a very heavy looking carrier bag, 'garages that sell booze, and twenty four hour opening to boot! The walk home will be far more pleasant than it used to be my friend, far more pleasant.'

'It will still be eight bastard miles long though won't it?' George gratefully accepted the can of extra-strong lager that Tim pushed into his hand and they walked off down the hill that led to the cycle path, hoping it was still there twenty-something years since they had last followed its winding trail home.

'Ah! Tramp juice,' Tim sounded supremely refreshed, 'I have not drunk this in a very long time. In fact, probably not since the last time me and you walked this way.' It had been a very long time, but back when they were teenagers, Tim and George had often walked home this way after a night out, having once been stranded after the last bus had left. They had had no money for a taxi, no floor, sofa (or willing bed) to fall back on and no other option. So they had walked the eight miles back, found it to be easier than they had thought, and, provided you were drunk enough, really quite fun. After this they had made a point of doing it at least as often as they didn't. George suspected Tim was trying to take his mind off everything with a trip down nostalgia street (which is a little like memory lane, only a bit more urban).

'Honestly, that girl looked just like a young Ant, George,' Tim began, 'I could almost fall for her if she weren't a her. Do you remember him when we first met?'

George nodded, and took another swig at his drink.

'Of course you do, he was beautiful, all that jet black hair all the way down to his arse, his lovely, young, pert arse. Dressed head to toe in black leather and velvet – and those lacey gloves he used to wear. It is such a shame we all have to get old and sensiblish isn't it? I know he's still the same person, but you know, I would not have fallen so madly in love with the round chap in the spectacles, with the neatly clipped hair. Especially in his eminently practical, lightweight, waterproof coat.' Tim practically spat these words as if ashamed to have them grace his tongue, 'He used to wear a huge wide-brimmed hat, like Carl McCoy from Fields of the Nephilim when he went out, the only hat he owns now is a fucking woolly beanie hat, to keep warm in the winter, I mean, why does everything have to be so fucking practical all the time?'

'Your winklepickers aren't are they?' George countered, 'or that coat you're wearing.' Tim had on a terribly thin, cream jacket with no pockets, it had flaps that looked like pockets, but no actual pockets, in case you put something in them that would ruin the lines of it apparently.

'Somebody has to continue to fly the flag of style my dear chap, and I will wear no hat, not while I still have this beautiful head of hair,' and he pointed to his deliberately dishevelled DA.

'Fair enough,' George replied, shoving his free hand deep into the pocket of his lovely warm anorak. He took another long swig of lager, pulled his beanie hat down a little further against the cold, and they walked on, Tim starting to shiver slightly.

'You know when you see a bloke with an enormous fat wife?' Tim went on, 'and you think to yourself, oh my, a chubby chaser, how marvellous.'

'What?' George enquired, incredulously.

'Bear with me, it's an interesting idea,' Tim replied, 'I always wonder to myself if they married a thin girl, and are now so in love that they don't care that she got fat. Or if they married a thin girl and are now too scared to leave the fat woman in case she sits on them. Or if they married a thin girl and didn't notice her putting on weight bit by bit, and are not quite sure why they no longer both fit in the bed like they used to. Or if they married a thin girl, but secretly liked fat girls, and fed her pies and pies and pies and pies and pies and pies until she looked how they wanted her to. Or if they are in permanent mourning for that thin girl they married and endlessly hope for her return while they lock themselves in the bathroom and wank over the wedding pictures. Or if they are, in fact, just chubby chasers.'

'Really? That's interesting to you?' George asked.

'Yep, do you not think so?'

'You are still, after all this time, the single most shallow, superficial human being it has ever been my misfortune to meet,' George declared.

'Long may it remain so,' Tim replied.

'Do you think we'd have stayed in contact if either of us had moved away from here?' George asked.

'Doubt it,' Tim replied, 'as you have said, I am incredibly shallow – I would not have given you a second thought.'

'So, according to you, the longevity of our friendship can be put down entirely to geography and convenience then?' George countered.

'Yep, the fact that the two of us have lived our entire lives in this wonderful little town, well that one over there,' Tim waved vaguely in the direction of the lights blinking in the distance, 'is the only reason that me and you are still friends. That and the fact that everyone else we knew moved away.'

'Thanks mate,' George said emptily, 'that means a lot.'

'Might be true, we'll never know though, since neither of us have the get up and go required to move somewhere else and start new lives. Not like Andy, remember him?'

'No... oh wait, was he the guy with the acne and the glasses?' George asked.

'The very same, he popped up on my Facebook feed the other day, he's in London, like all the other twats, loads of cash, shiny children, blah blah blah blah.' Tim said.

'I got a request from Tom the other day as well,' George said, 'similar, and Martin, and Darren, and – fuck, actually loads of guys from back then.'

'All twats now, except our dear Elaine, because she came back,' Tim nodded sagely, 'the rest of them can fuck off though, even if they do come back to breed. Some of them have you know, but you don't see them out do you?'

'Who?' George asked.

'Colin the cock is back, and big bad Dom, according to the internet anyway, only live round the corner, sold up their tiny flats in London and bought big posh-nob houses up in College Green with the curtain twitchers. Probably why we never see them,' Tim explained.

'Never liked those two anyway, twats.'

'Twats indeed, we are infinitely better off than them, money and shiny things are overrated. Were it not for the marvel of social media, we would not give them a second thought. I do not care if we are only still friends because we are the only guys left in town, at least we *are* still friends, now get that down you,' they clinked their near empty cans together in camaraderie, drained what was left in them and threw them towards the river. George immediately felt bad about that and ran to pick up their litter, sinking up to his knees in tidal mud.

'Fuck 'em, there's a lot worse than that goes in that river every day mate,' Tim stated as he pulled George out, 'here have another.'

George took the proffered can once he had got to his feet, and drank hard, 'why do they always leave me Tim?'

'Because you are a whiny twat, that's why,' Tim put his friend in a mock headlock, rubbed his head and then released him, 'remember the mantra Georgie boy.'

George remembered it well, when they were kids, any time one of them was dumped they would go for a drink, and the one who had not been dumped would say, in the blandest monotone they could muster, and all in one unpunctuated sentence as Tim did now: 'plenty more fish she/he wasn't good enough for you anyway blah blah blah cheer up old stick let's have a drink,' and no more would be said about it.

'But we're not kids any more Tim, and I am just a stupid old man who was dumb enough to think that a beautiful, smart young thing like that might actually like me, and not just be after a place to stay and somebody to blag money off and I can't believe I didn't see it, and I feel old, bald, fat and stupid, and I am not sure if there are any fish left now anyway, or at least, any that I might like, I fucking hate fish Tim, they taste like crap, and they suck other people's dicks.'

'You are not stupid George, you're just an endless optimist,' Tim replied, 'you always want people to be better than they are – for which I am eternally grateful by the way,' he wrapped George up into a massive bear hug as George began crying into Tim's shoulder, 'you are old, fat and bald though, dear, sorry to break it to you,' Tim chuckled. They stood like that until George had cried all the embarrassment out of his system.

CHAPTER 24

'Sorry,' said the man in the bed opposite George as he let out yet another very loud fart. This happened every couple of minutes, and not just to the man opposite. George too was regularly breaking wind, as were the other five gentlemen in the room. This was the recovery ward for the colonoscopy department, and the little jet of air that helps the camera find its way inside you without tearing the lining of your intestines has an amusing side effect. All that air has to find its way out again, and the rest of your day will be spent expelling it at five minute intervals or less. Sadly, men are really just little boys at heart, and, if you put seven of them in the same room while they are all parping, there will mostly be sniggering and giggling as well. Especially if they are in there while the painkillers wear off after a minor surgical procedure. George reflected that this might be intentional, as it helped take their mind from their more obvious worries.

As he lay in the bed, chuckling at the other trumping men, George considered the last week. It had stunk almost as much as this room did. He had forgotten all about lunch with Linda the day after his and Tim's ill-advised walk home, and had had both a filthy hangover, and a stinking cold as a result of his wading through the mud. None of that compared to how terrible he felt as a result of the Verity revelation. It was akin to a morning after when you see all the wonderful things you think you did the night before in a sober light and realise you were acting a complete tit. This is often accompanied by an attempt to eat your own fist as visions of yourself falling over, pouring coffee on your hostess and urinating in the cupboard under the stairs keep on coming. George could not believe he had been so stupid, and wished he had a way to go back and erase the last month of his life.

Linda had come round to see him the evening after the missed lunch – after an angry phone call resulted in him claiming the filthy cold had made him forget to ring and let her know he couldn't make it. As ever, she had forgiven him and he had spent the evening with his daughter, desperately wanting to talk to her about everything that had happened, but painfully aware of just how awkward it would make her life. His chronic embarrassment helped make his decision not to tell her a lot less selfless than it seemed. It had been a difficult evening as Linda did nothing but extol the virtues of her new flatmate. Apparently, Verity could do no wrong in that department. Although George continually tried to drag the subject round to something else, it didn't work, and he had had to pretend that he and Verity were still the very best of friends.

After work on Monday, things had taken another turn for the weird, as – during a long telephone conversation – Malcolm claimed that he had done the whole thing for George's own good. George was not entirely convinced of this, but it seemed the only explanation that made any sense from Malcolm's point of view. George had rung Malcolm to inform him that he would be leaving the band, he really didn't want to have to spend his free time with the two people who had made him more unhappy than he could ever have believed possible. He was also coming round to the fact that it just wasn't the same band without Bill, and it might never recover from his departure.

Malcolm had asked, well nearly begged, him to hang on until they could find a replacement for him. He wouldn't have to rehearse, he could just turn up to gigs, like Gavin. Having seen the trouble Bill's sudden departure had caused, George decided to be a pro about it, and agreed to cover all the gigs they had booked until another bassist could be found. Besides, the local music scene was a very small world – and if he walked out just like that, over what might seem like nothing to anybody else, he could probably forget about ever getting into another band ever again. While at the moment he didn't think that would be a bad thing, he was aware that he might not always feel that way, and George was nothing if not practical.

The lovely nurse, who had so kindly given George a barium enema earlier that morning, came in and told him he could get dressed now and go through to see the Doctor with his results. Ten minutes later, he was sitting opposite a tired looking man in a white coat, staring at a printed diagram of an intestinal system with some crosses drawn on it.

'Well, you are probably going to be okay, but, as you know, we did find a lump in there,' the Doctor said to George, who just nodded in reply, 'We cut it out of you, as you are also aware, and we've sent it off for tests. Hopefully, and we're pretty sure it is, it will prove to have just been a cyst – in which case we don't need to worry anymore, and you are indeed all clear. Apart from the haemorrhoids obviously.'

'How long 'til I know Doc?' George asked, pointedly ignoring the reference to his less serious problem.

'We'll ring you with the results as soon as we get them through, shouldn't be more than a week, maybe a week and a half, two weeks tops,' George couldn't help thinking of Monty Python's famous 'Spanish Inquisition' sketch as the Doctor kept refining his estimate, and tried not to laugh, though it may just have been a side effect of the painkillers he had been given, 'and of course we'll send it to you in writing – special delivery – as soon as possible.'

Sitting on the bench outside the hospital, George wondered if things could get any worse. He had lost the girl he had fallen madly in love with, his dignity, his band, and pretty much everything he had done to make his life better over the last year in less than a week. He just wanted to go home, curl up into a ball and die – which was fortunate, because if that lump proved to be something worse, and malignant, that might be exactly what he was going to do. It was either lucky or unlucky, depending on what mood he was in, that he was not allowed to drive himself home after the procedure, and had therefore finally had to tell somebody about his condition. He was not sure he had made the best choice of confidante, but he could not have taken the string of bum jokes he would have received from Tim, and he had no intention of burdening Linda with any of this.

'You look like you need a drink,' Elaine said, as her car pulled up alongside his bench, 'get in.'

George duly obliged and got in, 'I am very glad that you are back in town again,' he said, 'how was London anyway?'

'Utter shit,' she replied, matter-of-factly, 'it's me that needs a drink, I care not one jot for you and your problems, which pub?'

'Pub? You might want to just help yourself to my drinks cabinet instead,' George suggested, 'I restocked it yesterday.'

'You are never turning down the offer of a trip to the pub?' Elaine looked shocked until George let out yet another blast of gas, then she just looked disgusted and wound down the window.

'Yep, that's why, I am filled with air,' he explained, 'and I am terrified that each one will have an unintentional follow through. Please don't make me shit myself in public.'

'As long as your legendary collection of funny-coloured spirits is intact, then we have a deal. Or is your "house guest" still there?' Elaine asked, making actual quote marks in the air and causing George to wince until she put her hands back on the steering wheel again, 'She might not like you bringing another girl home to get her drunk.'

George suddenly realised that Elaine didn't know. He hadn't spoken to anybody in the last week, and she had been away in London visiting her son. He had arranged for her to come and pick him up from his hospital appointment before she had left. She knew nothing of his current troubles, even Tim and Ant would not have told her since they had been sworn to secrecy – and occasionally they kept their word.

'Ah, not-so-funny story about that,' he began, and filled her in on the changes in his life as she drove him home.

'And you're still playing in the band with them?' Elaine shouted through the kitchen door at him while he prepared a jugful of booze that would have made Tim proud.

'Yeah, can't really think of a decent way round that yet,' he replied, 'cloudy lemonade in the top?'

'Yes, that amount of alcohol mixed together will need something to take the edge off it. Cloudy lemonade will work. Please stop avoiding the issue,' Elaine's voice sounded strained, as if telling off an unrelenting child.

'So you haven't told me how things went in London,' George said, bringing the jug in and setting it down on the coffee table in front of them, 'how's the ex problem going?'

'Well, I am now two weeks of travelodging poorer, and in need of some actual friends up there with spare rooms. Honestly, I can't remember what I ever saw in that arsehole, and he still has Jack convinced that I live in the middle of nowhere, so he won't come down to stay,' she ranted, 'I mean I agreed with him that it was better for Jack to stay up there, I am in no position to have him live with me anyway – my flat is tiny, I am working constantly to pay for it, and I am always very angry. But he is making me out to be some kind of witch. I think if I hadn't gone up there – and taken the time off from working to relax and become more pleasant – my own son would actually have ended up hating me, and... hey, nice deflection – well played,' she clinked her glass against his, 'and seriously, are you sure you can cope playing in that band every weekend after that?'

'I don't know, to be honest,' George sighed, 'but it can't be for too long – they must know a hundred bass players out there looking for a gig. And my reputation will remain intact.'

'You have no reputation,' Elaine replied flatly, pouring herself a very large glass of their pick-me-up cocktail, 'except as a first class doormat. She is still using you, even if you aren't talking to her.'

George let out another nasty bout of flatulence in reply to this.

'Oh dear god,' Elaine said, 'I do hope you didn't follow through that time.'

'No, at least, I don't think so,' George replied, 'it's the indignity of everything that is getting to me at the moment really, and I don't just mean all this farting. Everybody who knew about the Verity thing told me this would happen eventually, even you tried to warn me,' Elaine opened her mouth to say something, but was waved aside by George, 'no, don't apologise, you were right, and you knew I wouldn't listen, and that's fine. I am an old, fat, bald idiot, and even though I only told you, Malcolm and Tim about it, just the fact that three people know what an utter arse I have been is enough to make me want to lock myself in a cupboard and never come out again.'

'Four – Tim tells Ant everything,' Elaine reminded him and took a swig from the terrifying cocktail.

'Four, yes,' George groaned, 'and I know it was a shitty way to go about it, but Malcolm did do me a favour really – showing me what she was really like, and cutting all my fantasies short. I mean, I knew they were fantasies, but I was enjoying the idea that she really liked me, and that me and her could maybe be together.'

'That has always been your problem George,' Elaine cut in, 'you always play for keeps, I've almost never seen you just have a casual thing, well, there was that dreadful Kaye woman, but that just proves that you are an all or nothing kind of guy.'

'Maybe you're right,' George sighed.

'Course I'm right,' Elaine nodded, pouring more of the jug into George's glass.

'And it's not just the Verity thing,' George started again, 'this

whole bowel thing is just embarrassing – I've lost count of the
amount of people who have stuck their fingers up my arse recently.'

Elaine stifled a small giggle.

'And well you may laugh, the worst of it is the fucking piles,'
George's voice went up a few tones with frustration, 'every morning
and every night, I have to rub cream for – and I quote the tube –
Chronic. Anal. Fissures – into my own bumhole.'

'I bet you wish you'd heard that before you named the band don't
you?' Elaine quipped.

'If we had been a punk band, maybe, yes, chronic anal fissures
would have been a good name, anyway, do you know what I do –
pretty much every time?'

'No, and I'm sure I don't want to,' Elaine replied.

'As I look at my finger, with its little creamy hat on, preparing to
violate me, I look myself right in the eye in the bathroom mirror, and
then, in the most sarcastic voice I can muster...'

'Wow, that must be pretty damn sarcastic,' Elaine cut in, in an
uncanny impression of the voice George was trying to describe.

'In the most sarcastic voice I can muster,' George continued, 'I
sing the first line of Tears for Fears' "Everybody Wants To Rule The
World" at myself, you know "*welcome to your life, there's no
turning back,*" I love that song, I even loved playing it in the band,
it's pretty much just one note, over and over and over again on the
bass, but I never cared, the moment that guitar solo kicks in,
everything is better – although not the way Gav plays it – just the
whole world. At least it was, now I have ruined it for myself forever
with a sarcastic mirror song. And I can't stop doing it. Because this is
my life: I am old now, whether I feel it or not, and there is no turning
back from having to apply various unpleasant creams in vaguely
unsanitary-seeming ways now, things can only go down from here.
This is the healthiest I will ever be again, right now.'

'Oh get over yourself and grow a pair of ovaries George,' Elaine
said, 'I'm a woman – we are constantly having our bits prodded about
by doctors with incredibly cold, scary, proddy things. And there is
nothing like a yeast infection to make you appreciate the finer things
in life. Shall I tell you a song I can't listen to any more?'

'Go on then,' George obliged.

'"Alison" – Elvis Costello.'

'Why's that then?' George asked.

'Because I always look at my finger wearing a little creamy hat, about to do something that should be fun, but is not going to be, and I change the words, and sing, "*Canesten, my aim is true.*"'

'You won't believe this Elaine,' George said, 'but I had a fungal infection a year or two ago – I know,' he added in reply to the disgusted look on her face, 'but these things happen, and I did the same thing, exactly the same song, same words, same everything.'

Elaine tried to suppress a laugh, until George could hold his in no more, and they both fell about laughing, before launching into a joint chorus of the aforementioned Elvis Costello classic with the new words.

The next day George went downstairs to his empty house, glad he had friends like Elaine and Tim to talk to. He decided he would tell Tim about the cancer scare next time he saw him, to hell with the bum jokes, he was his friend.

CHAPTER 25

The next two weeks were a bit of a daze for George, he went to
work – same as usual; watched TV, ate his food and did all the
things he usually did, but took no joy in any of it. Even his favourite
records seemed to have lost any semblance of what used to make
them magic for him, he picked up Danny and Alice from school on
the days he was supposed to, and spent those afternoons playing
multi-player games on his new Xbox one with them, hoping against
hope that he would still be able to do this with them as adults. The
whole world suddenly felt dreadfully hollow, and in his darker
moments he wanted the news to be bad, just so that he could stop
this feeling that life was just killing time – waiting around for time to
kill him.

He knew full well that it was almost certainly just a cyst, and that
he had nothing to worry about, but there was always that little
nagging doubt. Even a one percent chance is still a chance – so he
felt his focus on the worst case scenario was entirely justified and
not just an extension of his pessimism. It was the waiting that was
driving him mad, he just wanted to know one way or the other
whether it was over or not, and he wanted the fairy in his ear to stop
singing 'bum cancer bum cancer bum cancer bum cancer bum cancer
bum cancer...'

He turned up to gigs, pretended none of what had happened
mattered to him, and laughed along with Gavin and Chris – well as
much as you could with Gavin and Chris, neither of them were
exactly a bundle of laughs at the best of times. He only spoke to
Verity or Malcolm if he had to, and he was avoiding Bryony, when
she was there, out of sheer embarrassment from their last
conversation. Each gig was a tiny torture session, apart from the
blissful release of just playing music to a willing audience. But even

the audiences were starting to notice the rifts building in the band, there were less and less dancers at the front, the applause was becoming ever more polite, and the obligatory encores ever more tenuous. It was having an effect on the sound, they were not the tight unit they had been before, things were coming apart.

Eventually, Verity cornered him after they had finished playing one night.

'Babes, I'm so sorry if you misunderstood,' she said, her face pushed in close to his, her breath warm against him, her scent filling his senses, her eyes – so deep and beautiful, holding his gaze until she allowed him to look away, 'I don't really do exclusive or monogamous, I thought everyone knew that. I really wish you weren't leaving though – are you sure there's nothing I can do to persuade you to stay with us,' she waggled her eyebrows suggestively.

'I'm cool with everything, really I am,' George replied, entirely untruthfully, 'I was a little old fashioned before, I get it now, really, but I just can't play in this band any more. We're too busy, I need more time with my kids – that thing on Danny's birthday was bad – but don't worry, I'll cover until you get a replacement, I'm cool, like I said,' he tried to give a self-assured grin, while internally reprimanding himself for saying he was cool, at his age.

Verity leaned in and kissed his cheek, 'Thanks,' she said breathily, 'for everything – I really appreciate it,' and she let her tongue run slowly over his earlobe before walking away, without breaking eye contact, all the way to the door.

George let out a sharp breath and considered this a lucky escape. He had nearly fallen for her charms again, and he was under no illusions that she wanted him. She just needed a bass player, and if that was the way to persuade him to stay, then that was what she would do. Except it was backfiring, George did not want to be dragged back into that situation again, especially now Verity was living with Linda, what would his daughter think of him if he became involved with Verity again, knowing full well that it was some kind of crazy open lack-of-relationship. He couldn't go back there, he just couldn't. He drove home feeling thoroughly miserable, especially now that he couldn't even just drop in and see his daughter anymore – since Linda would know immediately she saw him and Verity together that something weird had gone on, he couldn't yet manage to completely mask the emotions from his face. And Linda was clever at spotting things like that, even without the psychology degree.

CHAPTER 26

It was little Nicky's birthday and, in their usual style, Tim and Ant had invited everybody they knew round for an enormous bash. George was looking forward to a Saturday without having to see any of the band. He had finally received his results from the doctor and was feeling a great deal happier than he had for a long time.

'So you haven't got African Bum Disease and you're not going to die?' Tim said, grinning from ear to ear as he pushed a multi-layered cocktail into George's hand.

'Really? You're going for racist and homophobic today are you?' George answered, looking bemused.

'No, you remember at primary school? We'd say have you got skill?' Tim recalled, 'and if they said yes, then you would say, "urgh, you've got african bum disease!" and it was hysterically funny, I thought since you had bum trouble I'd bring it back.'

'For fuck's sake Tim!' Ant said from behind him, and then apologised sheepishly to a waspish mother holding a baby nearby, 'you do know that was AIDS don't you?'

'What!' Tim went white as a sheet, 'I haven't really thought about it since school, never really occurred to me, I just thought it was funny.'

'Well done, you managed to be a homophobic homo,' Ant giggled, 'though since it is born entirely of ignorance, and it is our only son's birthday, I will forgive you,' and he kissed Tim on the cheek and went off with a tray of canapés.

'I really never thought about it,' Tim laughed, 'lucky I've got you and Ant around to point this stuff out to me.'

'You'd be lynched without us mate,' George said.

'Well, at least you are not dying of whatever the hell it was you thought you had, so you can continue to be my conscience and advisor – like that horrible bug thing out of Pinnochio,' Tim said raising his glass, 'here's to you not dying, old chap.'

'Never before has a man been so glad to be told he's got piles,' George agreed and he and Tim clinked glasses and drained them off. It was going to be one of those children's parties.

'Ah, this might make things a little more awkward. Don't look now, but your daughter's brought an unwelcome guest,' Tim said, with some urgency. Linda had just entered the party with Verity, 'I suppose I did say she could bring anyone she liked, but I had rather hoped it would be one of her mopey beardy friends – Ant does so enjoy them.'

George's face fell, and his previous enthusiasm for the day's festivities was replaced with a sense of terrible foreboding. He made eye contact with Elaine across the room, and received a sympathetic groaning face with a fake hanging noose gesture in reply. It was going to be a long day.

Later on, George was talking to Linda, – Verity having mercifully disappeared in the throng, doubtlessly being admired by one of the many parents in attendance.

'Are Danny and Alice having a good time then?' she asked him.

'Must be, I've barely seen them all day,' he replied, 'have you not spoken to them yet?'

'I tried to, but Danny could not be torn away from the bouncy castle, while Alice and Matt and Donna's girls have set up some kind of makeover salon by the ball pool, and I am slightly scared that they might want to experiment on me, so I just waved from a distance,' Linda explained. 'I have, however, sent Verity over to see them without any prior warning of what they are up to. Poor girl's never met Fiona and Willow, I doubt she has any idea of what Alice turns into when she's with them,' Linda had a mischievous glint in her eye as she recounted this, 'hopefully they won't make her look too strange.'

'Anyhow,' George said, trying desperately to get the subject away from Verity, 'how's the job going?' Linda had managed to finally land herself a decent job with a private mental health practice nearby.

'Utterly shite,' she quickly retorted, 'it is nothing like I expected, I'm a glorified office assistant – I make tea, I do photocopying, and I have to stay late and answer phones when nobody else wants to.'

'Well, we all have to do things we don't like to make ends meet sweetheart,' George put his arm round his daughter to comfort her, 'it won't be forever, you'll soon get up the next rung on the ladder, and then you can get the next poor sap to do all the crap you don't like.'

Linda giggled and then her face went utterly straight again, 'well Dad, not really you see, the recession has bitten again, I'm doing my month's notice already, they laid me off. So actually – even shitter than I may have made out at first.'

'I'm sorry love,' George hugged her closer, 'I'll be alright on my own now if you want to move away,' he grinned, reminding her of her earlier reasoning.

'Oh, ha ha,' she hugged him back, and the two of them comforted each other, although only one of them knew they were doing the comforting.

'Did you hear about Joan though Dad?' Linda said, into his armpit.

'What about Joan?' George was intrigued, and broke off the embrace.

'She and Robin broke up,' Linda replied, 'apparently he can't stand your children, so he left. She's really upset, by all accounts.'

'I saw her this morning when I picked the kids up,' George said, taken aback, 'she didn't say anything.'

'Well, she thinks you'll just gloat,' Linda said, 'you've always been good at holding grudges, I saw it coming back at Danny's birthday party when he didn't show up, but she wouldn't listen to me then. I managed not to do an "I told you so" when I spoke to her the other day though, she seemed pretty cut up.'

George had a brief flash of revenge-driven joy, before realising he felt pretty bad for Joan if she was feeling any bit as miserable as he did right now. The sympathy was unexpected, the revenge had tasted bitter, and he had a terrible feeling that he might finally be growing up.

Suddenly there was the sound of shouting from across the garden, which made everyone instantly silent – listening for the sounds of scandal.

'Seriously! What is your problem with me you old hag?' Verity was shouting.

'Problem? I'm not the one with the problem,' came Elaine's calm, measured voice in response, 'paranoid much?'

'It is not paranoid if you really are being stalked,' Verity screamed back, 'you've been looking at me like you scraped me off of your shoe all day, everywhere I've been, there you are – watching me like some stalky old grandma.'

'I think you might have had a few too many of Tim's cocktails dear,' Elaine said in her best patronising voice, 'they're not really for children.'

'You dried up old bitch,' Verity shouted back, and stepped forward to slap Elaine, who stepped nimbly back – allowing Verity to gracelessly slip on one of her impractically high heels and fall face first onto the ground instead, Tim appeared from nowhere, and helped Verity back to her feet.

'Maybe you have had a bit too much, sweetie,' he said, passing her over to Linda to hold up, 'she's right about my cocktails, they are a little strong for the uninitiated.'

'Oh, both of you now is it?' she continued, 'you're no better you fucking queen, looking down your massive nose at me whenever you get the chance. You're both just jealous old fruitcakes, because neither of you can have George, and I have very much had him, in ways neither of you could ever possibly imagine, and you can't take the fact that I am young and beautiful, and he wants me, not you. And trust me, he really, really wants me still – whatever he says.'

There was a stony silence as she once again landed heavily on the ground, gaining a huge grass stain down the other, unstained, side of her once pristine, clinging white mini-dress. Linda had pushed her away, and looked stone-faced at her father.

'Is this true?' she exclaimed, 'Have you been fucking my flatmate without me knowing about it?'

'Well,' George shuffled his feet and looked guiltily at her, 'it's not as simple as that.'

'I don't believe you, it's all lies, all the time isn't it Dad?' she said, tears running down her face, 'Well you can tell them to someone else this time.' She turned on her heel and left.

Verity was still lying on the ground, drooling slightly from the left side of her mouth, and clearly suffering from the sleepy effects of Tim's cocktails. She was not going anywhere any time soon.

CHAPTER 27

It was much later the same night, and the party continued for those who were able. Most of the hangers on and parents of Nicky's friends had had to leave, some of them had been a little upset by the drama earlier, and had made a hasty exit, but most of them were used to that sort of thing, and came to expect it at Tim and Ant's parties. Danny was sleeping over with Nicky anyway, and Alice, Fiona and Willow would not be left out of the arrangement. This left Tim, Ant, Matt, Donna, Elaine and George in Tim and Ant's living room being made to drink coffee for an hour by Ant before going back to the booze – in the vain hope that it would help them to communicate in a comprehensible manner for the rest of the evening. Tim and Elaine managed to piece together the whole sorry tale of George's recent misfortunes and had filled everyone else in on it while George inadvisedly drove Verity home and tried to find Linda.

'Well, I'm glad you didn't kill yourself you twat,' Donna exclaimed, as George came into the room.

'It's only round the corner, and all the police are in the middle of town on a Saturday night, he was fine,' Tim stuck up for his friend for once, feeling that it was quite a noble thing George had done: risking his driving licence to make sure the woman who had all but destroyed his heart got home in one piece. Everybody else just saw George running around after a pretty young girl despite all she had done – like a lovesick teenager. George himself had thought of it more as an excuse to go round to Linda's and explain himself, not that he should have needed an excuse, but he couldn't help trying to over-justify his every move. It may have proven to be a terrible idea had it worked out. She really was very angry, and taking the cause of that anger back to her home could not be a good idea. However, he really didn't want Verity hanging around after that, and couldn't think of any other way to remove an unconscious drunken woman that wasn't illegal, or at least terribly worrying. It had been, in some ways, a relief to find that Linda was not at home.

'S'alright, nobody stopped me,' George defended himself, 'I know it was stupid, but did you lot want to spend all night holding her hair back while she chucks up the last of Tim's not-quite-Mojitos?'

They all nodded sagely, it would not have been a pleasant end to the evening, looking after a girl that they had all decided they definitely hated over the last few hours.

'Lin's disappeared anyway, no sign of her at her place,' George sighed, 'I am not entirely sure how I am going to come back from this one. I even rang her mum to ask if she'd seen her – didn't tell her why of course, but no sign there either.'

'Well, since you've spent most of the last year or so apologising to her,' Ant began, wagging his finger, 'and most of it has been because of her friend Verity. I reckon you should just stay away from Verity, simple as that mate.'

'Yeah, but it isn't that simple is it?' George responded, 'there's the band to think of, I said I wouldn't leave them in the lurch, and I don't intend to. I can turn up, play, and leave again without throwing myself at her for a few more weeks, and then they'll have a new bassist, and I'll be free.'

'Really?' Matt said, 'she wasn't a little bit right with her parting shot then? You remember: "he really, really wants me, no matter what he says" – nobody would blame you George, she is proper fit.'

'Oi you!' Donna retorted, punching him playfully on the arm, 'you shouldn't be noticing that sort of thing.'

'Yes, I know,' George said, 'that's what got me in all this trouble in the first place.' He briefly recalled how their first night together had been born of his worrying about her drunken state, just as this evening's humiliating journey had been, however, this time he had felt no remorse in leaving her alone on her living room floor in the recovery position. She had had enough presence of mind to look him in the eye, attempt to slap him round the face and call him a prick before he had left, so he was pretty sure she wasn't going to die. 'I will have you lot know that just a couple of weeks ago I turned down some very exotic offers from her, I am not doing that again. I have learned from my mistake – and her claim is no more true than her statement that Tim and Elaine were driven to try and kill her with sharp looks by jealousy.'

Elaine and Tim shared a wry grin with each other and both reached over to claw at his legs, 'Oh but George, we do so love you, we love you, let us have you please!' they chanted almost in unison while mock tearing at his clothes. 'One at a time, or both together, I just don't care anymore!' Tim screamed, pulling his orange corduroy jacket off in mock excitement.

'Very funny,' Ant cut in, 'but we all know that Tim has been in love with you his entire life George, even I know that. Second fiddle to your endless unrequited love affair – that is the role I am happy to play.'

'But of course I love George,' Tim said, plainly, 'but not like that: George is like my brother – only not a bank manager, or an unutterable tosser, in fact nothing like my actual brother, who I barely like, let alone love – I have known George these near forty years, we have been through everything together, and, and I hope George will back me up on this, I have never so much as made a pass at him, as I have never, ever thought of him in that way.'

George nodded, as Tim hung his head dramatically, 'S'true, he never has, and I too love Tim dearly for all the reasons he said, and more. I have often reflected that life would have been much simpler if I had turned out gay and we'd ended up together.'

'Do you not get it George?' Tim said, 'I have never fancied you, even before you got fat and bald, it would be like some kind of weird incest, and I am not into that kind of thing at all thank you. Honestly, much as I love you, you have never really understood the gay thing have you? Any more than you, my darling,' and here he looked pointedly at Ant, 'have understood that men can be friends with other men without wanting to fuck them ragged.'

Ant shrugged and waved at Matt across the room, 'Hello friend,' he said, winking. The tension in the room drained away in raucous laughter and George tried to enjoy the rest of the evening without worrying about Linda, or Verity, or the band, at least he no longer had to worry about the bum cancer fairy singing in his ear all the time anymore.

CHAPTER 28

It had been nearly three months since George had caught Verity and Malcolm *in flagrante delicto* and he was starting to dread dragging his gear into the car and driving off to yet another night of awkward silences and difficult conversations. In all this time they had still failed to find a suitable replacement for him, which he was finding both flattering and exasperating, as it was harder and harder to spend time with Verity. It wasn't that he was still in love with her, it was just the burning shame that she brought out in him.

Equally, it wasn't even the awkwardness of playing with Verity and Malcolm that was bringing him down any more. The whole thing was starting to grate, he still loved playing, but the hanging around waiting to play – and the continual and never ending loading and unloading of gear in and out of cars and venues – was less exciting now. He remembered when they first started it had seemed exotic and exciting when strange drunken women had tried to get on the stage and sing down his microphone, now he just wanted them to get out of his way and stop having such a good time. He was beginning to feel little more than contempt for the audiences, how dare they enjoy this show, it was nothing like as good as they had been before, they were a shadow of their former selves – and it was only ever a covers band anyway, why on earth would people enjoy that? He barely recognised himself from the guy who was so excited about playing in a band less than a year ago. He wasn't sure now if he would even bother joining another band if they ever let him leave this one. He was starting to get the feeling they were just marking time until he changed his mind – it seemed to be working on Gavin.

In a rare conversation with Malcolm he told him he was thinking of jacking the whole thing in.

'Ah, George, we all feel like that some days, but you try a few months without it, you'll get itchy fingers and you'll be back out on the circuit before you know it. It gets in your blood, know what I mean?' Malcolm had replied.

'Maybe that's true for you mate,' George continued, 'but you've been doing this for so long you don't know how to do anything else. I've not been doing it a whole year yet. I still remember Saturday nights in front of the telly. Maybe I'm not cut out for this? Perhaps I'm just going through a phase?'

'Doubt it George, I doubt it very much,' Malcolm assured him, 'I've seen your face when you're playing – you love it too much, you don't get that feeling playing in your bedroom. Trust me, I know this stuff.'

George nodded, 'Yeah, I guess you might be right, there's just so much politics involved. Walking on eggshells around Chris in case he gets angry, listening to Gavin go on and on about when he met whichever famous person he is claiming to have played with this week without telling him to shut up, dealing with what you and Verity did,' he looked pointedly at Malcolm at this point, as if daring him to justify it again, 'and all the time wanting you all to just find my replacement so it can all be over. I actually miss Saturday night TV now you know?'

'Sorry mate, I know – though I will never understand why anyone would want to watch that shite, isn't it all quiz shows and Noel Edmonds still?' Malcolm replied, 'and I know you still don't want to believe I was trying to help you with Verity, but I was. We haven't even found a proper replacement for Bill yet, we are trying, really we are, but it's not easy. I mean, being in a band is not what it used to be any more, and it makes me really pissed off. It's a proper shame you're leaving, cos it's been like it used to be again – being in a band with your mates.'

'What on earth do you mean?' George asked.

'Well, back when I was first doing this, you had a bunch of mates who all wanted to be in a band, so you all learned an instrument, and you started a band. Or you met guys in a pub, or at proper old style jam nights – not like the fucking whiny-bastard-show-off sessions that you get at open mic nights these days – and you all wanted to do the same sort of thing, so you started a band. You know, you were all mates already, nowadays everyone's answered a fucking advert, and it's like a proper job. The guys who can play are never your mates any more, but your actual mates can't fucking play and it's

168

proper shit. I like you George, and you can fucking play, and that's rare these days – I can barely tolerate Gav at the best of times, and he's no great shakes on guitar either, but he always turns up when you ask him, and that's about the best I can ask for really.' He looked at the floor, shaking his head.

'I suppose I should be flattered by that really,' George replied, 'but I'm still leaving – and you were still a total shit to me.'

'Look, I did what I did in the hope that we could avoid you having to leave, I didn't know you were that into Verity, I thought if you saw what she was really like, then we could all move on, and everything would be fine. I'm sorry, I don't know how many more times I'm going to have to say that to you. You know, you could have joined in at the other end, she's into threesomes – we could probably get one after tonight's show if you want?' Malcolm seemed genuine in his offer, with an eager face like a puppy who's just seen your plate-carrying hand start to slip.

'See, this is not my world,' George replied, draining the last of his drink and walking away, 'and that's why I have to leave. I can't ever be like that.'

He walked into the dressing room to change into his stage clothes where he bumped into Gavin, hunched over the windowsill.

'Alright George?' he chirped, wiping powder from his nose, 'fancy a toot on this? Same stuff as Keith Richards buys apparently, I got it off his roadie – old mate of mine.'

'No thanks,' George mumbled, trying to find a corner to change in where he might not have to listen to Gavin, whose casual use of cocaine to calm his nerves always seemed to backfire, and lead to him talking even more bollocks than usual.

They did yet another show, playing the same old tunes – Gavin stumbled and missed as many notes as usual, and George made more mistakes than he normally would, since he was so busy listening out for Gavin's fluffs and trying to compensate that he missed his own cues. Chris had become more half-hearted in his drumming as a result of this lack of cohesion, and everything was a little more lacklustre than it had been a few short months ago, before everything started to fall apart.

CHAPTER 29

'So she's in Bristol now?' Elaine said, 'and she's got a job that she really likes finally?'

'Yes, she's a counsellor at a sixth form college, but still not talking to me I'm afraid,' George replied. He and Elaine had gone out together for Friday night drinks, she had sent him a text message as she finished work explaining that she needed a drink and nobody else was available to come out, so would he do her a massive favour and meet her at the pub. Since he wasn't playing that night, and his current post round gave him Saturday mornings off, he hadn't even had to think about it. They had met at the Swan at five-thirty and were already two drinks in by six.

'I found out from her step-dad a few weeks ago,' George continued, 'I ran into him in the All Seasons at an open mic night – we're doing those now, by the way, every Tuesday, we're the house band, nobody ever wants to play bass, so I'm pretty much on all night, it's a proper gig night now. They told me it would be a really good way to find my replacement, and yet it's actually just another bloody night where I am not watching telly with my feet up. Interestingly, Gavin is getting a bit protective of his spot now, he slates every guitar player that gets up to play, especially if they're better than him. I think he secretly wants to be in the band, but can't bring himself to admit that he likes playing covers.'

'George,' Elaine exclaimed, 'we're talking about Linda! Your daughter, stop moaning about that bloody band!'

'Sorry,' George apologised, 'I rarely go out with anybody that's not the band now, so I am venting at you a bit, sorry again, anyway – Lin's step-dad, yes. I saw him in the pub, and he basically told me that Linda had told him everything about me and Verity – which was kind of awkward for a bit – but he didn't think it was fair of her to not tell me what she was up to, even though she had asked him not to tell me either. He reckoned that whatever I had done or not done was none of his business, but it was cruel of Linda not to let me know where she was. Her bloody mother wouldn't tell me anything, I rang her enough times, and she just told me that Lin was okay, but she was not at liberty to tell me anything else, and I shouldn't bother asking. Even though I've heard nothing from her since Nicky's birthday.'

'So you know she's alright, and you know where she is, but you aren't able to see her, talk to her, or even admit that you know where she is?' Elaine summarised, 'that is pretty shitty. I mean I know Pete has been trying to persuade Jack that I am the devil, but it's not working, and I know where he is, and I can talk to him any time I like. In fact, I am going up to see him tomorrow, which is why I am drinking tonight.'

'Celebration? Dutch Courage? Or because you don't want to drink while you're up there?' George asked.

'Bit of all three really,' Elaine replied, 'truly, I do not want to drink in front of him – as it will just give Pete ammunition to claim I am an unfit alcoholic mother. Despite the fact I am nothing of the kind, as you well know,' she aimed a sly wink at George as he was hailing the barmaid for the third round of drinks, 'also, I do need to get my courage up, since I see him so rarely now that I get nervous our time together will not be good enough and he won't want to see me any more. And finally, I am celebrating the fact that my old friend Shirley has moved back to London again, and has a spare room that she says I can use any time I like, so that's a great deal of money saved.' She raised her fresh glass, and her and George chinked glasses and drank to her good fortune.

'That is pretty good,' George replied, 'I am happy for you.'

'You could come along you know? Shirley's away, but she's loaned me her keys, so you won't even have to meet new people. Weekend up in the smoke might do you some good,' she suggested, 'you don't have to hang out with me and Jack – you can go to Denmark St and play with the guitars, or whatever. We're doing art galleries though, if you fancy some culture.'

'Can't,' George sighed, 'got a gig, some awful birthday party at a yacht club somewhere miles away from here. It will be awful I'm sure.'

'Fine, keep on martyring yourself to those tossers,' Elaine said, 'they're never letting you leave by the way – just so you know.' She stretched her arms out and yawned loudly, 'ooh, I haven't eaten, have you eaten?'

George shook his head, he hadn't eaten yet.

'Chips? You want chips? Chips with curry sauce? Down on the Quay? We can throw chips at the pigeons and the seagulls and start a war – it'll be just like the old days. Then we can carry on, this feels like it's going to be one of those nights, and we will need ballast. Tomorrow I have to pretend to be responsible, and you need to look happy in front of strangers – I think we deserve a night of drunken fun.'

It was a good suggestion, they downed their drinks, and headed off over the bridge to the Blue Dolphin for a couple of bags of chips, a pot of curry sauce and some scrumps (or scribbles, scraps, scrapings, fishbits, batterbites – whatever you call them where you're from – regional variations apply). It was what they used to do back when they were young and stupid. They would spend Saturday afternoons crawling from pub to pub, and at around five or six o'clock they would need to fall into a chip shop for something to soak up the booze so they could continue. The throwback to the old days was just what George needed, he and Elaine sat on the Quay eating their chips and throwing the black bits at the birds.

'Hello mate, how's it going?' came a voice from behind the bench they were sitting on. They turned around and saw Bill and a woman they had never seen before but assumed must be his wife.

'Hello Bill, how have you been?' George asked, with genuine warmth – he had missed him more than he realised since he had left the band.

'Not so bad mate, not so bad, have you met my wife before?' he indicated the woman with him, 'Anna, this is George, he used to play bass with us in the Badgers.' Anna frowned at the mention of the band.

'And this is my friend Elaine,' George waved in her general direction with his styrofoam box of chips, 'I can't remember if you two ever met before.'

'I would have remembered,' Bill said, that old devilish glint appearing in his eyes as he shook her hand, she just gave him a withering look as he smiled his most winning smile at her, 'pleased to meet you.' Turning to George, he said, 'How's the band going then? I see ads for gigs still, but haven't managed to make it along to one yet, sorry.'

'Oh, it's still going, yeah, not the same as it was with you though mate. I'm leaving anyway, I think I've had enough.' George explained, without going into the Verity thing.

'That's a shame, you're a tidy little bassist, if that's not too patronising,' Bill replied, 'if I ever go back to it you'd be my first call now – we worked well together.'

'We did,' George agreed, 'if you did, I might consider coming back to it.'

'Listen, are you getting your share of the money for those lights back?' Bill asked, ''cos when I spoke to Malcolm about it, he denied that we ever agreed to buy anybody's share out when they left. He was kind of a dick about it actually, I mean it's not like I need the money – but it's the principle isn't it? We made an agreement.'

'Verbal contract Bill, you know what they say,' George replied, he had forgotten all about the agreement over the lights, he was too busy just trying to get out of the band, and now there was another reason to stay in contact with them, great.

'Not worth the paper it's written on, yeah, I suppose you're right, it's happened to me enough times before, musicians always stiff you over money, especially once they know you've got enough,' Bill sighed, 'I thought Malc was alright though. Mind you, it's exactly the sort of shit I'd expect from Chris, he never even looked like he was enjoying himself once did he? I always wondered why on earth he was doing it.'

'I thought the same thing,' George said, 'in fact, I asked him about it last weekend, I said "Chris, you moan about every last little thing that we do, you complain that it is not worth the hassle for the tiny amount of money that we get, you moan that the gig isn't big enough, or that it is too big, that it is too near, too far, everything! Why do you do it still? Why don't you just quit?" – and do you know what he said?'

Bill looked quizzically at George, 'No, but I'd like to, I'd imagine the secret to life, the universe and everything could be hidden in Chris's reasoning.'

'Not really, he just shrugged, said "TV's shit on a Saturday night, better to get out and get paid" necked the rest of his dutch courage tequila shot, and then we went on – so I'm none the wiser really.'

'That is a shame,' Bill said, 'I had hoped for so much more. Oh! Did I tell you though, I found the sound – the one in my head, finally.'

'Really?' George was surprised, 'what was it, how much did it cost?'

'You'll laugh, really,' Bill said, 'I was going through my stuff in the loft, and I found my first guitar at the back of it all, some weird old seventies thing from Japan, not even any name on it – I remember hating it for being so cheap and getting something better as fast as I could. Haven't even looked at it in years, let alone played it.' George nodded, that sounded like the sort of thing Bill would do, 'but I always kept it for sentimental reasons you know? Anyway, I plugged it in a few weeks back, and there it was. That sound I've been trying to find all along. Sat up in the loft, under my nose all the time. Could have saved myself a lot of money and trouble if I'd noticed that in the first place.'

'That it would mate, I am glad I have stuck to my Precision all along, it does what I want it to.' George replied.

'Yeah, wish I'd thought like you did.' Bill said, 'anyway, maybe I will go and see you guys again, see if I can find out more about Chris.'

'You should, and maybe once I'm out we should start a new band together – with a less miserable drummer,' George suggested.

'Yeah, won't be for a while, I'm very much enjoying all these free weekends now, we're going to the cinema tonight, and off on a day trip to the moors tomorrow, it's going to be lovely,' Bill said.

George could not tell if Bill was being entirely honest, since he knew that he had been made to leave the band under duress. However, he did feel a mite jealous, as he would like to be doing anything but playing a gig the next evening.

'I am very much looking forward to that – if they ever manage to replace me – it's been ages now,' George complained.

'Ah, you've been caught in the stand-in trap have you?' Bill nodded knowingly, and whispered conspiratorially, 'between you and me, I made the situation out to be a lot worse than it really was to Malcolm, I just didn't want to get caught in the endless waiting that goes on. I feel for you, just go, or Malc will keep you there forever, I know what he can be like.' Bill's words sounded a little hollow, and George thought he might just be trying to put up a front.

'Yeah, I know – oh, did you ever find out about the Guacamole Window reunion?' George asked.

'Yes, funnily enough I ran into their singer at a work thing,' Bill said, 'it turns out that they didn't want Malcolm back because one of them came down here ages back, heard about that friend of your daughter's he was shacked up with and immediately didn't want him around his own daughters. So they didn't get him back – bit paranoid really.'

George agreed it seemed paranoid, but couldn't help feeling it was a sensible precaution.

He could tell Bill was missing the band, he got a hungry, excited look once they had brought it up, which went away again as soon as his wife pointed at her watch and rolled her eyes at him.

'Got to go George,' Bill sighed, his face sinking back to normal again, 'film starts soon, good to see you though, we must catch up properly some time, nice to meet you Elaine.'

'Yeah, we must have a drink together again, maybe you could come to a gig?' George replied, fairly certain that there was no way Anna would let him do that, 'nice to meet you Anna, see you again.' Bill and Anna walked away, leaving them to finish their chips.

'I have met him before,' Elaine quipped as she launched a chip at the side of a seagull's head, 'loads of times, slimy git.'

It was a good deal later on, though not as late as it felt, George and Elaine found themselves in the Patch and Parrot, mostly because they knew there was almost always a good chance of a lock-in in there. They had slowed their drinking pace considerably, and had been nursing the same drinks for a good hour.

'We are definitely getting old now,' George said, looking at his half-full glass, 'back in the old days, we would have necked half a dozen of these by now. I don't think I could manage that now.'

'Speak for yourself,' Elaine teased, 'I'm just holding back so as not to embarrass you. Drink up – my round next.' This was plainly a bluff, as she was also feeling that any more and she would be too drunk. Once you have reached a certain age, then too drunk is not a state you wish to reach any more, not least because the next day, or possibly two days will be utterly lost to you.

'Really?' George had a look of despair in his eyes as he glanced at the clock which claimed that it was only ten o'clock, it could not possibly be only ten o'clock, 'I have done enough stupid shit this last year as a result of this stuff. I would like to remain in control of my faculties for once if that's okay? By the way – is it really only ten o'clock or is this clock wrong?'

'It is indeed only ten o'clock,' Elaine said, momentarily taken aback, 'but well done, you seem to be learning. Shall we blow off waiting for this lock in and go back to mine? It's nearer than yours, and I have better coffee than you do.'

'Coffee?' George raised an eyebrow, 'by which you mean...'

'Coffee you daft twat,' Elaine slapped him playfully on the thigh, 'I've got a train to catch in the morning, and you need to not have a splitting headache if you're going to go to this yacht club. Bugger the old days, we can't drink like this any more and function as human beings. So come back with me, and we can carry on talking – which I am enjoying very much, and stop pouring alcohol into our bloodstream – which I am not any more.'

George sighed, and grudgingly agreed. They left the pub and trudged through the streets, which were filled with the young and foolish, winding their way from pub to club, some casually vomiting into shop doorways on the way and others fighting, hugging, shouting, and swapping bodily fluids in almost equal measures with utter abandon. Both George and Elaine were filled with a mixture of jealousy at their youth, and gratitude that they didn't have to go through all of that again.

'Would you like to be that young and stupid again?' George asked, once they were happily settled in on her sofa drinking freshly ground Columbian coffee.

'God no,' she replied, 'all that screaming about nothing, and crying over good-looking idiots? I don't miss it.'

'But we had great times back then didn't we?' he said, 'I mean we were out all the time, we were drunk most of the time, and we did a whole lot of stupid shit. I have not put a traffic cone on that statue's head in a very long time, we should have done that tonight.' He paused for a minute, with his eyes closed deep in thought before continuing, 'Do you remember when we used to go right out past the car park on the Quay, out on the river bank?'

'Heh, yeah, do you remember when Tim slipped over and fell in the sewage outlet?' Elaine chuckled.

'Ha! Yes, and he wouldn't go home and change, and we all went to that nightclub later. He went in bold as brass, and covered in shit. The bouncers went to stop him, and he just took the two cans of lager out of his pockets, handed them over, apologised for them and walked straight past. I'm pretty sure they were too shocked to stop him, don't you miss doing stuff like that?'

'Yes, but while I miss it George, I really wouldn't want to do it again. Not now, these days I just want to sit here, watch a movie and maybe have a glass of wine or two.'

'Me too really,' said George, 'and that sometimes just pisses me off, I know it's stupid, but I miss the chubby nerdy kid with the stupid quiff that I was. I sometimes think he had it right you know, pretending to be in a band was a lot more fun than actually being in one.'

'I miss him too – I had a bit of a crush on him actually,' Elaine grinned at George and shuffled across the sofa towards him.

'Did you?' George replied, slightly unnerved at this revelation, 'I had a bit of a thing for that crazy girl with the dungarees as well. Even if she did drink pints, and everybody thought she was a lezza.'

'Did they now?' Elaine said, with mock hurt in her voice, 'I wasn't you know, not then, and not now, Lindsay should have been a clue.'

'Everybody just figured Lindsay was as close to a girl as you could get without causing a proper scandal,' George joked, 'he did have a girl's name.'

'Very funny, so how come you never acted on this thing?'

'We were mates, we were really good mates. Still are – which I am very glad of – I didn't want to fuck that up. I mean a shag is a shag and all well and good, but a good mate is hard to come by – and I've only got a few. I did not, and do not, want to lose you to the complications of a sexual relationship.' George sipped at his coffee, slightly uncomfortable that this subject had come up. It was making things much more difficult than he wanted this evening to be.

'Yeah, but I'm willing to risk it if you are,' Elaine said, 'I know you need it spelling out so here it is. There is a genuine chance that I will sleep with you at this point. Now, are you going to fuck? Or fuck off? I am tired of being alone – and I was always saving you for later, until it turned out to be too late. It's not too late anymore, and after all, as you say, a shag is a shag, and if it proves to be a mistake, I promise never to bring it up again. We will never speak of it, and we will go back to being the mates we always were. Don't you ever wonder what it would be like? Me and you? Like in your *Sliders* thingy – don't you reckon there's a parallel universe where me and you got together, and we are incredibly happy, and none of the shite we've been through ever happened to us, because it turns out that mates can be lovers, and might be the best kind?'

George was gobsmacked, as he looked at Elaine he realised that nothing much had really changed in the last twenty years or so. He had always had a bit of a thing for her back then, though his reasons for not acting on them were genuine, and he had blocked out his feelings – persuading himself that they were nothing more than friends. A wall came down inside his head, and all the old forbidden thoughts came flooding out, this was a chance to act out a teenage fantasy, no strings attached, no promises, no problems. It was perfect.

'Well, yeah, I had always put you in the parallel universe game, but I wasn't going to tell you about it, because me and you, we've always been mates, and I didn't want to jeopardise that, because I love you like I love Tim, and he genuinely has never tried it on with me, and...'

'Shut up now,' Elaine said, and took his head in her hands, kissing him hungrily. He kissed her back, and before they knew it they had fallen into one another completely, holding onto each other with a fear that all this might be a dream and not really happening. George moved his hands from behind Elaine, and began clumsily trying to unbutton the front of her dress. He was pretty sure that he did not love her in the same way as he loved Tim now.

'Not down here, not like this,' Elaine whispered into his ear, 'we are grown-ups now after all,' and she got up from the sofa, straightened her dress, took George by the hand and led him upstairs to the bedroom.

CHAPTER 30

George opened his eyes. He was once again in an unfamiliar bedroom. He could see daylight streaming through the curtains; and on his left he could see Elaine's smiling face. She was still asleep, but smiling nonetheless – and just the smile made George incredibly happy.

Last night had been everything he had been looking for for as long as he could remember, how could he have been so stupid for so long. Elaine had been under his nose all this time, one of his oldest and best friends, and he had never realised that that was, in fact, a really good reason to embark on a relationship with someone, rather than the opposite. He positively ached with feelings of unexpected love and happy memories of their night together. It had been like living the fantasies of his youth, she was right. They may both be a little older, a little plumper and a great deal less idealistic than they had been – but he had just got to sleep with the crazy girl in the dungarees he remembered from school, and it was every bit as wonderful as he had imagined in his fevered teenage dreams. He could not for the life of him remember why he had pushed those teenage lusts away.

They had reached the bedroom, and George had begun the frenzied gropings of the adolescent boy whose fantasies he was acting out. As he had begun pawing at Elaine's bra straps through her dress she had stopped him, pushed him away, and calmly explained to him, that there was, in fact, very little sexy about trying to remove each other's clothes. She had then begun to undress herself, and motioned him to do the same. She did it in the unhurried style of somebody preparing themselves for bed, without breaking eye contact with him, and George could honestly say that watching her was far more erotic to him than the usual attempts at finding out which way a girl's bra fastened, and the inevitable pinched skin and lost buttons of over excited and lustful rending of cloth.

She had slowly stepped out of her dress in the most unselfconscious way George could recall seeing, while lecturing him on how Hollywood movies have ruined sex for everyone. Her theory was that everybody expected to be able to easily peel off each others clothes – without all the ripping, accidental squeezing of tender parts and embarrassing lack of mechanical underwear knowledge that goes along with it – and a great deal of precious time was lost from the erotic act itself just trying to get the wrappers off; and that was before you even started on all the unrealistic expectations generated by the aesthetics of movie sex. She removed her last piece of underwear, and smiled at George. He thought her naked body was probably the most beautiful thing he had ever seen – stretch marks, cellulite and all. He quickly followed suit, eagerly throwing his clothes across the room, and the night was lost to them making up for the missing years.

It had been the single most beautiful night he could remember. It was everything he could have hoped for in a romantic encounter – practically, erotically, and just conversationally. Everything, in fact, that he had been hoping to get from Verity – who had merely been young, and not the actual object of any of his genuine young lusts. He realised now just how foolish he had been in trying to recapture his youth with somebody young enough to be his daughter. If you really want to recapture a lost moment in time, he realised now, it was far better to do it with someone who was there.

'Morning you,' Elaine said, looking over at him and still smiling, 'any regrets?'

'Not a one, how about you?' George replied.

'Nope, what time is your gig later?'

'Do you know, I don't think I give a shit any more, can I borrow your phone?' he asked, suddenly gripped with a courage and self assertion that had been completely absent for a long time.

'Of course.'

George got out of bed, and disappeared downstairs, this had been a long time coming, and he wasn't putting up with it anymore. Twenty minutes later, he reappeared with a grin on his face.

'Well, that's the end of that,' he said, 'what time is our train?'

'Are you serious? Have you just quit the band?' Elaine said, with a shocked look on her face.

'I think we can consider those bridges well and truly burned,' he chuckled, feeling like a great weight had been lifted from his shoulders – he owed them nothing, if only he had realised it earlier. 'There may have been some swearing, now, what time are we going to London, I feel a need to see some art.'

'We've a couple of hours yet, get back in here.'

He did, and they picked up where they had left off the night before.

EPILOGUE

It was Danny's seventh birthday, and everybody had come to
George's for a lavish party. He felt it was the least he could do after
what had happened the year before. Most of the children had been
taken home by their respective parents by this time, and Joan had
gone home alone without Danny and Alice (though she had confided
in George that she was actually going out on a date – he was
genuinely hoping things would work out for her). They were staying
over with everybody else, as after Nicky's birthday party and the big
sleepovers of the year before, the children were pretty insistent that
all parties now had to end in a sleepover.

'Dad, you're playing it wrong – that's an A minor, not major,'
Danny complained, he had wanted a guitar for Christmas, and had
received it from his thrilled father. The lessons with Bill were
definitely working out, he was already miles ahead of George as a
musician. George was just pleased that they could play together
when Danny came round, it had brought them closer together, and
last year's birthday problems were all forgotten now. He sighed, and
changed what he was playing to suit Danny's part.

'Are you two going to be doing that all evening?' Elaine enquired
from the other side of the living room, 'only we do have guests you
know? And you need to set up the dining room for all these kids
George,' George knew this, and had been hoping that Elaine had
already done it. Because of the size of his house, he needed to fit all
the boys that were sleeping over into the dining room. He was going
to set up the Xbox and a TV in there, and move all the furniture out
of the way to accommodate Danny, Nicky, Jack and Paddy from
school (who Danny now insisted had always been his friend, and had
never been a liar, as if nothing had ever happened).

Things had been a great deal better for George since he and Elaine had finally got together. He hadn't missed the band at all, and he spent all his free time with her, they went on day trips with the children, and Jack had taken such a liking to George (and Danny) that he was coming down to stay with them as often as he could now that George and Elaine were sharing a house. It meant that George's spare rooms were in a constant state of flux, but he didn't care. They were living the domestic dream – though George had no intention of messing it all up by getting married this time, and Elaine had no intention of letting him. They were happy as they were, taking it one thing at a time.

George put his bass down, patted his son on the head, and wandered through to the dining room to get everything ready. Noticing that Jack had picked up his bass to take over – with Danny pointing at the notes he should play – he smiled a rueful smile.

'So Dad,' said Linda, who was already in the dining room, moving chairs to the sides of the room, 'You had a good day?'

'Yeah, I think so,' George smiled, 'I have, thank you for coming down, I really appreciate it, and I know the kids do as well.'

'Wouldn't miss it Dad,' she said, 'you seem to have managed to go quite a long stretch without doing anything stupid for once. Perhaps you are finally growing up?' she winked at him as she swung a chair past his face.

'Ha! Never,' he replied, grinning, 'but I think you may have been right – you remember way back when you said I was lonely, and I needed a real somebody?'

'I did?' she looked blankly at him, 'you actually needed somebody to tell you that? Surely that's obvious to everyone?'

'Thanks for that, yes, I did it seems, but at least I have a real somebody now,' he retorted, 'anyway, after that you told me that joining a band was a good idea – and we all know how that ended, so you're not that good.'

She grinned at him, waving away the criticism with her hand, 'all worked out though didn't it? If you hadn't done all that, you might not have ended up with Elaine – and happy, I might add – and I might never have been angry enough to run away to Bristol, so I wouldn't have fallen into this job, or met Brian.'

'Who is Brian? And when are you bringing him to meet me?' George turned very quickly into the defensive father.

'Oh, he's just a guy,' she replied, 'oh shit, look it's seven-thirty, quick, it's starting.'

They both quickly finished setting up, and went back into the living room.

'Turn those guitars off for a bit boys,' George said, 'that new singing show's starting tonight – everyone's up for watching that yeah?'

The general consensus mumbled and agreed that yes they were, and the TV went on. As the opening credits began Jack turned round to George and said, 'You know something? You and Danny are pretty good playing together, why don't you start a band?'

George smiled, and replied, 'I think he might be better with you Jack, I'm done with all that thanks,' he took a long swig of his cup of tea, put his arm around Elaine and his feet up on his footstool, and they settled down for an evening in front of the TV.

THE END

If you enjoyed this book then please leave a glowing review on amazon or goodreads – helping it to reach more people.

Dave Holwill is online at:-
www.daveholwill.com
www.facebook.com/daveholwill100
davedoesntwriteanythingever.blogspot.co.uk
and @davenotthecat on twitter

17534683R00112

Printed in Great Britain
by Amazon